DIVORCING THE DEVIL

DIVORCING THE DEVIL

A novel by

Dwan Abrams

www.urbanchristianonline.net

Urban Books
1199 Straight Path
West Babylon, NY 11704

ISBN-13: 978-1-60162-960-9
ISBN-10: 1-60162-960-5

First Printing May 2008

Printed in the United States of America

10 9 8 7 6 5 4 3 2

This is a work of fiction. Any references or similarities to actual events, real people, living, or dead, or to real locales are intended to give the novel a sense of reality. Any similarity in other names, characters, places, and incidents is entirely coincidental.

Submit Wholesale Orders to:
Kensington Publishing Corp.
C/O Penguin Group (USA) Inc.
Attention: Order Processing
405 Murray Hill Parkway
East Rutherford, NJ 07073-2316
Phone: 1-800-526-0275
Fax: 1-800-227-9604

This book is dedicated to Nia

Acknowledgments

First and foremost, I want to thank God for blessing me with the gift of writing. I consider my writing a gift, and I cherish it.

I'm thankful to have such a loving and supportive family. Thanks to my parents, Gwendolyn Fields and Gary Abrams, for encouraging me to be the best person that I can be.

Thanks to my daughter, Nia, for being a source of constant joy. Thanks to Alex for being such a good man. He's my photographer, chauffer, and life companion.

To my siblings: Ireana, her husband, Kerryngton, Garet, and Grant—I love you.

To my grandmother, a.k.a. "Mother," I send all my love.

To my aunts: Deborah, Valerie, Wanda, Gail and Gwen andy my uncles: Willie T. Jr., Roderick and Handy Jr. I love you all. Sadly, both of my parents' youngest brothers, Narward and Anthony, are no longer with us. I'll always love them and cherish their memories.

To my extended family: Ceola, Alex II, Cordella, Marisa, Jerome, Lena, and Palestine—it's an honor to be a member of your family. I love you.

I've been blessed to have friendships that have stood the test of time. New friendships are nice, but old friends are the best. I met my dear friend, Juanita Matthews, when we were in high school. We've experienced the highs and the lows. I love you. I met my other dear friend, Aleta Barnes, while I was in college. We've been through it all and have been there for each other every step of the way. I love you. Margherita Graham and Yolanda Bowens are my cousins, but they also fall into the best girlfriends' category. I love you guys.

As an avid reader, I admire many writers, including Eric Jerome Dickey, E. Lynn Harris, Pearl Cleage, Marissa Monteilh and Mary Monroe. I was blessed to participate in a Christian anthology titled, *The Midnight Clear: Stories of Love, Hope and Inspiration.* For the anthology, I was fortunate to work with Kendra Norman-Bellamy, my writing mentor, Tia McCollors, Stacy Hawkins Adams, Patricia Haley, and sixteen other writers. It was a wonderful experience.

I want to thank my editor, Joylynn Jossel, for welcoming me into the Urban Christian family. And a special thanks to Marielle Marne for always giving me a little extra.

Thanks to all the readers and book clubs that have embraced my work. I greatly appreciate it.

Thanks to the media: ATLANTA LIVE TV show on WATC TV 57, *Booking Matters* magazine, and Marguerite Press.

CHAPTER ONE
Skyler

I felt so good this morning—like a kitten after someone has scratched under his chin and given him a bowl of chilled milk. My body tingled as I thought about the night of passion my husband, Donovan, and I shared. I loved watching him sleep. The way the satin cover draped over his trim waist, exposing just a hint of his toned thighs. Dreadlocks scattered in different directions over the pillow. Skin the color of pecans. He was sexy with a capital "S."

Donovan opened his chestnut brown eyes and yawned. Rubbing the stubble on his chin, he cooed, "Good morning, baby."

I loved his Jamaican accent. I gave him a naughty smile, letting him know I was very pleased with last night's performance.

"Good morning yourself. Sleep well?" I kissed him on the lips and caressed his muscular chest.

"Like a bear in hibernation." He stretched and yawned. "You got any appointments today?"

It was Monday morning and I had two clients who had regular appointments with me every Monday, Wednesday, and Friday. Their times changed depending on their schedules, but the days remained the same. I rolled over and glanced at the clock. It read 7:30 AM

"I actually have one at nine o'clock."

"Too bad. I was hoping we could continue where we left off." He wrapped his arms around me.

"Later."

I kissed him again and freed myself from his embrace. I stretched my arms and legs before placing my bare feet on the cold hardwood floor. I went into the bathroom and brushed my teeth before stepping into a hot shower. The pulsating water kneaded against my flesh like a million little fingers. It felt so good I didn't want to get out. That's exactly what I needed to wake up because there was something about Monday mornings that made getting out of bed more difficult. Especially on Sundays, since Donovan and I usually went to mid-morning worship service and brunch immediately afterward.

My eyes were closed as I tilted my head back and allowed the water to dance against my neck. Then I heard the glass shower door open. A sudden surge of cold air clung to my body like the plastic sweat suits people wore in the eighties for rapid weight loss.

"Hey," I said as I opened my eyes and turned my head in the same direction as the breeze.

Donovan stepped into the shower. Rather than complaining about the sweltering water like he usually did, he turned the knob to a cooler temperature. I didn't say anything. I could tell he was feeling amorous by the way he touched me. Ordinarily, I would never leave my husband in such a state, but I had an appointment. I had to go. As a psychoanalyst, I realized that the male ego was fragile. This situation needed to be handled with tender, loving care.

I turned to face him. "Donovan, I would like nothing better than to spend the entire day in your arms."

The water began to mist on his wheat-colored dread-locks. I looked at his six-pack and lost my train of thought. *If I leave this fine man alone, I'll be the one needing a therapist.* I quickly reeled myself back in, reminding myself that my patients depended on me. Being responsible wasn't an option, it was a job requirement.

So I said, "I'll be home early. We can have a romantic dinner and pick up where we left off."

A romantic dinner for us meant sitting down at the same time and eating food that wasn't take-out or delivery.

He pursed his lips, pretended to pout, and asked, "What's your definition of early?"

"No later than six o'clock."

"I'm gonna hold you to it." He pointed sternly.

I smiled, grabbed my towel, and stepped out of the shower. Donovan remained behind. I stayed in the bathroom while I put light makeup on my tawny-colored skin, smeared gloss on my thin lips, and pulled my long, jet black hair into a tight bun. I usually blow-dried my hair straight, but today I left it in its naturally curly state.

While studying my reflection in the mirror, I noticed that my sharp features and high cheekbones looked more European than black. Donovan says I look like Mariah Carey. Like most women though, I could point out numerous things about my appearance that I'd love to change, and my lips are one. I think they're too thin. I'd love to have those full, luscious lips like Angelina Jolie.

Donovan finished showering and started shaving. I went into the Victorian-style bedroom and put on sexy lingerie underneath my black silk *crepe de chine* flapper dress with ecru collar and cuffs and completed the ensemble with a pearl necklace. I usually wore lingerie underneath my work attire because it made me feel sexy. It reminded me not to take myself too seriously and enjoy life. And the fact that Donovan loved it didn't hurt either.

I returned to the bathroom just as Donovan was spitting his mouthwash into the sink. He dried his mouth with a hand towel.

"You look too good to leave the house." Donovan smiled, revealing beautiful white teeth.

I couldn't stop the blush. After three years of marriage, he still had a way of making me feel giddy.

"Thanks." I kissed him on the lips. His breath was cool and smelled like mint. "Have a good day."

"You too. And what time are you going to be home again?"

Our eyes connected. He reminded me because he knew that my schedule was erratic.

"By six." I reiterated my point by holding up six fingers.

I walked downstairs into the family room where my designer all-in-one briefcase-handbag-purse waited for me at the door like a puppy needing to go out. I picked it up along with my keys and left.

While driving in my BMW 325 along Peachtree Street in Atlanta, I noticed the brilliance of the sky. It reminded me of a day when I was around five or six years old, and I asked my dad why the sky was blue. He replied, "A clear sky on a sunny day appears blue because of Rayleigh scattering of the light from the sun." My dad had a PhD and was a rocket scientist. Those types of answers weren't uncommon coming from him.

I realized at an early age that I liked smart men and that I wanted to be smart. My dad and I would read the newspaper together and discuss current events. He would tell me that there was nothing more attractive than a beautiful woman with brains. That stuck with me. I studied hard and graduated from high school when I was fourteen years old. I went straight to college at my mom's alma mater.

After graduating from New York University, I attended the NYU School of Medicine. Then I enrolled in the NYU Psychoanalytic Institute. I decided to become a psychoanalyst because the human mind fascinated me. I liked thinking outside of the box and helping people. It gave me a sense of accomplishment. I felt as if my life had purpose, meaning.

Donovan and I met four years ago while we were both living in New York. I was twenty-eight and he was thirty. I was working as an assistant clinical professor at NYU. We were at a Jewish deli located on Second Avenue in the East Village. While we were waiting for our lunch orders, we struck up casual conversation and ended up sitting together at one of the plain white tables lining the wall. Donovan told me that his family had migrated from Jamaica to New York during the Jamaican slave trade. He had a PhD and worked as a product development chemist. I was immediately attracted to him because—it's true—women are attracted to men who remind them of their fathers. Since I held my father in high esteem, my standards for a mate were equally lofty.

Donovan's family lived in New York, and I had met his parents, four brothers, three sisters, and a slew of nieces and nephews. I loved his family. Donovan was the youngest child and didn't have any children from his previous relationships. As an only child, I always dreamed of having a big family. His family "adopted" me, and I adored them. It warmed my heart to hear his nieces and nephews refer to me as "Aunty."

Donovan and I had been dating for six months before I took him home to Boca Raton, Florida to meet my parents. Donovan insisted on meeting my parents because he said he wanted to marry me. We went to visit my parents during the Christmas holidays. My dad had retired from NASA and my mom owned a dance studio. He was the only guy I had ever taken home. I had devoted so much of my time to studying that Donovan was the first serious relationship I ever had.

When my parents met Donovan, they fell in love with him too. I knew Donovan would end up being my husband when my dad told me I had a good guy on my hands. We got married in Florida at my parents' church. Not long afterward, Donovan and I relocated from New York to Atlanta because Donovan got a job at Coca-Cola.

I arrived at my office fifteen minutes early and Yahkie, my assistant, greeted me. My stomach was grumbling, and I was famished. I wished I had grabbed a bagel or something.

"Good morning, boss lady," Yahkie said, sounding chipper and handing me a cup of freshly brewed coffee. "Just the way you like it: black with two sugars. I left you a Chick-Fil-A chicken biscuit on your desk, too."

I couldn't help but smile.

"How did you know I'd be hungry?" I tried to play it off.

"Are you kidding me? You're always hungry, but you hate to cook breakfast. You don't like to wake up early. You'd rather spend your time sleeping or getting to know your fine husband in the Biblical sense. You know I know you."

I couldn't resist laughing. Yahkie had been my assistant since I started my practice two years ago. I'll never forget the way he came into my office for his interview. It was summertime and he wore a blue-and-white seersucker suit. He looked chic. Even though he tried to tone down his flamboyant ways for the interview, I could tell he would let loose once given the opportunity. He was the most fashionable man I had ever met. His appearance was always meticulous. From his neatly cut hair to his manicured fingers, he was a vision of togetherness. Even beyond the physical, he was highly organized and took initiative. I was impressed with him the first day we met, and he had exceeded my expectations.

"Thanks for breakfast. I'll try to finish in time for my nine o'clock," I promised as I walked into my suite. A wooden bookcase lined with hardcover books ranging from the

Greek classics to textbooks to self-help books greeted me when I entered.

I placed my mug on top of my oak desk and slid my case underneath. Then I sat down on a soft, black leather, high-back chair and ate. The breakfast sandwich hit the spot. I dabbed the corners of my mouth and checked my Omega. The time was 9:28 AM. A couple of minutes later my intercom buzzed. It was Yahkie telling me that Monday Jackson, my new patient, had arrived. I was glad she showed up on time because late arrivals threw off my schedule. I dumped my trash in the receptacle located on the side of my desk and told him to send her in.

I walked from behind my desk and extended my hand to her. "Monday, I'm Dr. Skyler Little. It's a pleasure to meet you."

We gave each other a firm handshake. She flashed a smile that revealed tiny teeth that looked like Chiclets. She appeared to be at least five foot six and weighed about 250 pounds. Although she was portly, she carried herself well. She wore a yellow shirt, black slacks, and black high heels. Her makeup was flawless.

"Nice to meet you, too," she replied.

I offered her a seat on the gray sofa as I sat next to her on a chaise decorated in a black-and-beige African design motif. The various animal prints, such as cheetah, leopard, and zebra, covering several chairs around my office revealed that I have a sanguine personality.

I told her that I preferred to record all of my sessions so that I could refer back to them if necessary. I assured her that the tapes were for my personal use and wouldn't be shared with anyone without her permission or a court order. Then I explained that I began and ended every session with prayer. She informed me that she attended church regularly and was perfectly fine with us praying together. So we proceeded.

We bowed our heads and closed our eyes as I prayed aloud.

"Heavenly Father, thank You for this day. I pray that You be with us during this meeting. Lord, use me as a vessel for the up-building of Your Kingdom. It is my humble prayer that I decrease so that You may increase. Let the meditations of my heart be pleasing and acceptable in Your sight. Remove any obstacle that could hinder me from being an effective witness for You. Forgive us for our sins of omission and commission. In Jesus' name, we pray, Amen." Then I asked, "So, what brings you here today?"

She pointed at a five-by-seven framed photo sitting on the corner of my desk and asked if it was a picture of me and my husband. I glanced at the photo and told her that we had taken it last year when we went to Jamaica for vacation.

"Nice. Is that where you're from?"

I was taken aback by her question. No one had ever asked me that before.

"Not me—my husband," I explained.

She nodded her head and smiled. "You make a lovely couple."

"Thanks." I asked her again to tell me why she came to see me. I wondered why she kept avoiding the question.

"May I call you Sky?" She shifted in her seat.

"Sure, whatever works for you. Lots of people call me that."

"Sky, I have a problem." She crossed her right leg over her left. It made her legs seem as long as stilts. "My boyfriend suggested I talk to someone because he can't seem to help me."

I acknowledged by nodding my head.

"I don't know where to begin."

I explained to her that counseling sessions were a process and that we weren't going to resolve her issues in one meeting. I asked her to tell me about her childhood and her parents.

"My family," she sighed, "is complicated. My mom and dad were married until I was five. After they divorced, I never saw my dad again."

"Before we continue," I said, "would you please tell me the names of your parents so that I won't have to keep referring to them as your mother and father?"

"Sure. Paige and Stan."

"Thanks. Please continue."

Monday told me that Paige and Stan's marriage began to deteriorate due to infidelity. She said they argued a lot. After Paige accused Stan of child molestation, they divorced.

"Did Stan molest you?" I rubbed the back of my neck with my right hand, indicating this wasn't easy for me to listen to. Every time one of my patients revealed that she had been molested, I could feel tension creeping its way into my neck like a cheating husband trying to slip into his marital bed undetected after he's been with his lover. I maintained my professional composure even though, deep inside, I felt angry. Children are innocent. The thought of someone violating them infuriated me. I fought back my disgust.

Monday uncrossed her legs. "Yes. He used to fondle me and actually penetrated me when I was . . . five." Her eyes welled with tears. I offered her a box of Kleenex. She pulled a couple of tissues out of the box and dabbed the corners of her sparkling eyes. "My mom flipped out when she found out," she continued. "Burned him on the arm with an iron. Threw him out of the house and then reported him to child services."

I rubbed my arm. I empathized with how painful it must've felt to be burned with an iron. I did not advocate or condone violence, but I could understand how a mother could be driven to such drastic behavior because of the love of her child. Then I asked, "Did he go to jail?"

"Yes. A social worker conducted an investigation, and I had to see a child psychiatrist."

"I see."

Not long afterward, the timer went off, notifying us our session had ended. There was so much more I wanted to say, but I told her we'd resume the conversation at our next appointment. We prayed, and she left.

I checked my inspirational desk calendar and noticed that I had a few minutes before my next appointment, so I called Donovan on his cell phone. As soon as he said, "'Ello," I puckered my lips and blew a short series of kisses into the receiver. Then I hung up. We called those "drive-bys." We did a drive-by whenever one of us was thinking about the other but didn't have enough time for a drawn-out conversation. It was an alternative to saying "I love you."

I had to purge my mind so that I could mentally prepare for my upcoming meeting with Ambrosia. She had been my patient for the past six months. Her father died when she was little, and her mother never remarried. When I met Ambrosia, she was in a relationship with a married man, and they had two children together. Her relationship had soured, and she needed someone to talk to. She came to see me because she figured I would listen without judging her.

Yahkie came barging into my office, interrupting my thoughts like he was a policeman making a drug bust before the suspects could get away.

"Boss lady!" He closed the door behind him, arms flailing in the air. "Ambrosia is in the lobby, and she looks a hot mess! She looks like she's been fighting with Iron Mike Tyson of old and lost! Bruises everywhere! Got on shades! I bet she got a black eye!"

My heart raced and I dipped my head in thought. I felt nervous. "Bring her back."

Yahkie left my office. My mind was on emotional over-load. I wrung my hands and paced the floor. As a profes-sional, I knew better than to get personally involved in the lives of my clients, but as a person, I couldn't help but care. When Ambrosia entered, I stopped pacing. Seeing her in that condition made my stomach drop, the same as riding a roller coaster ride at Six Flags and without holding your breath. The Jackie O.-type shades she wore covered half her oval-shaped face and were in direct contrast with her milky white skin. I didn't ask her to take them off, even though I could see blotchy red spots on her cheeks and that her bot-tom lip was swollen. The thought of what hid behind those glasses scared me. I didn't want to see because I knew I'd get more upset than I already was. I took a deep breath. She closed the door behind her. I exhaled.

"What happened?" I asked.

Silence.

I walked over to Ambrosia and wrapped my arms around her. Even though I'm five foot six, athletic, and have an "apple bottom," as Donovan would say, standing next to Ambrosia's shapely but petite self, I felt like an Amazon. She clung to me the way a baby black howler monkey clings to its mother's fur. She sobbed on my shoulder so hard that her body shook. I closed my eyes and told her to let it out. As she continued to cry, I prayed silently for her. I stroked her highlighted auburn hair. She didn't have to tell me what was wrong be-cause experience had taught me it had something to do with her babies' daddy.

CHAPTER TWO
Skyler

By the time I finished consoling Ambrosia, I was ready to call it a day. Mentally, I was exhausted. Ambrosia left without ever telling me what happened. I was glad when Yahkie gave me the message that my afternoon appointment canceled. It gave me time to clear my mind and get some much needed psychological air. Worry consumed me. I had a laundry list of questions—*What happened? Who attacked her? Is she all right? Did she call the police?* More than anything, I feared for her safety.

The air in my office suddenly seemed stale. I tried to calm my nerves. I grabbed my handbag-briefcase and told Yahkie I was leaving for the remainder of the day. He understood.

While in my car, I couldn't get the image of a bruised and visibly shaken Ambrosia out of my head. I called her from my cell phone. I got her voice mail and left a message. My inability to reach Ambrosia intensified my fears. I prayed and finished up by saying aloud, "Lord, grant me the serenity to accept the things I cannot change, the courage to change the things that I can, and the wisdom to know the difference."

On my way home, I picked up Donovan's and my dry cleaning. Then I stopped off at the grocery store and bought some tilapia filets and a bag of salad.

When I got home, I left the dry cleaning on the leather sofa and set the groceries on the marble kitchen countertop. I grabbed a bottle of Evian from the stainless steel refrigerator, went into my bedroom, and changed into my sweats and sneakers. In my home gym, I hit the treadmill hard. For ten minutes, I ran as fast as I could without passing out. I wiped the excess perspiration from my face with a towel and commenced lifting weights.

Breathing heavily, I gulped down my bottled water like a parched camel who had discovered a hidden oasis. I went into my bathroom and ran a warm bubble bath. I took off my clothes and stepped into the garden-style tub. Soaking felt so good. I rested my head on my bath pillow and closed my eyes. Images of Ambrosia appeared on the screen of my mind as frequently as the video depicting the Rodney King beating had played on the news all those years ago. I quickly popped my eyes open and refused to think about Ambrosia. I reminded myself of my prayer. Then I thought about the saying, "If you're going to worry, why pray? If you're going to pray, why worry?" I chose the latter.

I finished bathing and dried off. I sprayed some "smell good" on my neck, stomach and thighs. Then I changed into a short bathrobe that cinched at the waist. I was about to go downstairs when my cell phone rang. It was Gabriella, my best friend. I answered and told her I'd call her back on the landline.

"Hey. How are you?" I said, talking on the cordless phone as I walked downstairs and into the kitchen.

"Good," she said with a Swedish accent. She had been living in Atlanta for nearly eleven years and her accent was less prominent as a result. Though still foreign, she had a better understanding of English. "Why you home so early?"

Due to patient confidentiality, I never discussed my clients in casual conversation, so I said, "My afternoon appointment canceled. I decided to come home and cook dinner."

I pressed the phone against my ear with my shoulder, took the groceries out of the bag, and rinsed off the fish. After I washed and dried my hands, I held the phone with my left hand, and seasoned the tilapia with my free one.

"I'm sure Donovan will love that."

I could tell by her tone that something was weighing heavily on her heart. I asked, "Is everything all right with you?"

She hesitated. "I–I found a note in Kevin's pant pocket a couple of weeks ago. It was from a woman."

Kevin was her husband and Donovan's best friend. I didn't want to assume the worst, because Kevin was a decent guy. From everything I knew about Kevin, he had a conscience and thought about the consequences of his actions.

I asked her to tell me what the note said.

"It talked about her being in love with him. She seemed angry. Like she was going off on him for not leaving me."

I was speechless. This situation could be volatile if handled incorrectly. "Are you sure you didn't misunderstand?"

"I'm sure. After I found the letter, I started listening to the messages on his cell phone."

I didn't like where this was going. Gabriella must've missed the memo that stated, "If you look for trouble, you'll find it."

"I heard her on his voice mail," Gabriella continued. "She was cussing him out. Said . . . said something about him coming over to her apartment. She wanted to know how he

DIVORCING THE DEVIL   15

could kiss her like that, tell her he loves her, and still come home to me. She said it wasn't fair. That they have so much fun together and I make him so unhappy." She paused and asked, "Can you believe that?"

I knew her question was rhetorical. She really didn't expect me to answer.

"I feel disgusted," Gabriella said. "What kind of woman does that? Messing with a married man. I mean, she's white trash. And him, I feel so betrayed. Like I can't trust him. You know?" She sighed and asked, "How can he talk about me with her?"

Even though she didn't raise her voice, I could tell she was angry.

"Have you confronted him with your newfound information?" I probed.

"Not yet."

She was a lot cooler than I would've been. There's no way I could've held on to that information.

Instead of asking, "Why haven't you told him?" I asked, "How do you know she's white?" Not like that made any difference. If her husband was being unfaithful, that was a bigger issue than the color of the woman's skin.

"I could tell by the sound of her voice. Besides, Kevin isn't attracted to black women. They've hurt him too many times in the past."

Her statement offended me. Kevin and I grew up together in Florida and had been best friends since we were in elementary school. Even though he was still in high school when I went away to college, we kept in touch. Ever since I had known him, he exclusively dated black women. Not just redbones either. Kevin was Nigerian, and he used to appreciate the beauty of all black women. It wasn't until a sister crushed him by cheating on him that all that changed. He took her back. She later aborted his child. At least she told him that it was his baby. That's when he ventured outside of his race and started dating foreign women, including Asians.

Kevin used to tell me about some of his friends who were making big bucks marrying women from other countries by helping them gain U.S. citizenship. When he told me he had eloped with Gabriella, I thought he did it for monetary gains. Why else would he marry someone I had never met and he never talked about? I was disappointed in him. I couldn't believe it. We used to be so close. I thought we shared everything. Apparently, I was wrong. Our friendship never fully recovered.

When I met Gabriella at their wedding reception ten years ago, she was already pregnant. I figured Kevin must've had genuine feelings for her because Gabriella didn't come from wealth. She didn't graduate from college, and she worked as a nanny. During Gabriella's pregnancy, we talked on the phone nearly every day and formed a friendship. In fact, the closer Gabriella and I became, the more distant Kevin and I became. I thought that when Donovan and I moved to Atlanta, Kevin and I could redevelop the friendship we once had. Things didn't work out that way. Kevin and I were cordial, but you'd never know we were once best friends. Donovan took my place as Kevin's "BOI" (Buddy Of Importance), and Gabriella replaced Kevin as my confidant.

"I don't understand those women," Gabriella continued, interrupting my thoughts.

"What women?"

"White women! They–they don't have any morals, values. They're nasty. You didn't know that?" She sounded shocked, as if it was common knowledge.

For some reason, Gabriella didn't consider herself white— at least not by American standards. In her mind, there was a difference between her and American white women. Maybe because she was married to a brother, she felt exempt from whiteness. That provided immunity for her whenever she wanted it. You couldn't tell by looking at her though. Bleached blond hair and eyes as blue as sapphires.

Amid everything I was dealing with, I wasn't about to start defending every American white woman. That was unrealistic. Besides, I thought Gabriella was only spewing venom because she was hurt and angry. And, I surmised, she may have felt inferior or inept in comparison to other white women, on a subconscious level.

Even though my mother was French Canadian and my father was black, in my house we subscribed to the "a dab will do you" philosophy. Therefore, I was a sister all the way.

"What are you going to do?" I asked.

"I–I'm going to talk to him. I want to hear what he has to say."

"And do you really think he's going to tell you the truth?"

"Yes. He knows how I feel about lying. I can forgive him for having sex with somebody. It's just sex. But if I ask him and he lies, I can't forgive him for that. It's disrespectful."

I dealt with other people's problems all day. I wasn't about to try to rationalize what she had just said.

"So, you don't care if he has sex with somebody else as long as he tells you about it?"

"I care, but I can forgive him. Right now, the trust . . . It's broken."

"I understand."

I didn't want to say much more than that because if I took the psychoanalytical approach, I'd help her see that if it walks like a duck and quacks like a duck, it's a duck. I could tell that a part of her wanted to believe that her husband wasn't cheating on her. I understood. That was natural. However, it wasn't my job to support a fantasy. Now, by no means would I have advocated divorce. I simply wished that Gabriella would deal with the facts. Women have come into my office after catching their husbands in bed with other women and told me that they weren't sure if they saw what they think they saw.

The mind is powerful, yet fragile. Given the right circumstances, we can convince ourselves of almost anything. A woman in love who wants to believe her unfaithful man is faithful can be swayed one way or the other based on what her man tells her.

"It doesn't make sense," Gabriella opined. "Why would he cheat on me?"

I imagined her shaking her head when she said it.

"If he is cheating on you, you shouldn't blame yourself." I tried to sound encouraging. I'd seen firsthand how so many women slipped into depression and assumed feelings of worthlessness after discovering that their husbands had stepped outside of their marriage and into the arms of another woman. "It's his decision to be unfaithful."

"I don't blame myself."

Her arrogance surprised me. She went on to tell me that Kevin constantly told her how beautiful she was. How he told her that she was everything he ever wanted. She explained how she helped Kevin become the man he was by encouraging him to go back to school to become a computer programmer.

She admitted that they went through a rough patch in their marriage after the births of their son and daughter (who were ten and eight, respectively.) She said that she devoted more time to the children and less time to Kevin. I could tell by her tone that she resented Kevin for being jealous of the time she spent with their children. That and the fact that she outright called him selfish.

I placed the fish in the skillet and prepared to blacken it. Gabriella asked me if I still talked to Kevin. I told her that I didn't speak with him very often. She knew that. She was grasping at straws. Then she asked if I would talk to him and see if he'd tell me anything about the affair. I seriously doubted that he would, especially since his wife was my best friend. Even if he would, I wouldn't breach our trust by telling Gabriella. I told her I'd talk to him. Not as a fishing expedition, rather as a concerned friend. She seemed to understand. We hung up, and I finished preparing dinner. I couldn't wait to see Donovan.

CHAPTER THREE

Skyler

I was in the living room watching a talk show about paternity test results when I heard the garage door open. As much as I hated to admit it, I watched this show to attempt to analyze the guests. Those young girls had men taking paternity tests by the droves. The sad part was that, as a society, we would shake our heads and point our fingers in dismay when we should really have tried to find out why those young women felt so worthless. All we saw was the cussing, fussing, and utter humiliation when the host held the test results in his hands and announced, "You are not the father." We didn't see or hear about the drug abuse, alcoholism, sexual abuse, rejection, or neglect that typically contributed to the promiscuous behavior. And those poor, innocent children. One day those babies would see those tapes. I wondered if they would have follow-up shows for the children involved in all that dysfunction.

Donovan's key jiggled in the lock for a few seconds before the door opened. He smiled when he saw me. I could tell he was pleasantly surprised that I beat him home. I stood up and greeted him with a hug and kiss. Being in his arms made me feel fortunate and secure. I felt like I was in a Calgon commercial, except, instead of Calgon, it would say, "Donovan, take me away." We broke our embrace when we heard screams coming from the TV. A heavyset black woman was sprawled out on the floor crying. The talk show host was trying to console her while a thin black guy danced a jig because he heard the magic words: "You are not the father."

"Why do you watch that? It's not real anyway," Donovan said, loosening his silk tie.

I explained that, whether it was staged or not, the show had found its niche and viewers enjoyed the drama. Besides, watching people publicly air their dirty laundry fascinated me. It often amazed me how many people appeared on national TV and exposed the most intimate details of their lives. Whether the guests wanted their fifteen minutes of fame or truly believed there was safety in numbers, I wondered what happened when they got home. *Were they ostracized by friends and family? Did they change their ways?*

We fixed our plates and Donovan blessed the food.

"Lord, thank You for the food which we're about to receive for the nourishment of our bodies. In Jesus' name, we pray. Amen."

We ate on serving trays in the living room. I turned down the volume on the TV. Over dinner, Donovan told me that the food was delicious and talked about a new product he was developing. I listened attentively because he was passionate about his profession, and his enthusiasm captivated me. Donovan enjoyed being a chemist. He liked experimenting with various ingredients and mixing formulas.

Then he asked me about my day. I didn't tell him about my drama with Ambrosia. But I did tell him about my conversation with Gabriella and her suspicions about Kevin possibly having an extramarital affair.

"Blood clot!" Donovan declared, squeezing the bridge of his nose with two of his fingers and thumb on his right hand. He mumbled something in broken English that I didn't understand.

"Does that mean you're surprised or no?"

I ate the last bit of tilapia on my plate. It practically melted in my mouth.

He removed his hand, shook his head, and exhaled. "What else did she say?"

"I told you everything. She said she found a letter and listened to some voice mail messages on his cell phone," I reiterated.

"What's she going to do?"

"She didn't say." I sounded frustrated. "And why are you evading the question? Did you know or didn't you?"

He was about to stuff some salad into his mouth, but he stopped midway. He placed his fork on the plate. "Baby, this is their business. You know better than anyone not to get involved in other people's marital problems."

"These are not just people. They're our friends."

"That's true. But what can we do?" There was a pregnant pause and Donovan continued, "Nothing! They have to work this out themselves."

I gave him an incredulous look and asked, "So you knew and didn't tell me? I thought we shared everything." I pretended to pout even though I knew full well that couples shouldn't tell each other everything. Having some secrecy was healthy. It helped keep the relationship interesting and allowed people to maintain their individuality.

He shook his head and leaned toward me. "No, I didn't know. I don't feel like talking about Gabriella and Kevin anymore. You and I have some unfinished business to tend to."

Whatever small amount of food remained on our plates didn't get eaten. We were too busy using the plush couch with oversized pillows as a bed. For the moment, thoughts about anyone other than Donovan didn't exist.

On Wednesday, I met with Monday again. We prayed before our session. I noticed that this time she wasn't wearing makeup and her hair was in a ponytail. Her skin had dark blemishes, predominantly on her cheeks.

"How have you been since our last meeting?" I asked.

"Fine." She folded her hands on her lap.

I pulled out a yellow legal pad on which I had transcribed some notes from our recorded conversation and said, "We left off with you telling me about Stan going to jail for molesting you. Tell me what happened after that."

"Do we really have to talk about him? Gosh!"

"Yes. It would greatly help me to understand what's going on in your life now. At some point, we're going to have to deal with this. Better now than later."

She laughed. "You remember those Now and Later candies from back in the day?"

"Yes, I do. That used to be one of my favorite candies." I smiled as I thought about the sweet taste of the strawberry, watermelon, cherry, and green apple flavored gooey treats.

"I'm sorry. I'm being silly. It's just that when you said 'better now than later' it reminded me of Now and Laters."

I deduced that Monday used humor as a way of hiding her feelings. Even though she was thirty-one years old, I could tell there were areas of her personality that weren't fully developed.

"Okay. What do you want to know?" Monday asked.

"What happened after Stan went away?"

"Well, it seemed like my mom blamed me for what happened. You know?"

"What do you mean?"

"Not like right away, but when I got older, it started to show. She would call me names and tell people I was fast."

She crossed her feet at the ankles. "Then when I was thirteen, I got pregnant."

I nodded. I always told people that the power of life and death were in the tongue. Our words could edify or destroy. The words we spoke into our lives and the lives of others had the ability to manifest. The subconscious mind couldn't know the difference between real and make-believe. All it knew was what had been programmed into it. Whenever someone said something negative about his condition or spoke death and damnation upon himself or others, I quickly reminded him not to claim it. If I found myself being negative, I audibly stated said "cancel-cancel" as a way of telling my subconscious mind not to accept it.

I asked, "Did you have the baby?"

"Uh-huh. Her name is Alexis. She's eighteen now."

"Did Paige help you with the baby?"

"She did a little bit after the baby was first born. But when I was pregnant, she acted crazy. She made it seem like I was fast all my life and that's why my father . . ." Her voice trailed off and she held her head down.

"Do you want a Kleenex?" I offered.

She declined. "Anyway, when I was fourteen, I altered my birth certificate so that I could get a job. I didn't like being on welfare, and I didn't want to depend on my mom."

"That was mighty ambitious of you. Especially at that age."

She sniffled and wiped a lingering tear with the back of her hand from her cheek. "Yeah, I did what I had to do."

"What about Alexis's father? Where's he?"

She waved her hand in a dismissing motion. "Whew." She gave a hearty laugh. "That's a whole 'nother story."

"Tell me about him. What's his name?"

"His name is Larry. He lives in Atlanta. We were both kids when we had Alexis. He didn't do a lot for her, but he did what he could for the first year of her life. After that . . . I . . . guess it got to be too much for him. He stopped coming around as much. I mean, he has somewhat of a relationship with Alexis, but he was never in her life consistently. Know what I mean?"

I nodded. Not long afterward, the timer went off.

Monday snapped her fingers. "Catch ya next time."

"I look forward to it."

We prayed and concluded the session. I thought the meeting with Monday went well. My hypothesis was that Monday's overeating was a direct result of being molested by her father. On a subconscious level, food had been a sort of comforter, a pacifier. Perhaps she used her weight as a control mechanism. If she was overweight, she may feel she was able to thwart advances from the opposite sex. Therefore, no dredging up painful memories of abuse. *I wonder if Monday's ever been married.* I shook my head. *No, I doubt it.*

And there was the issue with Paige. If I were a betting woman, I would have ventured to say there was a love-hate relationship there. Monday seemed torn. She loved her mother, yet she resented her. Based on what Monday told me about Paige, my guess was that the feelings were mutual.

I scribbled some notes on my legal pad before buzzing Yahkie and asking him to come into my office.

"Have you heard from Ambrosia?" I asked.

"Not a word. You?"

"Nothing." I sighed and tapped my pen on the desk, pondering my next statement. "You think she'll show up for her appointment today?"

"I don't see why not. She's really good about making her appointments. And whenever she's had to cancel, she always calls."

I bit my lower lip. "I suppose you're right."

"Boss lady, that's your problem: you worry too much. Let go and let God. Like my grandma always says, 'What's gon' be, gon' be.'"

"You're right."

"Now don't get me wrong; one of the things I love about you is your big heart. You care about people. But in your profession, you can't afford to take on everyone's problems. If you do, you'll get burnt out and you won't be no kinda good. Then you can't help anybody."

I nodded my head.

"I have some filing I need to catch up on. You need a hug?" he asked.

I chuckled. "No, I'm okay."

"You sure? You know I don't mind."

"I'm sure. But if you hear from Ambrosia . . ."

"I know, I know. I'll let you know." He walked out.

Since I had some time before my appointment with Ambrosia, I typed my handwritten notes into a Word document on the computer. I was relieved when Yahkie buzzed me to tell me that Ambrosia had arrived. I saved the file and turned off the computer monitor.

When Ambrosia walked through the door, she had on heavier makeup than I was used to seeing her wear. As she walked closer, I noticed that she was attempting to conceal a bruised eye that appeared to be a few days old. The additional luggage underneath her eyes revealed that she hadn't gotten much sleep either.

"I'm glad to see you," I admitted. "I was worried about you."

We sat down.

Her bottom lip began to quiver as if she was fighting back tears. I slid my chair closer to her seat on the couch and placed my hand on top of hers.

"Tell me what's wrong," I said. "What's going on?"

Silence. Then an outpouring of tears. I got up and grabbed

a box of tissue from the corner of my desk and handed it to her. She pulled a couple of tissues from the box and patted her face. I sat down next to her on the couch and wrapped my arm around her shoulders. I prayed that she would open up and tell me what was going on.

"Dr. Little," Ambrosia said. "I thought I was ready to talk about it, but I can't." She buried her face in between my chest and shoulder.

Not knowing was driving me crazy. I couldn't wait a couple more days until our next appointment. I refused to let her leave without telling me something.

I patted her head. "We need to talk about this. Let's get it on the table. I'm here to help you. Remember?"

"I . . . I . . . I didn't see this coming."

"What? You didn't see what coming?"

"Laron."

Laron was the father of her children. She lifted her head, and I removed my arm from her shoulders. She turned to face me.

"Tell me what he did to you."

The frightened look in her eyes made the fine hairs on my arm stand from my own consternation.

"He's dangerous. I hate him. I'll never forgive him for what he did to me."

Finally. Progress.

"Laron did this to you? Why?"

Ambrosia shook her head and covered her mouth with her left hand. She started crying again. "I've got to get out of here." She grabbed her clutch purse and stood up.

"Wait," I said, standing. "I can't let you leave like this."

"I'll be fine. I'm just not ready to talk about it. I'll see you on Friday. Promise."

"Ambrosia, if anything comes up . . . if you need anything—and I do mean anything—don't you hesitate to call me."

Ambrosia left and I threw my hands in the air, exasperated. I feared for her safety. I couldn't stand not knowing the entire story. I wanted to help her, to protect her. She seemed so vulnerable. Deep within, I knew that things would get worse before they got better.

CHAPTER FOUR

Ambrosia

Ambrosia Thompson arrived at the Christian daycare center to pick up her three-year-old son, Mateo, and one-year-old daughter, Destiny. She tried to open the glass door to the building, but it was locked. *Great*, she thought. *Just great*. Was anything going to go her way? She thought about the recent episode with Laron, and her eyes became misty. She rolled her eyes to the top of her head. When she was convinced she wasn't going to cry, she refocused straight ahead. Frustrated, she mumbled a few expletives and took a step back from the door as the receptionist pressed a button behind her desk and unlocked it. As soon as she heard the clicking sound, Ambrosia yanked the door open and hurried in. The young lady sitting behind the metal desk greeted Ambrosia with a smile.

"Hey, Puquesha. How you doin'?" Ambrosia greeted her.

"Fine."

Ambrosia was taken aback by Puquesha's freshly dyed hair. It was a reddish, orangish blond. *Her hair wasn't like that yesterday*, Ambrosia thought. She tried to conceal her shock. She walked to the computer sitting on the desk and punched in her personal code so that she could check her children out of daycare.

After she finished entering her code, Ambrosia turned around and saw the infants' room through the glass window on the right side of her. She stood still as she stared at the daycare worker cuddling an adorable brown baby. She remembered how happy she was when her children were born. They both weighed more than nine pounds at birth. Their skin was so soft and smooth. Those were happier times. She inhaled deeply and imagined the sweet scents of Johnson and Johnson Baby Powder and Chamomile-Lavender Lotion. She loved the way her children smelled after she gave them a bath.

Ambrosia realized that she was staring at nothing in particular and blinked a couple of times, as if she were snapping herself out of a daze. By then, another parent had arrived, so she walked briskly down the hall and into Mateo's classroom.

In the three-year-olds' room, the children were instructed to color pictures and stay within the lines. Some of the children were coloring, others were scribbling, and some were doing their own thing. There were fifteen children in the room and one teacher walking around. Ambrosia did a quick scan until her eyes landed on Mateo dressed in a green shirt and khaki shorts. She thought he was the cutest kid in the room. He had wavy brown hair and gray eyes. When Mateo was a baby, Ambrosia wondered how two brown-eyed people could have a gray-eyed baby. According to Ambrosia's mother, Mateo inherited his eye color from his great-grandfather. The corners of her lips curled upward when she saw him. She knelt down with one knee touching the ground and her arms open wide.

"Mateo!"

"Mommy!" Mateo squealed while he ran and thrust himself into her arms.

Mateo's forty-pound body could have knocked her over, but she braced herself. She wrapped her arms around him like a python and squeezed him tightly. Planting wet kisses on his cheeks, Ambrosia said, "I missed you today."

He giggled and wiggled free from his mother's embrace. Ambrosia stood up and waved at the heavyset teacher, who gave her a toothy grin.

"Hey, Ms. Munroe."

"How are you?"

"Good. Good. Thanks for asking."

Ambrosia grabbed Mateo's backpack from his wooden cubby, adjusted the straps around his shoulder blades, and held his hand as they walked two classrooms down the hall to get Destiny.

Most of the children in Destiny's room were sitting on mats playing with or trying to eat plastic blocks and other soft toys. Others were crying, some were crawling, and a few wobbled as they walked with their "new" legs. Ambrosia stepped carefully, and Mateo stayed close. She didn't want to accidentally step on any of the little people. There were several cribs lined against the wall, one of which held Destiny like a prisoner.

"Hi, Kathryn," Ambrosia said to the tall, skinny daycare worker who reminded her of a black version of Calista Flockhart, the actress who starred on the hit TV show, *Ally McBeal.*

"How're you?"

"I'm good. Did Destiny have a good day?"

"She always has a good day." Kathryn laughed, handing Ambrosia a diaper bag.

Ambrosia released Mateo's hand and placed the bag on her left shoulder. She turned to face him and said, "Stay right here."

Ambrosia practically walked on her tip-toes over to Destiny's crib and swooped down to pick her up. She pressed

Destiny's chubby cheek against the side of her face and in-haled. Destiny still had that baby smell that Ambrosia loved so much. Ambrosia stroked Destiny's silky brown hair. She held Destiny in the air, looked into her large, light-colored eyes, and said, "Hey, my baby."

Ambrosia kissed her on the cheek. Destiny cooed, drooled, and laughed. All of Ambrosia's problems seemed unimportant at the moment. Seeing her children always uplifted her. At least a little. In addition to Dr. Little, Ambrosia depended on her children for emotional support. Without Mateo and Destiny, Ambrosia was like an uncharged battery. Somehow, her children recharged her every time. They gave her the strength to move on, to do things she didn't necessarily want to do, but that she knew she had to do.

The children were securely strapped in their car seats as Ambrosia drove her Toyota Camry home. Occasionally, she would glance at the children through her rearview mirror to see what they were doing in the backseat. Mateo took sips from his sippy cup and played with Destiny's fingers, making her giggle. Ambrosia smiled as she thought about how much she loved her children and how beautiful they were.

Once she arrived at her gated apartment complex in Cham-blee, she entered her security code and waited for the gate to open slowly. She checked her rearview mirror to ensure that no one—more specifically Laron, the father of her chil-dren—was following her before she carefully drove over the speed bump. Then she checked . . . again. She hated feel-ing paranoid, but she wouldn't put anything past Laron. She considered him a threat to her safety.

As soon as she got inside of her second-story apartment, the beeping sound of the security system greeted her. She turned on the lights, placed Destiny on the carpeted floor along with the diaper bag and purse that she was carrying, and deactivated the alarm. Immediately, she reset the alarm to "at home" mode and locked the door.

She kneeled down to Mateo's eye level. "Mommy will be right back. Stay right here and watch your sister," she instructed.

Ambrosia grabbed the baseball bat that she kept in the hall closet and checked the small kitchen. Besides the few dirty dishes in the sink and dish rag on the countertop, nothing seemed to be out of place. After exchanging the bat for a butcher knife that she grabbed from the kitchen drawer, she inspected the living room. Floral-printed sofa with matching love seat, wooden coffee table, TV, large artificial plant in the corner, family pictures on the fireplace mantel, and toys on the floor. Nothing unusual.

She looked over her shoulder at her children and noticed that they seemed to be getting a little restless, so she reminded them to stay put. The dining room was directly across from the living room. From where she stood, she could see that the four-seater dinette was exactly as she left it, with magazines strewn on top.

She flipped on the light switch in the master bedroom. Her queen-sized bed was unmade with a few articles of clothing scattered in various places. First, she checked the crowded walk-in closet filled with suits, dresses, shirts, skirts, and pants individually grouped together and sorted by color. Rows of shoes faced the same direction. She had read a book about feng shui and organized her closet accordingly. Even though it wasn't as neat as she wanted, at least she had the principle down pat. Then she got down on one knee and looked underneath the bed. Nothing.

Next, she turned on the light in the children's room. Their bunk beds were unkempt. Toys covered the floor. There was no need to check their closet because it was too cluttered. Every time she opened it, stuff fell out. She was

certain that no one could hide in that closet without removing everything in it first.

Last, she checked the children's bathroom, which was
decorated like the sea. A step stool was conveniently located in front of the sink. Pictures of fish adorned the walls.
The shower curtain was transparent with fish swimming in
water at the bottom. The only things in the tub were a couple of rubber duckies, plastic blocks, and foam toys.

Breathing a sigh of relief, Ambrosia went back to the
front of the apartment where her children were waiting for
her. She was thankful that her children obeyed her. So
often she had seen children disobeying their parents, and
she didn't like it. By no means were her children perfect,
but she was glad that they listened to her. She taught them
early to obey her. And when they didn't, they got the
wooden spoon. Also known as Woody, it was a tradition in
her family. Her German grandmother used to use it on her
children whenever they stepped out of line. Although un-
conventional, Woody proved to be quite effective. Now, all
she had to do was threaten to get Woody, and her children
would straighten up.

"You guys can go into the living room and watch TV while
I fix dinner," Ambrosia said.

"Are you all right, Mommy?" Mateo asked.

"Mommy's fine," she lied, trying to reassure him. *Sometimes Mateo seems so much wiser than his years*.

Ambrosia moved the bags from the hallway and into the
children's room while Mateo and Destiny watched Nick, Jr.
She went into the kitchen and heated up a can of ravioli in
a copper pot on the stove.

Even though there was no sign of an intruder, Ambrosia
still felt jittery. She had other things on her mind, like how
her relationship with Laron had gone from a fairytale to a
nightmare.

She remembered how they met: at a nightclub in Buck-

head. He bought her a drink before coming over to introduce himself. Unbeknownst to him, Ambrosia was only
eighteen. He seemed to be the perfect gentleman, not to
mention good looking. His skin was as black and smooth as
a panther's hide and his teeth were sparkling white. He
wore a dark-colored three-piece suit with a French cuff
shirt and cufflinks. His conversation . . . intelligent. He even
showed an appreciation for a wide range of music including
jazz, blues, classical, world, rap, heavy metal, and house.
She'd never met a black guy who listened to heavy metal or
classical music. She was immediately attracted to him.

"Mommy," she heard Mateo say, interrupting her
thoughts.

"Huh?"

"Are you burning something?"

She realized that she had left the ravioli on too long. The
food hadn't burned beyond edibility, but it was bubbling
and the pasta was sticking to the bottom of the pot. She
swiftly removed the food and turned off the stove.

"Sorry, honey. Mommy wasn't paying attention," she
yelled into the other room.

She grabbed a saucer for Mateo and small plastic bowl for
Destiny from the cabinet and scraped food onto each.

"Mateo, go wash your hands, please," she instructed.

She placed the saucer, along with a toddler fork, on the
coffee table in the living room. Mateo liked to watch TV
while eating dinner. She picked Destiny up and washed her
hands in the kitchen sink before placing a bib around her
neck and sitting her in a high-chair in the kitchen. When
Mateo returned, he picked up his miniature chair from the
side of the couch and set it in front of his food.

"The food may be hot, so make sure you blow on it," Ambrosia warned him.

Ambrosia waited a couple of minutes before placing the
bowl in front of Destiny. She figured the food would be cool

enough for Destiny to eat by then. She spoon-fed Destiny the first couple of mouthfuls after which she set the spoon down and let Destiny feed herself with her fingers. It was messy. Sauce ended up on Destiny's face, hands, and bib; the serving tray and the floor. Ambrosia didn't mind because she knew Destiny was learning self-help skills.

When Mateo and Destiny finished eating, Ambrosia poured them each a glass of milk. After cleaning up the kitchen and turning off the lights there and in the living room, Ambrosia gave the children a bath and put on their pajamas. Mateo insisted on dressing himself, reminding Ambrosia that children are only babies for a season. *They grow up so fast. Too fast. Where has the time gone?* She brushed their teeth before reading them a bedtime story and tucking them into bed. She kissed them good night and turned off the light.

"It's too dark, Mommy," Mateo whimpered.

Ambrosia smiled and plugged in the nightlight. It wasn't too bright, but it illuminated the room enough to keep the boogeyman away.

"Is that better?"

"Mm-hmm."

"I love you. Sleep tight. Don't let the bed bugs bite."

She left the door ajar and went into her bedroom. She left a trail of clothing: shoes, shirt, bra, jeans, and panties leading from the bedroom to the master bathroom. By the time she got to the shower, she was ready to step in.

When she finished, she went back into her bedroom and pulled out an extra-large T-shirt and panties from the dresser drawer to sleep in. She preferred comfort over lingerie. Then she walked back into the bathroom where she washed her face and brushed her teeth.

Ambrosia was enervated. She sat on her bed and contemplated resuming a nasty habit that she had successfully kicked six months ago. The cancer sticks hidden in the nightstand next to her bed seemed to be calling her name.

It was hard for her to resist, considering how those long, slow drags used to calm her nerves. Or at least that was what she thought.

Ambrosia thought she must've been imagining things. She could clearly see a devil dressed in red with horns and a pitch-fork sitting on the left of her telling her to go for it. "Smoke that cigarette." On her right, a winged angel dressed in white with a halo advised, "Don't do it." Ambrosia rubbed her eyes and said to no one in particular, "I must really be tired." The illusions went away, and she decided to leave the cigarettes alone. She had come too far. *Besides, if I developed lung or throat cancer because of smoking, who would take care of Mateo and Destiny?* As far as she was concerned, no one could take better care of her children than she could. She wasn't about to do anything that would take her away from them.

She turned on the TV and turned off the light. There was nothing on that she wanted to watch. She turned down the volume and exhaled. She wondered how she had ended up here; "here" being twenty-three years old and unmarried with two children. If someone had told her that this would be her life, she would've told them they were crazy.

She had attended a Catholic high school and graduated with honors. Her freshman year at Auburn University in Alabama, she was a cheerleader. All of that changed when she came to Atlanta with some girlfriends—Mitzi, Barbi and Charlotte—to hang out at some clubs. That's when she met Laron. Back then she thought they were destined to be together. He was the first and only black guy she ever dated. In fact, he was her first and only lover. He pursued her for months, calling her long distance, writing letters, and visiting her in Alabama. He even paid for her transportation and lodging whenever she visited him in Atlanta.

Laron treated her like a queen. He bought her expensive gifts and took her to upscale restaurants. She waited several months before becoming intimate with him. Initially, she wanted to wait until marriage before having sex because she was a devout Catholic. She had been taught in church that sex outside of marriage was a sin. She had also read First Corinthians 6:18 which states, "Shun immorality and all sexual looseness. Any other sin which a man commits is one outside the body, but he who commits sexual immorality sins against his own body." But, she had fallen in love with him. And he said he loved her, too. The timing seemed right.

Not long afterward, she became pregnant with Mateo. Laron insisted she move to Atlanta to be with him. Laron seemed happy about the baby. She thought they were going to get married, and Laron promised her they would. So Ambrosia dropped out of school and moved into an apartment Laron got for her in Chamblee.

Ambrosia thought that she and Laron were going to live together. She had no idea that Laron was already married. She was hurt and angry when he didn't move in. Laron explained to her that their relationship was out of order. He convinced her that they should wait until they were married before living together.

She was thankful to have a job at a major law firm as a clerk. Her boss liked her, and she was studying to become a paralegal. Ambrosia struggled financially, but she managed. She refused to get on any type of government assistance.

What's that? Ambrosia wondered, listening attentively. Her body tensed and her heartbeat sped up. She could've sworn she'd heard a loud thud come from the children's room. It was probably Mateo, she reasoned. Perhaps he fell on the floor again. He was a wild sleeper and sometimes he ended up out of his bed. Or maybe he had to go to the bathroom. While still in her bed, she looked into the hallway to see if Mateo was going to go into the bathroom, but he didn't. She dismissed it, figuring she had already checked the apartment. If someone had entered from the outside, the alarm would've sounded.

She positioned herself on her side, leaving the TV on with the volume muted, trying to fall asleep.

"Amber," a familiar voice sounded.

Omigod! She didn't know whether to call 911 or get up fighting. *He'd better not have hurt Mateo or Destiny.* Beads of sweat formed on her forehead and her heart raced. She grabbed the butcher knife that she kept securely tucked underneath her pillow and hopped out of bed. If she had to, she was prepared to slay the "boogeyman."

CHAPTER FIVE

Kevin

Kevin James drove his Range Rover up I-20, heading toward Decatur, feeling as if his world were spinning out of control. He knew he shouldn't have broken into Amber's apartment, but he thought he had no choice. Amber had stopped taking his calls, and he was tired of leaving messages. Besides, he wanted to apologize for hitting her. That wasn't him. He wasn't a batterer. Never before had he hit a woman. It was just that when she threatened to take him to court for child support, he lost it. He couldn't figure out what would've made her do that. It's not like he didn't take care of his children. Whatever they needed, he got it. He paid half of their tuition at the expensive Christian daycare that Amber just had to put Mateo and Destiny in. He even paid for Mateo's uniforms.

To Kevin, being ordered by a court to pay child support meant that he wasn't doing his job as a father. He didn't want that stigma attached to him. Especially since it wasn't true. Not only did he voluntarily and consistently pay child support, he was actively involved in Mateo and Destiny's lives. Kevin was convinced that whomever Amber was listening to was giving her bad advice, because he was not a deadbeat dad.

His cell phone vibrated. He checked caller ID, and it was his wife.

"Hello," he said, adjusting the earpiece to fit more snuggly in his ear.

"Where are you?"

"I'm on my way home. Whassup?"

"Nothing. I was wondering, you know, where you were."

"Well, I'm not that far away."

He was about to hang up when he heard, "I love you."

"Yeah, love you, too," Kevin replied. Then he hung up and felt guilty. What would Gabriella do if she knew he had a secret life? She didn't deserve that. And what about his children with Gabriella? He was convinced that if his wife ever found out he had tipped around on her, it would be like soup on a piece of bread—a hot mess. He couldn't let that happen. That's why he needed to talk some sense into Amber.

He picked up the phone and dialed Amber's number. It rang a couple of times before she answered. He let out a sigh of relief.

"Amber, don't hang up."

"What do you want?"

"I just wanted to thank you for not calling the police on me."

"For what? Kicking my behind or breaking into my house?"

"Both. I know you probably hate me, and I understand. A black man arrested for anything ain't no joke. Let alone a domestic disturbance with a white woman. You're a good person, and I never should've laid a finger on you. I'm sorry."

"Whatever."

"Come on, don't act like that. I told you before I know

too many brothas who've lost their livelihood because they couldn't stop their women from calling the police. I want you to know it means something to me that you didn't do that. I owe you."

Amber sighed and said, "I have to go."

"Wait, you still love me?" The phone clicked. "Amber . . . Amber?"

He checked the display and it stated that the call had disconnected. *I know she didn't just hang up on me!* He was tempted to call her back but didn't want to press his luck. Heat rose in his cheeks. He flung the phone on the seat and pressed his right foot on the gas pedal.

Kevin parked his car in the garage of his three-bedroom home in Decatur. Before going inside, he sat quietly, reflecting on his current state. *Why did I allow myself to get involved with Amber in the first place?* He shook his head and took his keys out of the ignition.

"Hey, you," Gabriella greeted once he was inside the house.

He kissed her on the cheek.

"Hi, Daddy," Kevin, Jr. said as he sat doing homework at the white-tiled kitchen table that was trimmed in wood.

"What's up, little man? How was school?" Kevin asked as he took a container of apple juice from the refrigerator and poured himself a glass.

"Okay."

"Whatchu working on?"

"Math."

After drinking his juice, Kevin walked over to his son and said, "I know you don't like math, but pay attention, son. Math is one of the most important classes you can take. That and English." Then he patted his son on the back. He turned to face Gabriella and asked, "Where's Imani?"

"Sleeping."

He checked his watch. "It's only eight o'clock."

"She had a tummy ache and fell asleep."

"Oh."

He went upstairs and checked on their daughter. She was sleeping peacefully in her princess-style bedroom. *She looks like an angel*, he thought. His eyes became wet. *How could I have been so selfish? You deserve a better man for a father than me. I'm so sorry, baby*. He bent down and kissed her on the forehead. Noticing that she must've removed her covers, he pulled the sheet neatly to her chest and left.

The following morning, Kevin left his house earlier than usual. He had a breakfast meeting at the Waffle House with Donovan, his best friend.

"Whassup, dude?" Kevin said to Donovan as they shook hands.

"Nothing much, man. Just hanging. You know."

The smell of eggs and bacon cooking on the grill filled their nostrils. Having seated themselves in a booth, they could hear meat sizzling on the stainless steel appliance as the cook—dressed in a white hat, shirt, pants and apron—flipped and scrambled the food. When the waitress arrived at their table, they both ordered scrambled cheese eggs, grits, bacon, raisin toast, and orange juice.

"Thanks for meeting up with me," Kevin said. "I got so much craziness going on."

"No problem. What's going on?"

"First, you gotta swear you won't tell Sky."

"Come on, man."

"Nah. This ain't negotiable."

Kevin hated putting Donovan in this predicament, but he needed someone to confide in. There was no one he trusted more than Donovan.

"Fine."

The elderly black waitress returned with two glasses of OJ. "Your order will be up shortly," she promised, placing two straws on the table.

"Thanks," they said automatically.

Before Kevin said anything else, he looked around the restaurant as if double-checking to make sure he didn't see anyone else he knew. "I messed up." He sighed loudly. "I've been cheating on Gabby."

"Aw man, why?"

"I . . . I . . . I . . . don't . . . know . . . why."

"Come on, man. That's weak. You're as crooked as scoliosis. You know why you did it."

They hardly noticed when the waitress returned and set their plates down. She must've noticed the intensity of their conversation and left quietly.

"When I first met Gabby, she was everything I wanted in a woman. Pretty. Sexy. Liked the same things I liked. And she thought like a dude. She was cool. Not like any other woman I had ever met. She wasn't even jealous. We used to go to the strip club together and just chill. After we had Jr., she started changing. Always tired . . . too tired for me."

"Come on, man. Give the woman a break. She had your baby."

"I know. You know how hard it is to admit you were jealous of your own child? I feel bad enough."

"Is that when you started having an affair?" Donovan ate a forkful of food.

Kevin shook his head. "Nah. Cheating on my wife was the farthest thing from my mind. I never wanted to be one of those brothas running around on his old lady. That wasn't me. It wasn't until after we had Imani that things started going downhill. Gabby lost interest in sex. And when we did get down, she didn't want to go down. That messed me up."

"Dang, man. It's like that?"

"Yeah, it's like that. A brotha's needs weren't being met. Gabby treated me like I didn't mean jack. Everything was about the kids. All she talked about were what the kids did, what the kids needed, and what we were going to do with the kids. There was no more us. It wouldn't have been so bad if Gabby had acted like she still wanted there to be an us, but she didn't. My needs came after Jr.'s and Imani's. No man wants to feel like he's at the bottom of his wife's priority list."

"So you're blaming Gabby for you having an affair?"

Kevin raised his brows. "I'm not blaming her. I'm just trying to explain to you how it happened." He nibbled on a strip of bacon.

"Oh, all right."

"The night I met Amber, my whole life changed." He shook his head. "She was gorgeous and fine. Dude, she was a white girl wit' a sistah booty. Blessed in the chest and face like a glamour model. I was like . . . 'what?' I know it was wrong, but I had to push up on her. The girl was baaad."

"Did you tell her you were married?"

He shook his head. "Nah. I didn't tell her."

"Man, that's foul."

"I know I shoulda told her, but I didn't think she'd get with me if she knew. She's classy, ya know? She was in college. And a virgin."

Donovan choked on his orange juice.

"Dude, you all right?" Kevin asked.

"Yeah. It just went down the wrong way."

"Anyway, I felt bad about deceiving Amber, and Gabby too, for that matter. I could hardly stand to look at myself in the mirror. Every time I did, I saw my father's reflection staring back at me."

"Huh?"

"Dude, my dad was a straight playa back in the day. He used to cheat on Moms left and right. The jacked up part is that Moms knew about it. Back then, women stood by their men. When I got older, I asked Moms why she stayed with Pops when she knew he was cheating. You know what she said?" He paused and continued. "She said, 'I stayed with your daddy because I took my vows seriously. When I got married, it was for life. And I wasn't going to let some woman take away my husband and my children's father.' Dude, that messed me up! I was like . . . 'whoa.' "

"So, are they still together?"

"Yep, but not in the traditional sense. See, after all the kids left the house, my parents separated. Or should I say Pops bounced. Even then, Moms refused to give him a divorce. They're legally married, living separate lives at different residences."

"That's deep, man."

Kevin lowered his voice and said, "All my life I wanted to be a better husband and father than Pops. And look at me . . . I'm no better than he is. Like father, like son."

"It doesn't have to be like that. You can still turn this around."

"Nah, dude. I'm in too deep."

"Whatchu mean?"

Sighing loudly, Kevin confessed, "Me and Amber got kids."

"What? Man, I know I didn't just hear you say you and Amber got kids. Plural? With an 's'?"

Kevin lowered his head. "You heard right."

"Aw, man. What were you thinking?"

"I got caught up. When I first got with Amber, I planned to hit it and quit it. Then when I found out she was a virgin . . ."

"You got whipped and lost your mind."

"Guilty as charged. I broke all the rules. Fell in love. Stopped using protection. At one point, I even thought about leaving Gabby to be with Amber."

"What stopped you?"

"You know Gabby. She would've straight flipped. Probably would've taken Jr. and Imani to Sweden. I never would've seen any of them ever again. I couldn't deal with that. I love my kids more than anything."

"How many kids do you and Amber have?"

"Two—a son and a daughter."

"How old are they?"

"They are three and one."

Donovan placed his fork on his clean plate and covered his face with his hands. Dropping his hands, he said, "What're you going to do?"

The waitress interrupted them by taking their plates and asking them if they wanted anything else. When they said, "no," she placed a bill on the table and left.

"Until recently, I didn't really have to worry about that," Kevin said. "But lately Amber's been talking to someone. I don't know who it is, but I wish I did. They've been giving her bad advice: telling her to break up with me and put me on court-ordered child support."

"I understand how you feel and why you'd think that was bad advice. But man, I gotta tell you, that's the best thing for her. You're not going to leave Gabby, are you?"

"No. But if she finds out, she'll leave me."

"You never know. If you cut off your intimate relationship with Amber, maybe you can work on your marriage. As long as you're still involved with Amber, you and Gabby don't stand a chance."

"You're right."

"Right now, you're being selfish. You want to have your cake and eat it too. You can't do that. If you care anything at all about this Amber, you gotta let her go. She deserves to be happy with a man who is free to love her. I know that's not what you want for her, but that's real. And as far as Gabby goes, you'd better start rekindling those romantic flames."

Kevin nodded his head.

"Man, is this your first affair?" Donovan said.

"Yes."

"I can only imagine what you're going through, but I got your back. Whenever you need to talk, I'm here." Donovan checked his watch. "I hate to leave you, but I have a meeting with marketing this morning."

"I understand. It's cool."

They left a tip on the table and walked up to the register to pay their tabs. As Kevin drove to work, he thought about Amber. He really cared about her and he blamed himself for ruining her life. Even though she assured him that her kids were the best things that ever happened to her, he still felt guilty for impregnating her out of wedlock. He regretted that they'd probably never get married.

Then Kevin thought about the day he received a notice at his job informing him that he had to appear in court because he was being sued for child support. His hands gripped the steering wheel. He remembered how angry he became. It angered him because his life with Gabriella was in danger. He knew it was foolish to think that he could keep his double life hidden indefinitely, but he could hope. Once the anger subsided, hurt seeped in. He never imagined Amber to be the vindictive type, and he thought they had an understanding. The court order caught him completely off guard. He was so upset that he confronted Amber. He knew that he should've waited until he calmed down, but he needed answers.

If he could take back what happened on that fateful day, he would. The children were visiting Amber's mother. He showed up at Amber's apartment intending to talk. Instead, they started yelling and things spiraled out of control. Amber pushed him and punched him in the chest. As a reflex, Kevin hit her in the eye. The moment it happened, he regretted it. He apologized profusely. When he tried to reach out to her, she turned away, tripped, and fell. Somehow she bit her lip. She blamed him for that, too. She cussed him out and called him everything but a child of God. His hands were trembling and sweat stained his shirt. All he could imagine was Amber calling the cops and the clinking sounds of handcuffs around his wrists. The scathing look in her eyes was more than he could bear. For the first time since he had known Amber, he saw hatred in her eyes. She might as well have doused him with acid. That's how painful it was for him.

Kevin snapped out of his reflective state when he felt a burning sensation in the pit of his stomach. It was his ulcer flaring up. Ever since he'd been living a double life, his health had begun to deteriorate. In addition to the ulcer, he suffered from high blood pressure and bouts of insomnia. He grabbed a bottle of Pepcid AC, which he left on the passenger seat, and drank straight from the container. He wiped his mouth with the back of his hand. *What am I doing? Amber or Gabby? Gabby or Amber? Who's it going to be?*

CHAPTER SIX

Monday

"Why, Alexis? Why?" Monday Jackson pleaded to her daughter. The walls of the family room seemed to be closing in on her. She stood up, hoping that would help the air flow to her brain.

"Mom, I never liked school," Alexis declared, smacking her chewing gum.

"How could you drop out of high school and not tell me?"

Monday's eyes welled with tears.

"I'ma get my GED."

"A GED? What about college?"

"I'm not going to college. I like doing hair. I wanna be a beautician."

"You still need to go to school for that."

Monday was at a loss for words. She had such high hopes and dreams for Alexis; yet Alexis refused to follow the script. Why wouldn't she listen? Didn't she realize that life was already hard enough without adding high school dropout to her credentials? Monday had a feeling that there was more going on than Alexis was telling her.

Wiping the tears streaming down her face, Monday asked, "What's really going on?"

"What do you mean?"

"Why do you really want to drop out of school? Does this have anything to do with your boyfriend, Derrick?"

"No. It's not about Derrick. Mom, I already told you. I don't like school." Alexis averted her eyes from her mother and said, "The kids pick at me."

Monday sat on the couch, wrapped her arms around Alexis's shoulders and held her close. Both of them cried.

"Baby," Monday said, "let me tell you something." She wiped her daughter's wet face, looked her in the eyes and said, "You're beautiful. There's nothing wrong with you."

Monday felt a twinge in the pit of her stomach. She felt responsible for what Alexis was going through. Had she not allowed her daughter to stay up late at night eating comfort foods with her whenever Monday was having man problems, perhaps Alexis wouldn't be forty pounds overweight. And maybe if Alexis hadn't eaten the wrong foods, she wouldn't have such bad acne.

She patted Alexis's head and said, "Baby, I hafta go to work. We'll talk about this later."

"Okay."

While driving in her Ford Focus, Monday couldn't stop crying. She felt like such a failure. *I'm a terrible parent. I can't even get my child through high school. How bad is that? What am I doing? Why am I going into a job that I can't stand? I don't feel like seeing those people. They get on my nerves. I hate my life.*

Sniffling snot and blinking away tears, Monday dialed Reggie's number. She hoped he'd make her feel better.

His voice mail answered. "Hey, it's Reggie. Leave a message."

Frustrated, she hung up. She didn't know why she wanted to talk to Reggie anyway. It's not like he was really her boyfriend. She wasn't even sure he cared about her. He had really been acting up lately. When they first got together, he was all compliments and seemed happy to spend time with her. As soon as she had sex with him, he hardly called her. She called him so much she felt like a stalker. Like most of the guys she had been involved with, he was probably seeing someone else. The signs were there, but she didn't want to admit it. He didn't call when he said he was going to call. He didn't come over when he said he was going to come over. When Reggie did see her, it was usually because she had to beg him to do it. She hated feeling like a booty call. It was as if she were at Reggie's mercy for sex simply because she was overweight and not attractive enough to be seen with during the daytime.

Whenever Monday made up her mind that she was going to leave Reggie alone, he'd come calling. "What's up, baby?" he'd ask. She knew his game; yet a part of her was vulnerable to him. She knew she deserved better. Or at least that's what her friends told her. All of her friends were skinny. They didn't have problems attracting men. Now, keeping them was a different story. Whenever she went out with her girls, she was the "fat girl." Admittedly, she wanted a better man, but men weren't exactly beating down her door.

Monday arrived thirty minutes late for her job as a manager at the phone company. She didn't even care. She went to her cubicle and didn't greet any of her subordinates as she usually did. Her computer booted up slowly.

" 'Bout time you showed up," Shanika, another manager, observed.

"Whatever, girl." Monday sucked air through her teeth. "You know I don't care nothing about this job."

"Keep your voice down."

As Shanika slid into the chair next to Monday's desk, Monday caught a whiff of the musty smell of cigarette smoke emanating from Shanika's clothes. It caused Monday to cough.

"Why?" Monday said. "I don't care who hears me. Shoot!"

"What's wrong with you this morning?"

"Girl, what's not wrong? Alexis told me she dropped out of school."

"What? Why she do that?"

"It don't even matter. I'm so outdone. I don't feel like talking about it or I'll start crying again. Anyway, what's up with you?"

"I got a date with this guy I met at the gym."

"For real? That's good." Monday feigned enthusiasm. Even though Shanika was her homegirl, it was hard to get excited about a possible new relationship for her when Monday's relationship was all screwed up.

"Excuse me, ladies," said Kyle, one of Monday's team members.

Monday and Shanika looked at him.

"What you want, Kyle?" Monday snapped. "You see me in here talking."

"I'm sorry to interrupt you, but did you want me to pass out the sales reports to the rest of the team?"

"Have you pulled them already?"

"Yes."

"Go ahead then. Thanks."

He turned away and left. Kyle was one of Monday's team members on the track to management. He was always looking for ways to help out, trying to take the initiative. One of the characteristics of a good manager, Monday had told him. Monday relied on him a lot more than she should have. Kyle did everything Monday didn't feel like doing and then some. He practically ran the team.

"I'll talk to you later," Shanika said.

"All right."

In between visitors, Monday spent most of the morning surfing the Internet. She hated being in the office. The only aspect that made it more tolerable was socializing with her co-workers. People always seemed to come to her for advice. She couldn't figure that part out, knowing how screwed up her own life was. But she listened and offered whatever constructive criticism she could muster.

Monday was glad to leave work early. She looked forward to her appointment with Skyler. It was one of the few bright spots in her day. *How pathetic is this?* The only thing she had to look forward to was talking to a shrink.

CHAPTER SEVEN

Skyler

"Ambrosia, are you ready to talk?"

"Yes."

We sat in my office drinking peppermint tea that Yahkie had brought for us. I noticed that her bruises were fading. She looked a lot better than the past couple of times I had seen her. Ambrosia proceeded to tell me about Laron breaking into her apartment, and the physical altercation she had with him regarding court-ordered child support. She explained that she was having doubts as to whether or not she had taken the right action in regards to pursuing the matter through the court system.

"Let me tell you something," I said. "Even though Laron takes care of his children financially, the fact still remains that he's a married man. Child support isn't about you. It's about the well-being of your children. You have to protect their interests. A lot of men take care of their children when they're in relationships with the mothers. As soon as they break up, a lot of those men break out. Those women find out the hard way that collecting child support becomes quite difficult. I don't want to see you in that situation."

"Dr. Little," Ambrosia said slowly with her eyes looking down in shame, "I ended up withdrawing my petition."

"Why did you do that?" I scrunched up my face.

"Because after I had a chance to think about it, I didn't wanna make it seem like Laron wasn't a good father, like he didn't take care of his kids."

"All right. That's not permanent. You can go always go back and open up a new claim. But what about him breaking into your home and subsequently hitting you?"

"I pushed him. Had I not provoked him, he never would've hit me. He's not the violent type. He's never hit me before."

I bit the left corner of my lip. I couldn't believe Ambrosia was sitting here defending Laron's actions. If she continued down this path, she'd end up right back in his arms.

"I hear you. Now I want you to hear me." The words spewed from my mouth. "The day you came into my office bruised and battered, you were terrified. You were a mere shell. Fragile. Vulnerable. That man scared the living daylights out of you. Previously, we agreed that you were going to end the affair. Right?"

"Mm-hmm." She nodded her head and sipped some tea.

"You were supposed to get court-ordered child support so that you wouldn't have to deal with him and you could establish visitation. Is that what we agreed upon?"

"Yes."

"And when you went through with it, he attacked you."

"He didn't attack me. I told you that."

"Fine. He reacted in an unexpected manner. Leaving you with a black eye. The police weren't called because you didn't want the father of your children to go to jail. Is that right?"

"Right."

"What about when he broke into your apartment? Weren't you scared?"

She shifted in her seat. "I was terrified."

"I'd imagine so."

"But he didn't hurt me or the kids. He didn't raise his voice and he didn't lay a finger on me."

I nodded and took a sip of tea. The smell of peppermint entertained my olfactory senses.

"Dr. Little, I know you think I'm softening up on him, but I'm not. He's outta my life. I'm not gonna take him back. Trust me. I can handle him."

I raised a brow and gave her a dubious look. I could tell she had made up her mind, and I hoped she had followed through. We sat silently for a few minutes, draining our cups. The timer buzzed, alerting us that the session was over. We prayed, and she left.

As soon as Ambrosia left, Yahkie stood at my door.

"Boss lady, you okay?"

"Yes, I'm fine." I exhaled.

"Meeting with Ambrosia upset you, huh?"

"A little."

Yahkie walked in and sat down. "It don't do any good to get upset about these women."

"Don't start."

He shooed his hand and kept talking. "I remember when I was eighteen years old. Stephanie, my older sister, had a boyfriend who hit her. She came to my momma's house all upset. Hysterical. Me and Darius, my younger brother, went to find that Negro. And when we did, we put a hurtin' on him. Now, here we go thinkin' we did the right thing: protecting our sister's honor. When Stephanie found out what we did, do you know what that heifer did?"

"No, what?"

"She cussed me and Darius out from sun up to sun down. Told us to mind our business. Said we shouldn't have gotten involved." He sucked air between his teeth. "I wanted to tell Stephanie that the next time she gets her behind whooped, not to come around us. Keep her behind home if she don't want nobody helpin' her. Well, you know what my momma told me and Darius?"

"No."

"She said, 'Y'all were right to want to help your sister. But y'all need to remember that blood may be thicker than water, but . . .' " Yahkie paused. "How can I say this tactfully? You're a doctor; you know what's thicker than blood." He burst out laughing, and I did, too. He stood up and said, "The worst thing a woman can do is to start feeling sorry for a man. Once she does that . . . humph . . . she can forget about it. He got her then."

Yahkie went back to his desk, and I thought about what he said. I checked my watch and noticed that I had enough time to grab a bite to eat before my appointment with Monday. I went out and picked up a grilled chicken salad and ate it at my desk.

After I finished eating, I went into the bathroom and brushed my teeth. Then I smeared a coat of lipstick across my lips.

"Monday's here," Yahkie announced over the intercom.

"Thanks. Send her back."

We exchanged pleasantries. A smile was etched across her face, but her eyes seemed sad.

"How are things going?" I asked.

"All right."

"What does 'all right' mean?"

Her eyes became wet. "Sky, I don't know how much more I can take."

"What's wrong?"

"Alexis. She . . . she dropped out of high school."

"Your daughter?" I leaned in toward her with right my hand resting on my chin.

"Yeah." She blinked and a couple of tears escaped.

"Why?"

Monday began to sob uncontrollably. I handed her a box of Kleenex. She dabbed her face and explained to me that she felt responsible for Alexis's self-esteem issues. She told me that Alexis was overweight and suffered from acne. Even though she had taken her to a dermatologist, Alexis still had breakouts.

"Monday, you are the adult here. You have the authority to make Alexis stay in school. Not only that, you're bound legally to see that she goes."

"But she's eighteen." She blew her nose.

"That doesn't matter. Enroll her in an alternative school. She's living in your house; therefore, she needs to be in school."

"I'll check into it." She wiped her nose and held the tissue in her hand.

"What are Alexis's talents? Her interests?"

"She likes to do hair."

"Well, if another school isn't possible or Alexis gives up and starts getting poor grades for spite, then there's always a bright side. *Any* education or training is a plus. She could go to school to become a cosmetologist. Just because Alexis dropped out of high school doesn't make you a bad parent. And it doesn't mean that her life is over either. Alexis can get a GED and take up a trade. Becoming a beautician is a noble profession with a lot of possibilities. Not only can she become a fabulous hairstylist, she can also learn how to do makeup. Who knows? She could become a celebrity stylist. There's big bucks in that. Not to mention the fact that she could one day own her own salon, making her an entrepreneur. So you don't have anything to feel bad about. Children are going to make mistakes. You just have to be there for her and give her Godly guidance when she needs it."

"Hearing you explain alternatives doesn't make it seem so bad."

I smiled.

Monday proceeded to tell me about her job and how much she hated it. She told me that she got her job dishonestly. Both she and her friend, Shanika, applied for jobs at the phone company. Shanika got scheduled for an interview, but Monday didn't. After successfully completing the initial screening process, Shanika was scheduled for training. Since Monday knew the date, time, and location of the training, she attended. When the training instructor advised Monday that her name wasn't on the list, Monday offered that there must've been a mistake, and added her own name to the list. That was four years ago. Since then Monday had been promoted from sales rep to sales manager.

I was speechless. Monday had chutzpah.

I gathered my thoughts and said, "Do you think the way you got your job has any bearing on why you don't like it?"

"I don't know. I never thought about it."

"Perhaps on a subconscious level you don't feel like you deserve to be there. Do you ever worry about being discovered?"

"I used to. I don't really think about it anymore. Now I just feel more like I'm not doing what I was called to do. I wake up feeling like 'what's the point?' You know?"

"Yes. I do know. You're feeling displaced. Unfulfilled. Monday, do you ever pray?"

"Mm-hmm. I pray."

"Do you believe in what you pray for?"

"I think so."

I nodded my head. "What's your passion?"

"You know, I've been thinking about that. I'm not sure, though."

I explained to Monday that she needed to pray and ask the Lord to reveal her purpose. I also told her to start keeping a journal to help her focus her thoughts and desires. She said she would go and buy a notebook. By the time our session concluded, I felt optimistic. Monday seemed to genuinely appreciate the advice I had given her about Alexis, as well as the idea to keep the journal.

Gabriella called me on my cell phone before I left the office to find out if we could meet at Starbucks in Stone Mountain, a suburb of Atlanta. I agreed. I called Donovan and told him that he should pick up dinner for us on his way home because I was meeting Gabriella. He understood.

Gabriella and I hugged when we saw each other.

"Nice to see you," I said.

"You too."

The restaurant wasn't crowded. We ordered two mochas. I heard a machine grinding coffee beans behind the counter. The smell of freshly brewed coffee permeated the air. We paid for our hot drinks and sat at a table for two.

"How are things going?" I asked.

She sighed. "I'm ready to talk to Kevin about my suspicions. I want to hear what he has to say."

I didn't say anything. I took a sip of java.

She ran her fingers through her hair, head tilted to the side, and said, "Kevin has been spending more time at home with me and the kids, and that's great. I'm glad he's home more. But, I still need answers."

"Of course." I nodded my head.

"I hope he tells me the truth, because I could not stand it if he lied." She took a sip of her drink.

I understood her plight and prayed that she and Kevin

would resolve their marital issues. "You know I'm here for you. If you need me, you can call me anytime."

She smiled knowingly. After we finished our mochas, we hugged again and left. In the car, I had an uneasy feeling in the pit of my stomach. I knew that something was wrong. I prayed silently for Gabriella and Kevin.

CHAPTER EIGHT
Gabriella

"Hey, baby," Kevin said, giving Gabriella a kiss on the lips as she entered the house.

Kevin told her that he had already fed the children dinner and had given them a bath. She was pleased. For so long, she had felt like a single parent. Usually, Kevin spent so much time at work and hanging out with friends that she had to do everything for Jr and Imani herself. Sometimes she was so tired and overwhelmed. She was glad to be able to come home, kick her shoes off, and relax for a moment.

"Hey." She kissed him back and thanked him for tending to the kids. Then she walked into the family room where her children were watching TV and hugged and kissed them.

"How was your day you two?" Gabriella asked.

"Good," they said in unison.

Gabriella asked if they had done their homework and they both said, "yes." She went upstairs to take a shower and get ready for bed. About thirty minutes later, she went back downstairs. She wanted to spend some time with her children before they turned in for the evening, so they watched TV together. At nine o'clock, Jr and Amani went to bed. Gabriella turned off the TV and she and Kevin went upstairs to their bedroom.

"We need to talk," Gabriella said to Kevin. She could tell by his expression that he dreaded hearing those words.

He sighed. "About what?"

She pulled out a piece of paper from her purse and handed it to him. He unfolded the paper and his eyes bucked.

"Are you having an affair?" Gabriella said, eyes glaring at him.

He crumpled up the paper and tossed it on the floor.

"It doesn't matter what I say. You've already made up your mind," Kevin said defensively.

Gabriella's eyes became misty. "That's not true. Tell me. Are you cheating on me?"

Kevin held her in his arms and stroked her hair. "No, baby." She sobbed in his chest. "Baby, I love you," he assured.

She cried harder and pulled away from him. "What about the letter and the messages? I heard her, Kevin! I don't understand why you do this. Tell me the truth!" Gabriella demanded.

"Baby! Baby, that girl is crazy! She's mad because I won't get with her. She knows I'm married. She leaves those jacked up messages hoping you'll listen to them."

"Why would she do that? I don't understand. That makes no sense to me."

"I don't know why. I put her in check and told her to stop."

"Did she?"

"Yep." He planted kisses on her forehead, cheeks, and then her lips. "Baby." He kissed her lips again. "You're the only woman I want. I love you."

He wouldn't cheat on me. She wanted to believe him. *Why would he? He said I'm everything he wants.*

He kissed away her tears and picked her up. Gabriella felt safe in his strong, muscular arms. He placed her on the bed and made love to her. All the while, he reassured her that he loved her and that she was the most beautiful woman in the world to him.

Gabriella let out a slight moan. "I love you, Kevin Laron James," she said.

CHAPTER NINE

Monday

It was Friday evening. Monday had gone to the gym to work out. She was determined to lose weight. Her mind was made up. She planned to go on a diet and stick with it. *Maintain a workout regimen and stick with it!* She was on her way home when her cell phone rang.

"Hello," Monday said in a breathy tone.

"Hey. Whatchu up to?" Reggie said.

"I'm just now leaving the gym." She used the keyless remote to unlock her car door. She threw her bag on the back seat.

"You going home?"

"Mm-hmm. Why you wanna know?" She placed her key in the ignition and cranked the car.

"Can I come over?"

She paused, pretending to think it over. "Sure. What time?"

"Gimme an hour."

"That's kinda soon, but okay."

They ended the call. Monday couldn't wait to see Reggie.

She was glad that he called her instead of it being the other way around. Maybe he was finally coming around.

When Monday got home, Alexis wasn't there, and the house wasn't clean. Monday wiped off the kitchen counter-tops and put the dirty dishes in the dishwasher. She ran the vacuum over the carpet in the family room. The pillows on the couch seemed flat, so she fluffed them. She placed the junk mail and bills cluttering the coffee table into the island drawer in the kitchen. Then she went upstairs and made up her bed.

After that, she took off her sweat clothes that fit a bit too snugly. She laughed when she thought about her high-water sweat pants. *Who cares? I'm not trying to impress nobody.* Then she took a shower. Her legs seemed a little hairy, so she shaved them. She got out of the shower and generously lotioned her body. She slipped into sexy, black laced lingerie, put on light makeup, and styled her hair into a bun.

Monday went into the kitchen and poured herself a glass of white zinfandel. She sipped the wine as she patiently waited for Reggie. Two hours passed before Monday dialed Reggie's digits. First she called his cell phone: no answer. Then she called his home phone: no answer. *Where is he?*

Thirty minutes later, she called his cell phone again, and left a message. By the time three hours had passed, Monday was in tears. "Why does he keep doing this to me?" she pleaded with a higher power. She drained the entire bottle of wine and couldn't stop crying. She wasn't hungry, but she popped some popcorn and added extra butter. The DVD *Phat Chickz* was already in the DVD player, so she turned it on and watched the movie. She liked that movie because she could relate.

"That's right, Mo'Nique," she slurred. "Go. Get. Yo. Man."

Not long afterward, she fell asleep on the couch. She never heard from Reggie.

CHAPTER TEN

Kevin

Kevin woke up feeling guilty—like a real jerk. As Gabriella lay next to him sleeping peacefully, he watched her chest rise. *I should've told her.* His eyes became misty as he leaned back on the pillow. He rubbed his hand over his face and exhaled. He considered waking her up and confessing to his affair.

"Dude, are you crazy?" a little voice inside his head admonished him. "If you tell her, you'll break her heart. She doesn't deserve that. You screwed up, so you fix it."

How can I fix it?

He eased his way out of bed, trying not to disturb Gabriella, and put on a T-shirt and lounge pants. Then he went into the bathroom and took a leak. Afterward, he washed his hands, brushed his teeth, and took some Pepcid. His stomach was bothering him. He figured that if Jr. and Imani weren't already awake, they would be soon, so he went downstairs and cooked scrambled eggs, grits, and bacon for breakfast.

"Good morning, Daddy," Imani said as she tugged at his pajama bottoms.

"Morning, love. Did you sleep well?" he said, giving his daughter a hug.

"Yes."

"Are you hungry?"

She nodded her head and smiled.

"Where's your brother?"

"He's still in the bed."

"Go get him." He patted her back, shooing her away.

"Okay." She went back upstairs.

Not long afterward, Jr. entered the kitchen with Imani trailing behind him. Kevin finished cooking and prepared three plates of food.

"Morning, Jr.," Kevin said. "Here." He handed him and Imani each a plate.

Kevin carried his plate as he led his children to the dining room table. He took a bite of eggs, and Imani interrupted him.

"Wait, Daddy," Imani said. "You didn't say grace."

"Oh, oh," Kevin said, putting down his fork. "Okay, you say it."

Imani and Jr. attended Swedish school on Sundays where they were taught Biblical principles, including prayer. They bowed their heads and closed their eyes. Imani said, "Lord, thank You for this food we're about to receive for the nourishment of our bodies. In Jesus' name, amen."

"Amen," Kevin and Jr. said in unison.

Eating a mouthful of eggs, Kevin looked at Jr. and said, "You got a girlfriend?"

Laughing, Jr. replied, "Nah, Daddy. I don't have a girlfriend."

Imani snickered and corrected, "Yes, you do."

"Shut up," Jr. said. His cheeks turned red.

"Don't talk to your sister like that. Come on now, tell me about this girl."

"She's not really my girlfriend."

"But you like her?" Kevin asked.

Jr. nodded his head and stuffed his mouth with food.

"Told you," Imani said, giggling.

Kevin smirked and continued to eat.

"Something sure smells good in here," Gabriella said, entering the kitchen and looking through the covered pots on the stove.

"Good morning," Kevin, Jr., and Imani said.

Gabriella fixed herself a plate and joined them at the table. Jr. and Imani had nearly finished eating their food and Kevin went back for seconds.

"Do you want juice?" Gabriella asked her children.

"Yes," they both replied.

Gabriella got up and fixed the kids both a glass of apple juice. Kevin stood behind her and wrapped his arms around her waist, resting his hands on her flat stomach. She smiled at him. He leaned over and kissed her on the cheek before releasing her so that she could put the container of juice back in the refrigerator. He grabbed his plate and went back to the table. Gabriella followed and placed the glasses in front of Jr. and Imani.

Before she sat back down, she asked Kevin if he wanted a cup of coffee. He told her that he would start the pot and for her to sit down before her food got cold. She took her seat. Kevin took a few more bites of food before getting up and putting on a pot of coffee. When he returned, he noticed that the children had gulped down their juice and cleaned their plates.

"The food is delicious," Gabriella said. "Thanks for cooking."

"You're welcome."

"Why didn't you wake me up?" Gabriella asked.

"For what? You looked so peaceful sleeping; I didn't want to disturb you."

Gabriella smiled. "What do you guys want to do today?" She looked at Jr., then Imani.

"Go to the mall," Imani suggested.

"Let's go to the park," Jr. said.

"Daddy," Gabriella said, knowing how much Kevin loved to hear her call him that. "What do you want to do today?"

"Hey, it doesn't matter to me. You all decide."

Since Kevin had purchased annual passes to the Georgia Aquarium, the James family spent most of the Saturday there. Jr. and Imani marveled at the 100,000 fish: whale sharks, toothy cubassa snappers, schools of predatory travally jacks, squadrons of small and large stingrays, an enormous grouper, and hammerhead sharks swimming overhead. Jr. joked about them "finding Nemo."

After leaving the aquarium, Kevin treated his family to dinner at Red Lobster. He loved his wife and children more than words could ever express. The thought of losing them because of his own selfish actions caused him to tear up. He blinked hard and fast to fight back the tears. That didn't quite work, so Kevin took a long, deep breath, which seemed to do the trick.

"You all right, Daddy?" Jr. said, sitting next to Imani and across from Kevin and Gabriella.

"I'm fine, son. Just fine." He sipped some ice water. "I was just thinking about how lucky I am." He placed his arm around Gabriella's shoulder and squeezed. "I have two terrific kids and a beautiful wife. What more could a man ask for?"

He wasn't a religious man, but he prayed that the Lord wouldn't strike him dead for saying that he only had two children when he knew full well that he had four. Denying Mateo and Destiny seemed unnatural, especially since he loved them just as much as he did Jr. and Imani. Every time he thought he couldn't sink any lower, he found a way to be more disgusting than gum on the bottom of a shoe.

The waitress arrived carrying a tray filled with steamed lobster, crab legs, and shrimp. The cleaned and deveined lobster was for Kevin. Gabriella had a pound of crab legs while Jr. and Imani ate an assortment of shrimp. Kevin felt a burning sensation in the pit of his stomach, so he removed his arm from around Gabriella's shoulders. He wasn't sure whether it was the ulcer or his guilty conscience. He popped a couple of Pepcid like candy before cracking the shell of the lobster. Hot melted butter trickled down his chin as Kevin devoured the sweet meat.

He realized that he couldn't change his situation at the moment, so he took pleasure in seeing the happy looks on the faces of his family. Thoughts about him being a jerk and living a lie were forced to the back of his mind as he tried to enjoy his succulent meal. Fighting hard to suppress the negative thoughts moving around in his mind like microorganisms under a microscope, Kevin still couldn't help but wonder whether he was loving on borrowed time. He looked over at Gabriella and thought, *I pray you never find out, but God help us if you do.*

CHAPTER ELEVEN

Skyler

Donovan and I went away to Destin, Florida for a romantic weekend. I loved the beautiful, white sandy beach. From the balcony, our condo had a perfect ocean view. We woke up early to watch the sunrise. That and watching the sunset were two of the most serene things I had ever witnessed. Like God bidding you good morning and good night.

After seeing the sunrise, Donovan and I prepared a delicious breakfast of scrambled eggs with red peppers and green peppers, cheese grits, thick cut bacon, French toast, and a side of assorted fruit. We took turns feeding each other as we sat out on the balcony in our bathrobes. I could hear the gentle waves splashing on the beach. The smell of salt water filled the air.

"Baby, I'm so glad we were able to get away," Donovan said.

"Me too." The food tasted so good I licked my lips. "I have something to tell you."

"What? You pregnant?" His face lit up.

"No, no, nothing like that." I shook my head vehemently.

The thought of us having a baby appealed to me because of my love for Donovan. However, the responsibility that comes along with being a mother intimidated me. There was something about being solely responsible for another person that scared me.

"Oh." He seemed disappointed. Even though we hadn't talked about having a baby in a while, judging by his expression, he'd been thinking about it. I was wondering if it was a subject we need to revisit.

"Anyway, Gabriella told me that she's going to confront Kevin about his affair."

He coughed into his fist. Then he wiped his mouth and hand with a napkin.

"Are you all right?" I said.

"Yeah. It went down the wrong way."

I could tell he was lying by the way he raised his brows, causing his forehead to wrinkle. I was curious to find out what he knew.

"Why're you looking at me like that?" He seemed uncomfortable, avoiding direct eye contact.

"Like what?" I eyed him suspiciously.

"You know. Staring at me."

"I was thinking how fortunate I am to have you." I grabbed his hand and held it.

"Yeah, I love you, too." He smirked.

"Donovan," I said seriously, looking him in the eye, "would you ever cheat on me?"

"Baby, I hate when you do that." He set his fork down and gazed directly into my eyes. "Every time one of your friends or clients has a problem, you start analyzing us. I'm committed to you. More than that, you're my ideal woman. When I fantasize about a woman, I see *you*. Whatever I can't get from you, I get from God. So you don't have to worry about my fidelity. I haven't and can't imagine anything or anyone who could ever make me stray."

I placed my hand on top of his. Couples were strolling along the beach hand-in-hand, children were laughing and playing, and seagulls were flying. There was something about the water that seemed so peaceful. It was impossible to be sad in the midst of nature's own meditation fountain.

"That's sweet," I said. "With so many marriages falling apart, sometimes it's hard to feel secure."

He nodded. "I understand, but I'm telling you, me without you is like soul food without hot sauce."

We both laughed.

It was starting to feel a little breezy on the terrace, so we took our empty plates inside and placed them in the kitchen sink. We took off our robes and went back to bed. The queen-sized bed felt quite comfortable. I nestled my head on Donovan's shoulder.

"Honey," I said. "Do you think Kevin and Gabriella's marriage will survive this?"

He let out a deep breath. "Baby, I don't know."

I decided not to probe any deeper because I didn't want to be put in an uncomfortable situation. It was difficult enough knowing that Kevin was having an affair. The fact that my husband knew the particulars was a bit disturbing. Yet, if he informed me of the details, I'd feel obligated to share the facts with Gabriella, which in turn would wreak havoc on all of our relationships. Therefore, I was better off getting my information from Gabriella. At least for right now.

We talked about having children for the umpteenth time. We had more discussions about having children before we got married than since. Neither one of us wanted a big family, but Donovan said he wanted at least two, maybe three. For me, one would be fine. Twins would be ideal. With twins both of us would be satisfied and I'd only have to go through pregnancy once.

Donovan told me that he wanted us to start trying right

away. I was taken aback. I thought we had at least another two years before we started seriously trying to conceive a baby. *Wow, a baby!* The thought tickled me. *I absolutely adore Jr. and Imani. They're my godchildren. I watched them grow up. Perhaps having a baby won't be so bad.* In fact, the more we talked about it, the more I could feel myself getting excited.

CHAPTER TWELVE
Skyler

The sound of a lawnmower jolted me out of my sleep. Nothing seemed to bother Donovan. He slept right through it. I looked outside my bedroom window and saw Reggie Owens, my lawn guy, mowing the lawn. He was earlier than usual. Ordinarily, he'd wait until later in the morning. I slipped on a bathrobe and went into the bathroom to wash my face and brush my teeth. My first appointment was a few hours away, so I went into the kitchen and brewed a pot of coffee. I could hear the lawnmower getting louder and louder. Reggie was working in the backyard. I opened up the backdoor and waved at Reggie. He turned off the mower and walked toward me.

"Mornin', Dr. Little. How you doin'?" Reggie inquired.

"I'm fine. And you?"

"I've been better." With the back of his hand, he wiped the sweat from his brow.

"What's the matter?"

"I need some advice."

Reggie didn't normally discuss his personal business with me. He knew that I was a psychoanalyst but our conversations were usually regarding lawn care and the weather. His shoulders slightly slumped over.

"Do you want to come inside? I made coffee."

"I don't wanna put cha out."

"It's no problem."

He removed his protective eye goggles, and we went inside. We sat at the island in the kitchen, sipping coffee and discussing his issues with women.

"Dr. Little," he said, shaking his head. "I don't get these women. I got this one girl who is real nice. We met at a club, and she seemed cool. We hooked up a few times, and I told her right off the bat that I wasn't looking for a serious relationship. She was cool with that until she thought I was seeing somebody else."

"Were you? Seeing someone else?"

"Yeah. But it shouldn't have mattered. We weren't kickin' it. We were just chillin'. Friends with benefits."

"Reggie, how old are you?"

"Thirty-eight."

"Okay. Let me explain something to you. Women are emotional creatures. Some women use their bodies to gain acceptance from men. Those are the ones who will agree to almost anything just to have a piece of a man they think they want. In your case, your friend agreed to having a sexual relationship with you because she was attracted to you. She most likely thought that by sleeping with you, you'd change your mind and want to have a relationship with her. You need to understand, if you become intimate with the average woman, she's going to develop feelings for you. The deeper her feelings, the less likely she is going to want to share you with anybody else."

"A grown woman should know the game. If a brotha says he just wants to kick it, he just wants to kick it. Don't go flippin' the script after the fact."

"I understand how you feel. It seems simple enough, especially from a man's point of view. Men don't equate sex with love. For men, the two are distinct and different from one another, whereas women don't see it that way. Regardless of what a woman may agree to on a conscious level, on a subconscious level she wants to be loved. Unless a woman is a prostitute, nymphomaniac, or has low self-esteem, she can't hop in and out of bed with men who don't mean anything to her."

"So because she changed her mind, I look like the villain?"

"Not necessarily. If you were honest in the beginning and didn't get your friend into bed under false pretenses, then you're not the villain. Besides, I don't think she set out to fall in love with you. She probably got caught up." I offered a wan smile.

"Ah, man. Love? I'm not wit' it."

"Have you been married before?" I took a sip of hot java.

"Yeah. How did you know?"

"Most people who are down on love have been scorned by it. A bitter divorce or an unfaithful mate can do it."

"I had both. I don't trust women as far as I can spit. No disrespect." He drank his coffee.

"None taken. But let me caution you. It's all right to hurt, but it's not all right to become bitter. You don't want your heart to become hardened. If you do, you'll miss the blessings God has in store for you."

He smiled and nodded his head. "You're all right, doc."

"Thanks. I'm curious, though. What are your intentions for these women?"

"I can't say, 'cause I don't know. The two women are so different from each other. The one that I told you about earlier is like my homegirl. She's there when I need her. Down for whatever. She's a big girl, but she sexy. Know how to make a brotha . . ." He cleared his throat. "Anyway, the other one has been hurt. She got some trust issues going on, too. But she's sweet. She got a good heart. I'm feelin' her."

I nodded. "Seems to me like you've got some decisions to make. I don't believe you want to hurt anyone, so continue being honest with both women. Give them the choice as to whether they play the game or not."

"Will do. Thanks for everything." He went back outside and shortly afterward the lawnmower noise resumed.

"Top of the morning to you, boss lady," Yahkie said from behind his desk as I entered the office.

"Top of the morning. Did you have a nice weekend?"

"I sure did. I finished reading a romantic suspense novel, *Only True Love Waits.* You should check it out. How was your trip to Destin Beach?"

I nodded. "It was wonderful. We watched the sunrise and sunset. You ever seen that before?"

"Yes. It's breathtaking. Simply gorgeous."

"Here." I handed him a souvenir spoon with *Destin, Florida* inscribed on it. He collected spoons whenever he or someone he knew visited a different state.

"Thank you." He looked at the gift and placed it in his desk drawer. "I'm up to thirty-five now."

"Impressive." I smiled and went into my office.

I checked my desk calendar to confirm my upcoming appointment with Monday and read the day's inspirational message: "Where I was born and how I lived is unimportant. It is what I have done with where I have been that should be of interest." I unlocked my desk drawer and removed her folder. Then I quickly reviewed the notes in her file. Monday arrived half an hour later. We prayed before beginning the session.

"Sky, what's wrong with me?"

"Why are you asking me that?"

She started crying. "Why is it so hard for me to find a good man?"

"Did something happen?"

She nodded her head. "I think my boyfriend is cheating on me."

"Really? Why?"

"We were supposed to get together this weekend, and he never showed up. When I tried to call him, he didn't answer. He finally called me Sunday night with some lame excuse: talking about his car was acting up and he was trying to get that taken care of. I knew he was lying."

"How do you know it was a lie?"

"Whatever, Sky. I'm not stupid. He coulda called me. If he really wanted to see me, he woulda asked me to come get him."

I nodded. "What are you going to do about it?"

She shrugged her shoulders. "I mean, what can I do?"

"There's a whole lot you can do. You can stop seeing him. You can make him responsible for his actions. You have options."

"I don't think I'm ready to stop seeing him. I really like Reggie."

Reggie? Humph. Small world. Couldn't be. Not my lawn man.

"Even though he disrespects you?" I said.

"Sky, I don't have a lot of guys trying to get at me since I've put on some weight. Don't get me wrong, I think I'm fly and all that. But I'm realistic. I see how guys treat big girls. They want us in private but not around their friends."

"Monday, there are plenty of men out there who appreciate the beauty and sensuality of a full-figured woman. Case in point, my husband is Jamaican. They love plus-sized women. When I go to New York to visit his family, I feel like an outcast. The women in his family all have a little something extra. Those women are confident and know what they're working with. And look at Mo'Nique. She's starting a revolution. You don't have to be with a man who doesn't find value in who you are. It's not strictly about the physical. If it were, goddesses like Halle Berry and Kimora Lee Simmons wouldn't have any man problems."

"I hear what you're saying, but it's hard in Atlanta. There are so many beautiful, successful women here. The guys know it and it's tough to compete."

"Atlanta isn't the only place on earth. If you think it's that rough, you can always move."

"True. I guess I'm frustrated. Your husband got any single brothers?"

We both laughed. "Everybody feels frustrated at one time or another," I said. "It's perfectly normal. . . . How's Alexis?"

She let out a loud sigh. "She's fine. I checked into her getting a GED. We're working it out."

"I'm glad to hear that."

We concluded our session with prayer. I wondered whether her Reggie was the same Reggie I knew. *What are the chances? If it is the same Reggie, my opinion would be biased, because I know that he really is seeing someone else. What to do?*

CHAPTER THIRTEEN
Ambrosia

Ambrosia had been fatigued for weeks. Because she was tired all of the time, she was unable to gather enough strength to exercise. Even walking short distances challenged her. She would breathe heavily. It was unusual for Ambrosia because she maintained a regular exercise routine. At first, she thought that maybe her potassium level was low, so she ate a banana every morning. It wasn't until she fainted that she made an appointment with Dr. Michaels for a check-up. Ambrosia thought she was dreaming when the doctor told her she had viral cardiomyopathy. She didn't quite understand what that meant. She felt melancholy that something was wrong with her, but she couldn't muster any tears or ask any questions.

The doctor explained that with viral cardiomyopathy there was a fifty-percent survival rate. After running more tests, Dr. Michaels told Ambrosia that she needed a heart transplant. *A heart transplant?* Ambrosia had heard the stories about the long waiting lists for people needing organ donations. That could take years. Listening to Dr. Michaels, Ambrosia didn't think she had years to wait.

Dear Lord, I'm going to die. She didn't know how much time she had left, but she knew she needed to get her house in order. She had so many questions. How had her heart become defective? Who would take care of her children? Thinking about not being there to raise them caused her to cry. She was well aware that life wasn't fair, but this? What was she going to do?

Dr. Michaels wanted to admit Ambrosia to the hospital right away, but Ambrosia refused. She was scared and knew that she had to get her affairs in order. For the first few days after her diagnosis, Ambrosia was depressed. She cried often and hardly got out of bed. She knew that she needed to sleep, but every time her head hit the pillow, she was afraid that she wouldn't wake up if she fell into a deep slumber.

Going to work was out of the question. Somehow her job no longer seemed important. Mateo and Destiny were the only bright spots in her now bleak existence. Her children gave her solace. Seeing their adorable faces, hugging them, and kissing them helped Ambrosia put on a brave front long enough to get them dressed and dropped off at daycare. After that, she would return home and go to bed. On the days she felt too sad to leave the house, she would ask her mom or sister to come and get the children.

It was Monday morning, and Ambrosia had just dropped the children off at daycare. Unable to deal with her own procrastination any longer, Ambrosia picked up the phone and called Laron and asked him to come over. Within thirty minutes, Laron was knocking at her door.

"You seemed upset over the phone," Laron said. "What's wrong?"

She looked him in the eyes.

"Let's go in the living room," she said, closing the door behind him.

"You been crying?" he asked, noticing her puffy, red eyes and tear-stained face.

Ambrosia nodded her head and began crying again. Laron wrapped his arms around her and said, "Are Mateo and Destiny all right? Tell me what's going on."

She sniffed and patted her eyes with the back of her hand. "I'm–I'm d . . . d . . . dying."

Laron released her and took a step back. "What did you say?" He furrowed his brows.

Ambrosia proceeded to tell him about her diagnosis. She explained to him that her condition was terminal. Laron sat down on the couch and covered his face with his hands. She realized that he was crying and wrapped her arm around his shoulder. She found herself consoling him.

"Amber, please tell me this isn't true." He wiped away the tears.

She looked away and shook her head. "I wish it wasn't true, but it is."

"What're we going to do?"

"That's what I wanted to talk to you about. You're Mateo and Destiny's father. They should be with you."

Laron focused his eyes past Amber. "You know I can't . . ."

"They're your children. They need you. I know you have a wife and other kids, but this is serious. When I'm gone, you'll be all they have left."

"That's not true. What about your mother? Can't she take care of them?"

Mrs. Wrey, Amber's mom, moved to Snellville after the birth of her first grandchild, Mateo. She had no idea that Laron was married. Ambrosia had neglected to tell her.

"She could," Ambrosia said, "but I don't want her to. I want you to get custody of them and raise them with Jr. and Imani. I want them to be a part of a family."

"This–this is a lot on me right now. Give me some time to process all of this."

"We don't have time. Don't you understand that? I'm . . . I'm . . ."

"Don't say that," he interrupted. "Doctors have been known to misdiagnose patients all the time. Did you get a second opinion?"

"Not yet."

"There you go." He threw his hands in the air, exasperated. "Wait until you get another opinion before we go making plans."

"I'm scared, Laron."

He hugged her tightly as she buried her face in his chest. "Me too," he said in a tone barely above a whisper.

"I'm afraid that once I'm gone, my children will lose their father."

"You never have to worry about that." He stroked her hair. "I love all of my kids. None more than the others. As long as I have breath in my body, I'll be there for them."

She removed her face from his chest and rested her head on his shoulder. "I hope that's true."

Laron held Ambrosia in his arms for a while, trying to console her. After Laron left, Ambrosia dried her tears and thought about all of the things she had to do to prepare for her death. She rummaged through the junk drawer in her bedroom and pulled out her life insurance policy. *I've got to get more organized,* she chastised herself. She scanned the policy, which was still active. Mateo and Destiny were the beneficiaries. In the event of her death, they would each receive $250,000. She realized that she needed a will. Having a last will and testament never seemed important until now. Previously, she always thought she had time. She had youth on her side. Besides, she assumed that if anything ever happened to her, Laron would take care of Mateo and Destiny.

The thought of missing her children grow up, go to their proms, graduate, get married, and have children of their own caused Ambrosia to cry yet again. Her heart began to flutter. She needed to calm down. She held her policy in her hand and called the number on the bottom. Then she placed the document on her dresser.

"Hello," Ambrosia said. "May I speak with Mr. Black?"

"Sure, hold one moment, please," the receptionist said with a smile in her voice.

"This is Earl."

"Hi, Earl. This is Ambrosia Wrey."

"Ambrosia, how are you?"

"Fine, fine. I was calling because I needed to do some estate planning. I was wondering if you would be able to assist me with that."

"Like wills?"

"Yes."

"I don't personally do that, but I have someone I can refer you to. Hang on one moment. Okay?"

"Okay." She heard a click, then soft elevator music. A few seconds later, Earl returned to the line.

"Thanks for holding," he said. Earl dictated the number and Ambrosia wrote it down.

"Thanks so much. I'll give Mr. Wright a call today."

"Great. Did you want to make any changes to your insurance policy?"

"No, I'm good. Thanks, though."

They disconnected the call, and Ambrosia dialed the number for Attorney Wright. He wasn't available, so she left him a message. Her head began to hurt. It was throbbing at the temples. She went into the bathroom and retrieved two Aleves from the medicine cabinet. She walked into the kitchen and grabbed a bottle of water from the refrigerator and washed down the pills. Her body was fatigued, but Ambrosia didn't feel like sleeping.

There were several framed photos of Mateo and Destiny on the mantel in the living room. She picked up one that showed both of them and studied it. The picture was taken only three months ago. She sat down on the couch, clenched the wooden frame in her hand, and sobbed. Her heart palpitated. She could feel the valves pumping at an irregular beat as she felt a shortness of breath. All she could think to do was call her doctor. Dr. Michaels told her to come in right away.

Ambrosia was terrified and couldn't stop the tears. *When are these Aleves going to kick in?* she wondered impatiently.

"Please, God. Don't let this be the end," Ambrosia pleaded before grabbing a few sheets of stationery from her notepad on the coffee table. She grabbed a pen from her purse and wrote a long, emotional letter. Once completed, she sealed the letter in an envelope and addressed it. She always kept a book of stamps in her wallet, so she affixed the postage to the envelope and stuck it in her purse. She removed a blank envelope from the box and scribbled the word "Insurance" on it, stuffed her policy inside and placed it in her purse, too.

Once at the hospital, Dr. Michaels admitted Ambrosia. She ran a series of tests and reiterated that Ambrosia needed a heart transplant. Ambrosia gasped. She felt like she was having an emotional meltdown. Even though Ambrosia knew she needed a heart transplant, hearing it this time seemed to make it more real, closer to home. Dr. Michaels then recommended a medically-induced coma. The word "coma" terrified Ambrosia. She was ready to run out of the hospital.

"I can't do this," Ambrosia said.

"Ambrosia," Dr. Michaels said, "we need to do this. There's too much strain on your heart. If we do this, you'll have a better chance of survival."

Ambrosia exhaled. "Let me call my mom. I need to talk to her. Tell her what's going on."

Dr. Michaels nodded and left Ambrosia alone in the room. She stared at the white wall for so long she began to see tiny dots floating in the air. She took several deep breaths before placing a call to her mother. Her mom answered, and Ambrosia was relieved. She told her mom about her condition and that she had been checked in to the hospital. Mrs. Wrey tried her best to assure Ambrosia that everything was going to be all right, but Ambrosia wasn't convinced. She could hear her mother's voice trembling as she spoke. Before they hung up, Mrs. Wrey told her not to worry about the children. She would get Anastasia, Ambrosia's older sister, to pick up Mateo and Destiny and watch them while she went to the hospital to be with Ambrosia.

Ambrosia couldn't help but worry about her children. They were the most important things in her life. She desperately wanted to see them, but she knew that they were too young to visit her in the hospital. Besides, she wasn't sure how much they'd remember about their childhood once they were all grown up, but she didn't want them to have sad memories of seeing their mom in the hospital.

Next, Ambrosia phoned Dr. Little.

"Hey, Dr. Little. It's me, Ambrosia."

"Hi, Ambrosia. How are you?"

Ambrosia sniffled and sat down on the side of the bed. "Apparently not so good."

"What's the matter?"

"I'm in the hospital. My doctor told me I have viral cardiomyopathy."

"Oh my God! How are you holding up? Who's watching your children?"

"I'm scared, Dr. Little. I need you."

Ambrosia provided Dr. Little with the hospital information.

"I'm on my way," Dr. Little promised. "And Ambrosia: 'Be

ye not afraid. Greater is he who is in Me than he who is in the world.' "

"Thanks. I needed to hear that." Ambrosia placed the phone on the cradle and thought about what she was going to do next.

CHAPTER FOURTEEN

Kevin

After leaving Amber, Kevin went to the gym to workout. He needed to relieve some stress. He pumped iron and reminded himself to breathe. His body dripped sweat. He looked around the room and noticed guys bench-pressing, doing squats and sit-ups, and running around the track. He wiped perspiration from his forehead with a face towel. Then he guzzled some bottled water before heading for the sauna.

Kevin was the only person sitting in the heat box. He was glad because he needed time to think. And he didn't feel like entertaining light-hearted conversation with anyone. He was so worried about Amber that he felt like a midget was dancing in his stomach. Since he was alone, he felt safe enough to cry. Besides, even if someone did join him, they'd just think he was sweating, he reasoned.

He thought about Mateo and Destiny. It wasn't their fault—the way in which they were conceived. They were innocent. They were his blood. His children. What if Amber did end up dying? The thought was too much for him to bear. He cried so hard his shoulders shook.

What am I going to do?

He wiped his face with his hands and leaned farther back on the bench. He thought about what would happen if he confessed his indiscretion to his wife. Thinking about hurting Gabriella caused his stomach to churn acid. He imagined the hurt look in her eyes. Tears. Cussing. Yelling. Lots of yelling. Knowing Gabriella the way he did, he was convinced she'd never forgive him. Trust meant everything to her. Not only did he breach her trust, he disregarded their relationship. Not one isolated incident, but countless times with the same woman. And those indiscretions resulted in a son *and* a daughter.

He never meant to hurt Gabriella. But how could he ever explain? He didn't just cross the line; he ran over it and erased it. For crying out loud, he had another family. The rich man's family. A son and a daughter. Two sons. Two daughters. Two women. How could he ever convince Gabriella that he loved her and was committed to their marriage? He couldn't. Because if he were, he never would've let things get this far. Especially having two children with somebody other than his wife.

He felt as if his mind was on overload. Something had to be done. Even though he suggested Amber allow the children live with her mother, he didn't mean it. That was a knee-jerk response. He felt like an insensitive jerk for even mentioning it. He was sure Amber probably thought he was some monster with ice running through his veins. In reality, he would love to see Mateo and Destiny every day. Deep down inside, he really wanted all of his children to be with him, raised in the same household. There was another pang in his stomach. Who was he kidding? If Gabriella found out about his affair, she'd probably take the children to Sweden and he'd never see any of them ever again.

"What's up, man?" Donovan said as he stepped into the sauna with a towel wrapped around his waist.

He and Kevin both had a membership to the same gym.

"Hey," Kevin replied.

"How you doin'?"

"Not so good."

Donovan sat down on the bench. "What's going on?"

"I got some bad news. Amber told me she has a heart problem. She thinks she's going to die."

"Aw, man, that's rough. Sorry to hear that. How you holding up?"

He shrugged his shoulders.

"Man, you know if there's anything I can do . . ." Donovan patted him on the back.

"She wants me to take the kids."

"That's deep, bro. What you gon' do?"

"I don't know."

Donovan seemed thoughtful. "Wait, when did she tell you this?"

"Today. Why?"

"Well, Sky had to go to the hospital a little while ago to be with one of her patients. Let me make sure I got this right. She said, 'Ambrosia's been admitted to the hospital for viral cardiomyopathy.' "

"What? Are you serious? Amber is Sky's patient?" He simultaneously squeezed his fists and closed his eyes.

"I'm not sure, but it seems like more than a coincidence to me."

Kevin swallowed hard. "I gotta bounce. I'll talk to you later."

Kevin hit the showers and changed into jeans and a muscle shirt. On his way home, Kevin popped a few Pepcids. He called Amber from his cell phone to check on her but got her answering machine. He was tempted to call Skyler to find out if her Ambrosia and his Amber were one in the same, but decided against it. If they weren't the same person, he wasn't prepared to explain why he was inquiring.

Even if they were the same, he could never offer a suitable explanation to Skyler. Either way, he was sliced and diced and tossed in an alcohol river.

He felt uneasy, as if something wasn't right. He decided to call information and get the phone numbers to some of the area hospitals. He wanted to see if Amber had been admitted. After some coaxing, the second hospital he called informed him that Amber was a patient. He nearly swerved off the road. Since he told the operator that he was Amber's fiancé, she provided him with Amber's room number. He declined the operator's offer to connect him to her room. Instead, he hung up the phone and wiped away the beads of sweat that had formed on his forehead.

When he arrived home, he was agitated. Jr. and Imani greeted him, but he hardly noticed them. He thought he asked them about their day, but when he saw the puzzled expressions on their faces, he realized that he had ignored them.

"Daddy, are you all right?" Jr. asked.

"Huh?"

"What's wrong?"

"Oh, I just had a long day. Sorry. How was your day?"

"It was cool."

"Good." He patted his son on top of his head. He turned to face his daughter and said, "Baby, how was your day?"

Imani smiled and said, "It was good. I got an A on my spelling test. See." She handed him a piece of paper with a large red "A" on top with a circle around it.

"That's great, baby. Daddy's real proud of you." He kneeled down and kissed her on the cheek. "Where's your momma?" He stood back up.

"Taking a bath," Jr. said.

Kevin hugged Jr. and Imani before going upstairs to the master bedroom. His mind was on Amber, Mateo, and Destiny. He wondered how Amber was doing. He wanted to be with her. His heart ached thinking about what Amber must have been going through. He wondered who was at the hospital with her and who was watching their children. *How am I going to get away? I've got to see her.*

Kevin stood in the doorway of the bathroom just as Gabriella stood up in the tub. Her body was firm and glistening.

"I didn't hear you come in," Gabriella said.

He couldn't help but stare and think about the vision of loveliness standing before him. He felt an arousal at the core of his manhood.

Gabriella grabbed a towel. "Why are you looking at me like that?"

"Oh, I was just thinking about how beautiful you are."

Smiling, Gabriella stepped out of the tub and walked toward him. "Are the children still downstairs?"

"Yeah. They're watching TV."

She brushed past him and went into the bedroom where she sat on the edge of her bed rubbing moisturizer into her skin.

"How was your day?" Gabriella asked. "I left you some pot roast for dinner."

"Thanks. Maybe I'll get some later." He was so worried about Amber that he couldn't even think about eating.

Gabriella slipped into a nightgown. "Are you all right?"

"Why you ask me that?"

"You seem distracted."

Kevin held both her hands. "Baby, I'm sorry. I have a lot on my mind." He released her hands. "You know what? I . . . I need some fresh air. I'll be back."

"You just got here. What's going on? Where are you going?"

"I can't talk about it right now. Trust me. I hafta do this. I'll be back." He kissed her on the lips. "I love you."

Gabriella called out after him, but he ignored her. He felt

as though he had been a coward long enough and wanted to "man up" to his actions. He knew that he was taking a risk by going to the hospital. What if Skyler was there? He dismissed the thought and reasoned that whatever happened would happen.

CHAPTER FIFTEEN

Skyler

I don't know how I managed to drive myself to the hospital to see Ambrosia without getting into an accident. My nerves were frayed from worry. *I feel so bad for Ambrosia. She's so young. I know she must be terrified right about now.*

I went to the nurse's station to get Ambrosia's room number. Ambrosia had a private room. When I got to her room, a woman who looked like she could be Ambrosia's mother was with her. The older woman strongly resembled Ambrosia, only she had bleached blond hair and fine lines in her face.

"Hi. You must be Mrs. Wrey." I extended my hand to her. "I'm Dr. Little."

"Nice to meet you, Dr. Little. Ambrosia's talked about you before."

I smiled and turned to face Ambrosia. "Hi, kiddo. How're you feeling?"

Her eyelids were red-rimmed. I could tell she had been crying. I noticed a framed photo of Mateo and Destiny displayed on the nightstand next to her bed. The picture appeared to be recent. *Such beautiful children.* I prayed that their mom wouldn't be taken away from them.

"I'm so scared," Ambrosia admitted.

I gave her a hug. "Everything'll be all right."

"Don't cry, baby," Mrs. Wrey said, stroking Ambrosia's hair.

"Mom," Ambrosia said. "Would you please give me a moment alone with Dr. Little?"

"Sure. I'll go into the break room and get a Sprite. Do either of you want anything?"

"No," we declined in unison.

As soon as Mrs. Wrey left, Ambrosia said, "Here." She handed me two envelopes.

"What's this?" I said, holding the envelopes in my hand.

"The nurse gave me some paper and an envelope. I wasn't able to draw up my will with an attorney, so I handwrote it and the nurse witnessed it. For my living will, I wrote in there that if I fall into a vegetative state and suffer brain damage, pull the plug on me. I don't want to live like that. I don't want to be a burden to my family."

"Ambrosia . . ."

"Let me finish. My life insurance policy is in the other envelope. I carried it with me after I spoke with Dr. Michaels. If I die, I want you to be responsible for overseeing Mateo and Destiny's inheritance. I wrote that in my will. Now I need to ask you a serious question."

"Anything. What is it?"

"If Laron doesn't step up to the plate and seek custody of my children, would you?"

"Would I what?"

"Raise them?"

"Me? You want me to raise your children? Have you told Laron about your condition?"

"I did, but he's worried about his wife. He doesn't want to destroy his marriage."

"What about your mom? Your sister?"

"Dr. Little, I want my kids to be raised by two parents who'll not only love them, but also love each other. I see the way your face lights up whenever you talk about your husband. You're committed to your marriage. And you're smart and decent. You're a Christian, so I know you'd raise Mateo and Destiny in the church. That's what I want. I know you'd raise them to pray, stay in school, and do something productive with their lives."

"I appreciate everything you're saying, and I'm honored that you trust me so much. But Ambrosia, this is major. Life changing! I'd have to seriously discuss it with Donovan."

"I thought he wanted to have children. Isn't that what you told me?"

"Well, yes, but . . . ."

"Please, Dr. Little. I can't go through with this medically-induced coma not knowing if my children will be taken care of."

"How do you think your mom would feel? Those are her only grandchildren. She'd be hurt that you didn't trust her enough to let her raise them."

"I don't care about that. I love my mom, but I love my kids more. I want the best for them, and right now, that's not her. She's single and she barely makes enough money to support herself."

"But your insurance money would help."

"That's the problem. My insurance money is for Mateo and Destiny. Not to help my mom come up."

"I can understand how you feel, but do you think that's fair? If something happened to you, your mom would lose a daughter. That's devastating for a parent. Think about it. If a woman loses her husband, she's a widow. If a man loses his wife, he's a widower. If a parent loses a child, there's no word for it. It's indescribable.

"Honestly, if Laron won't raise your children, you should allow your mother to do it. There's a love grandparents share with their grandchildren that's even greater than the love they have for their own children. I don't think you should take that away from your mom. She's a decent person. She may not have a whole lot of money, but she has good character. It's not like she's a drug addict or alcoholic. I'm sure if you share with your mother your desires regarding how you want your children to be raised, she'd honor your wishes. And besides, no matter who has custody of Mateo and Destiny, they will still need some money from the insurance policy to help support them: food, clothes, co-payments for doctor's visits, prescriptions, school expenses, daycare, after school activities, and the list goes on."

Ambrosia nodded her head as a single tear trickled down her cheek. I gave her a hug and faint smile.

"Now," I continued, "if neither your mom nor Laron want to take the children into their homes, which I seriously doubt, then we can revisit this."

I stared at the white wall behind Ambrosia's bed. There was a knock at the door. She squeezed my hand.

"Laron," Ambrosia said, sounding surprised. "What are you doing here?"

I turned around. My mouth fell open. *Laron? This can't be happening.* It was hard to conceal the shock that was frozen on my face like a tattoo.

"Hey," Laron said. "These are for you." He handed her a bouquet of red roses.

Ambrosia smelled the flowers and placed them on the stand. "They're beautiful. Thank you."

He nodded.

"Sky," he said, averting his eyes.

"How do you know Dr. Little?" Ambrosia asked.

"I'm friends with her husband," Laron said.

"Wow. What are the chances?" Ambrosia looked at me then back at Kevin—I mean "Laron." There was an uncomfortable silence.

"Knock, knock," Mrs. Wrey said. "May I come in?"

"Come on in, Mom," Ambrosia said.

Mrs. Wrey entered carrying a Sprite in one hand and a bag of potato chips in the other. "Laron, what a pleasant surprise." She gave Kevin a hug. "Can you believe what's happening to my baby?" She broke the embrace and her eyes became misty.

"No. I was hoping it wasn't true." He looked at Ambrosia and said, "So what happened since I saw you earlier? Why are you here?"

"I had difficulty breathing and my heart seemed to be racing, so I called Dr. Michaels and she told me to come in. When I got here, they said I needed a heart transplant and she wanted to put me into a medically-induced coma."

"A coma?" He plopped down on the bed. He began to tremble. In all the years I had known him, I had never seen him cry. I hugged him, and he wrapped his arms around my waist and continued to cry. Even though it was a devastating situation for all parties involved, I couldn't help but feel conflicted. Somehow comforting Kevin over his mistress while his wife was my best friend felt unnatural.

"Laron, please try to be strong. Ambrosia needs your strength," I said.

"I can't take it," he said.

I could only imagine the stress he must've been under. He appeared worn and emotionally drained. When I looked around, I noticed that Ambrosia and Mrs. Wrey were crying, too. Dr. Michaels entered. Kevin released me and wiped his face with his right hand.

"Hi," Dr. Michaels said. "I'm coming to check on Ambrosia." She used the stethoscope hanging around her neck to check Ambrosia's heartbeat. She jotted some notes on the chart she carried on her clipboard.

"How is she?" Mrs. Wrey asked.

"The same." Dr. Michaels then said to Ambrosia, "Is this your family?"

Ambrosia introduced her mother, Kevin, and me to Dr. Michaels.

"Nice to meet you all. Sorry it had to be under these circumstances. Ambrosia, be sure to get some rest. We're going to begin medicating you tomorrow."

"Yeah, right. I doubt I'll get any sleep."

"I'll be back in the morning to check on you," Dr. Michaels advised. "I know it's hard, but the rest of you should get some sleep as well." She looked at each of us and offered a weak smile.

"Doctor," Mrs. Wrey said. "What exactly is a medically-induced coma? How long will Ambrosia need to be in one? And how will you get my baby out of it?"

"Ambrosia's condition is considered terminal," Dr. Michaels answered.

Mrs. Wrey covered her mouth and began to cry.

"Wait. Viral cardiomyopathy usually has a fifty-percent survival rate. However, since Ambrosia needs a heart transplant, we're going to give her sedatives to help her brain to sleep. There have been reported cases of patients that, after going into medically-induced comas for a couple of months and being on heart and lung machines, their hearts repaired themselves. I'm hoping that will be the case with Ambrosia."

"A couple of months? What if it doesn't work? What if you can't find a heart donor?" Mrs. Wrey said.

"We'll cross that bridge if and when we get to it. In the meantime, pray," Dr. Michaels offered.

After Dr. Michaels left, I suggested we pray. Not a usual prayer. Since we wanted a miracle, I figured we needed a radical, heartfelt prayer. We gathered around Ambrosia's bed, held hands with each other, and closed our eyes.

I said, "Heavenly Father, we need Your help today. In Your Word You said that where two or more are gathered in Your name, You are there in their midst. Father, protect us by Your power as we divorce the devil today."

I cleared my throat and continued. "Devil, you've had your time with Ambrosia. You lulled her into a false sense of security. You made her think that you cared about her when in actuality you only wanted to kill, maim, and destroy her. Well, I'm here to tell you today that you can't have her. She's got a new man and his name is Jesus. That's right. She's divorcing you. You are no longer welcome in her life or the lives of her children. You can't have her because Jesus has already claimed her. Now release the hold you have on her in Jesus' name. We plead the blood of Jesus over her. We command you to flee. Go back to the pits of hell where you belong so that you can't hurt anyone else. In Jesus' name. Amen."

Then I let go of Ambrosia's hand and placed my right hand over her heart and said, "In the name of Jesus, you are healed. Do you hear me? I said you are healed." I opened my eyes and tears were streaming down Ambrosia's cheeks but her eyes were still closed. I said, "Open your eyes and give God the glory. Claim your victory right now. Accept your healing."

Ambrosia opened her eyes, and we hugged. I could hear her mother in the background praising the Lord and shouting, "Hallelujah!"

Kevin sniffled and said, "Thank you, Lord."

I hugged Kevin and then Mrs. Wrey. I told them that I was

leaving but that I would continue to pray for Ambrosia. I asked them both not only to continue to pray, but to have faith. More than anything, we all needed to believe in what we were asking God to do. We had to trust and know in our hearts that His will would be done, regardless.

Kevin excused himself and walked out with me.

"I know you have a million questions," he said.

"Not really. I only have one . . . Why?"

"It's complicated. I didn't intend to have an affair, it just happened."

"Affairs don't 'just happen,' Kevin. You had to think about it first. Before every action, there's a thought."

"You're right. I messed up, and I don't know how to fix it."

"Do you want to come into my office sometime and discuss it?"

"Could I?"

"Yes. I care about you, Ambrosia, and Gabriella. I don't want to see any of you hurt, but I know it's inevitable. However, I will do my best to help each of you through this difficult time."

"You're not going to tell Gabby, are you?"

"Of course not. Ambrosia's my patient. And if you come to see me, you'll be my patient, too."

He hugged me again. "Sky, I'm sorry. I know that doesn't mean anything right now, but I am. I never meant to hurt anybody. I can't explain it, but I love Gabby and Amber."

"Good night." I didn't feel like addressing his last statement.

I got in my car. My mind was on overload. I thought about Gabriella and how she would react once she found out about "Laron's" affair. I shook my head. Thinking about her reaction caused the fine hairs on my arm to cower at the imagined wrath Gabriella would likely have when she learned Kevin had strayed. Then I thought about all of those children: Jr., Imani, Mateo, and Destiny. They should know each other. I wanted to help Kevin. Helping him would, in turn, help his wife and all of his children. The children were innocent. As far as I was concerned, there were no illegitimate children, only illegitimate parents.

CHAPTER SIXTEEN

Monday

"Reggie, we need to talk," Monday said, getting out of the bed and wrapping a robe around her body.

Alexis had spent the evening at a friend's house, so Reggie spent the night. Reggie sighed. He seemed to dread the coming conversation.

Monday sat down, propped her back against the headboard and stretched both of her legs out on the mattress. "Look, I have a lot going on right now, and I've been feeling sort of depressed."

"I'm sorry to hear that. I thought things were getting better." He sat up in the bed with the sheet covering his lower body.

"Yeah. Alexis dropped out of school, and I've been checking into getting her to go to one of those alternative schools."

"What? Why she do that?" He rubbed at his left eyebrow.

"It's a bunch of stuff. Mostly peer pressure. Anyway, I took your advice and started going to see Dr. Skyler Little."

"For real? My advice? I don't remember telling you to go see her."

"Well, you did. You told me that you did her lawn and landscaping. Remember?"

"I think I remember that conversation." Reggie's palms began to sweat. He rubbed them on the sheet. *Oh God, I confided in Dr. Little. What if she tells Monday? It's not like I'm her client. What to do, what to do?*

"You're so silly." She laughed.

"How's it going?"

"The sessions? It's going, but it's going to take a while. I have a lot of issues that I need to work out."

"If anybody can help, Dr. Little can. She has a good professional reputation."

Monday nodded. "But that's not what I wanted to talk to you about."

"Here we go." Reggie placed his large, calloused hand on his forehead.

Monday playfully removed his hand from his face. "Don't do that," she teased. "Reggie, what are we?"

"Last time I checked we were two human beings."

"Got jokes. Ha ha. Real funny. I'm serious. How would you categorize our relationship?"

"Why you have to take it there? We were having a good time."

"That's just it, Reggie. I'm tired of having just a 'good time.' I want more."

"Right now, I can't give you more. I told you that from jump."

"You can't or you won't?"

"Don't do this." Reggie got out of bed and put on boxer shorts. He stood approximately five foot ten, and his body was toned. No six-pack or bulging muscles, but fit. He grew a beard because he was tired of dealing with razor bumps. Monday wasn't crazy about the beard because it irritated her whenever it brushed up against the side of her face. But she loved Reggie's bald head. His head was as smooth as an ostrich egg.

"Don't do what?" Monday said.

"Monday, I care about you, but you're still searching. I wouldn't mind kickin' it with you, but like you said, you got issues. This isn't the time to focus on a relationship." He pulled his undershirt over his head.

"Tell the truth, Reggie. Are you seeing somebody else?"

"What if I were? What difference would it make? You and I aren't rolling like that."

Tears began to stream down Monday's cheeks. Reggie walked over to her and held her in his arms. "Come on, Monday. Don't cry. I hate to see a woman cry."

She sniffed. "I can't help it. I feel so used."

He wiped a tear away from her cheek with his thumb. "Used? You know I'm not using you."

"I don't know. You don't call when you say you're going to call. And you don't come over as often as you used to."

"That's because I've been working more. Business has picked up." He released her and continued to get dressed. He put on a pair of jeans and a polo shirt.

"Can I ask you a question?"

He shrugged his shoulders. "Knock yourself out."

"What do you see in me?"

"Are you serious? See, that's what I'm talking about. You don't even know what you have going for yourself. You don't need me to answer that question."

"Yes, I do. I want to know."

"Fine." He plopped down on the side of the bed. "You're funny. You're independent: got your own job, your own house and car. You're ambitious, you want to have thangs. And you freaky. Happy now?"

"Whatever, boy."

He laughed.

"If you like all of those things about me," Monday said, "then why won't you be my man . . . exclusively?"

"Already told you."

"What? That I have issues?"

"That, and you're insecure."

Monday couldn't deny the obvious. She was insecure, but she hated hearing Reggie say it. She wondered whether being insecure made her less attractive to Reggie. Her weight didn't seem to be a problem for him. He seemed to love seeing her in lingerie and appreciated whenever she opened the door wearing nothing but a coat and high heels.

Monday stood up and faced Reggie. "When am I going to see you again?"

He smiled and kissed her on the forehead. "Soon. I'll call you."

"How original."

"Nah, for real. I'll call you."

When Reggie left, Monday appreciated the time alone. She took Dr. Little's suggestion and jotted notes in her journal. She wrote:

Today, Reggie called me insecure. And he's right. If he doesn't call me, then I call him. Repeatedly. It's almost like I'm obsessing over him. I don't blame him for not wanting to commit to me. I wouldn't want to commit to me either. But I can't seem to help myself. I haven't told Reggie yet, but I love him. He used to treat me so good. We laughed a lot. He listened to my problems. He even referred me to Dr. Little. I really believed that he cared. When we would go out in public, he always held my hand or wrapped his arm around me. Never did he seem ashamed to be seen with me. With him, I felt beautiful. Like my weight didn't matter. For once, it was a non-issue.

Then something happened. I'm not sure what, but he started calling less. And his visits became fewer and fewer. I assumed he met someone else. Probably some skinny, beautiful chick.

Monday put her pen down. She pondered over the words on the page. *Bump that. I'm beautiful.* She picked the pen back up and started writing again.

What do I like about Reggie? His brown eyes and long lashes. His eyes seem so sincere. And his lips. Those full, sexy lips. He's nice. He listens. He has a good job. Whenever we go out, he pays.

What can I do to better myself? I love to bake. Maybe I should take a cake decorating class. One day I'd like to own my own bakery. I want to bake cakes for celebrities. That would be cool.

She flipped the page and continued to write.

Spiritually I've got to do better. I mean, I attend a mega church. I buy and listen to spiritual tapes. I even abstained from sex for two years before meeting Reggie. The problem is . . . I'm not involved in any ministry. I need to get involved. Maybe I should join the intercessory prayer committee. Why not? I like to pray. Especially for other people. I'll check on that.

And Alexis. I feel like I failed her. I've had to be both mother and father to her since Larry is so inconsistent. I worry about her. I wonder what she's doing. I pray she turns out all right.

That's all for now. 'Til next time. Good-bye for now.

She closed the journal and placed it in the nightstand next to her bed. "Sky was right. Writing is therapeutic," she said aloud. She went into the bathroom and splashed water on her face. In the mirror she saw a distorted image. She saw herself as a scared little girl with tears streaming down her cheeks. She pat-dried her face with a hand towel and shook her head. Blinking slowly, she opened her eyes and looked in the mirror, again. This time she appeared as her present-day self.

"I'm not going to let you do this to me, Stan. You hear me?" She yelled. "Not again." Monday threw the towel on the vanity and stormed out of the bathroom.

CHAPTER SEVENTEEN
Gabriella

Gabriella was so upset with Kevin that she couldn't think clearly. Her thoughts were canceling each other out—not allowing her to concentrate on any one notion. She still had not gotten over the fact that Kevin left the house without offering her so much as an explanation. When he finally did come home, he was aloof. He said he "didn't feel like talking." It was late, so she did not press the issue. Instead she decided to wait until the morning to discuss. To her surprise, when she awoke, Kevin had left her a note on his pillow telling her that he had taken the children to breakfast at IHOP. She needed to talk to someone, so she called Skyler.

"Hello," Skyler answered on the second ring.

"Hi, it's me. Is this a good time for you to talk?"

"Sure. What's going on?"

Gabriella sighed heavily into the receiver. She proceeded to tell Skyler about Kevin leaving without explanation not long after he got home. Gabriella explained that Kevin's behavior was bizarre and concerned her. She expressed her suspicion that Kevin might be having an affair.

"I need to know what's happening with him," Gabriella said.

"Sure, that's understandable."

She thought that working out might help alleviate some stress, take her mind off her troubles. Gabriella checked the alarm clock next to her bed. "I'm about to go to the gym and do yoga. If I hurry, I can make the next class."

"Gabriella, are you all right?"

"Yes, I'm fine."

"Just curious . . . If Kevin were having an affair, what would you do?"

There was a pregnant pause. "I don't know what I would do. We have children together, you know? That would be difficult because I'm still in love with him. It would be different if I weren't in love with him. There is a difference between being in love with someone and loving someone, you know? One of my friends, Constance, you remember her?"

"Yes, I remember her."

"She's not in love with her husband, but she loves him. They aren't happy. They live like roommates. Their marriage is more like one of convenience. I don't think I could live like that. It's hard, you know?"

"A lot of people live like that. They stay together in a loveless marriage for the sake of their children, financial security, or to keep up appearances. "

"Yes, but it doesn't seem right. Anyhow, I'll call you later."

"Sure. Enjoy your class."

"Thanks. Bye."

Once at the gym, Gabriella joined the yoga class that was about to begin. Individual mats were placed on the hardwood floor. The sound of a serenity-type water fountain could be heard in the background. The instructor warmed up the class with stretching exercises before lulling them into a meditative state. At the end of class, Gabriella decided to do some upper-body weight-training and cardio exercises.

"Hey, Gabriella. How you doin'?" The soulful voice sounded like Barry White.

"Hi, Caleb. I'm fine. And you?"

Caleb was a personal trainer at the gym. He wore a tight muscle shirt that showed off every perfectly cut muscle on his chest, stomach, and arms. His golden bronze skin glistened.

"Good, good. Thanks for asking. How's your workout coming along?"

"You know." Gabriella chuckled. "It's a workout. Not my favorite thing, but you gotta do what you gotta do. Right?"

"True, true. You need any help?"

"That would be nice." She smiled.

He held her feet while she did crunches, and occasionally touched her stomach to feel the strain. Caleb showed her the proper way to use the lightweight barbells for some arm curls and extensions.

When Gabriella finished her workout, she thanked Caleb for helping her.

"No problem," Caleb said. "It was my pleasure." He paused and continued, "Would you like to go out to lunch or for coffee sometime?"

Gabriella was surprised, yet flattered. Since she had been married to Kevin, she had taken her vows seriously. She had not gone out with any other men without Kevin.

"I don't know what to say."

"Hey, it's not like a date or anything. I just like talking to you." He smiled, revealing beautiful, full, white teeth.

Gabriella figured that she wasn't doing anything wrong. Lots of people went on innocent lunch dates. The thought of Kevin's possible infidelity appalled her. She looked at Caleb and thought about how attractive he was. Very attractive. Thinking about another man that way caused her to blush. She felt the heat rising in her cheeks and felt guilty.

"Well?" Caleb asked, looking at her.

"Oh, sure." Gabriella handed him her cell phone, which she carried with her at all times in case of an emergency, and let him program his number into it. After he finished entering the information into the memory, he handed it back to her. "I'll call you," she said.

"You do that," he said before leaving.

Gabriella felt a rush. Having another man pay attention to her felt good. *Maybe it will help Kevin appreciate what he has*. It reminded her that in addition to being a wife and a mother, she was still a desirable woman. With all of the stress surrounding her marriage, she had forgotten just how desirable she really was.

By the time Gabriella returned home, Kevin, Jr., and Imani were already there. They were in the living room watching TV.

"Hey," Gabriella said in a sing-song sort of way.

"Hi, Mom," Jr. and Imani said in unison. They popped up out of their seats on the couch like popcorn in a microwave. Jr. hugged her around her waist, and Imani wrapped her arms around Gabriella's leg.

Gabriella patted both of them on the back. "Did you have a good time with your dad?"

"Yes," Imani said. "I ate chocolate chip pancakes."

"Was it yummy?"

"Mm-hmm." Imani nodded and released Gabriella's leg.

"And what did you have?" Gabriella asked Jr., patting him on the head.

"French toast," he said, letting go of Gabriella's waist.

"That sounds yummy too."

"Where you been?" Kevin queried.

"I went to the gym." She walked over and kissed him on the cheek.

The nerve of him. Asking me where I've been when he up and leaves whenever he feels like it. Well, not anymore. The tables have turned, and I'm no longer your doormat.

CHAPTER EIGHTEEN

Skyler

"Morning, Yahkie," I said as I walked into my office. "Good morning, boss lady. I'm surprised to see you. Why aren't you at the hospital with Ambrosia?"

"I'm about to go. I came in to get a file so that I can work on it at home."

"Oh," he said, following me into my office. "On your behalf, I sent a prayer plant to Ambrosia in the hospital."

"Thanks. I really appreciate it. You think of everything." I unlocked my desk drawer and browsed through the files.

"That's why you pay me the big bucks. Anywho, do you think you'll be up for recording the public service announcement for the Sky's the Limit Foundation later today?"

I closed my eyes and smacked my forehead. "I forgot all about it." I closed the drawer and stood up.

The Sky's the Limit Foundation was an organization that I founded and chaired. The purpose of the foundation was to teach young girls about self-esteem and respect for their bodies. We encouraged young women to remain virgins until marriage.

"No sweat. I can call and reschedule," he said.

"No, don't do that. I'd rather get it out of the way instead of procrastinating. What time is the appointment?"

He checked his watch. "It's at eleven o'clock."

"That's two hours away. I'd better head out." I locked the drawer and clutched the folder in my hand.

"Break a leg. And when you see Ambrosia, give her my love." He smiled.

"I sure will. Hold it down. Call if you need me." I waved goodbye and left.

When I arrived at the TV station to record the PSA, the producer came out to greet me. Her hair was jet black and she was casually dressed in jeans and an oversized shirt.

"Hello! I'm Kayla, Kayla Phillips." She extended her hand to me.

"Nice to meet you, Ms. Phillips." I shook her hand.

"You can call me Kayla. Follow me."

She led me to a conference room that held a long table, twelve plush chairs, and a TV sitting on a rolling stand in the corner. We discussed my thirty-second script and she offered me a cup of coffee or bottled water. I accepted the water. Kayla excused herself and came back with the drink. Then she left me alone in the room. In her absence, I rehearsed my lines.

When Kayla returned, she took me on a tour of the studio. It was interesting to see the different sets for several talk shows. Some were fancy, like the custom-made set consisting of a purple velvet couch, colorful paintings, and a back staircase. Other sets were more conservative, mostly made up of a floral print couch, chair, coffee table, and plant. We finally arrived at the set where I'd be filming my PSA. It was very basic. No furniture. Only a lime green projector screen in the background and a camera with bright lights in front of me.

Kayla introduced me to Nick, the cameraman, before she departed.

"I'm a little nervous," I confessed.

"Most people are, but don't be. We'll do this until we get it right." He smiled, making me feel more secure.

Nick gave me instructions on where to stand, where to look, and when to begin. After he counted down for me to start, I said, "Hi, I'm Dr. Skyler Little. I'm founder and president of the Sky's the Limit Foundation. Our organization is committed to making a difference in the lives of young girls. We have programs dedicated to abstinence, academic excellence, and spiritual guidance. Our staff includes certified counselors and other professionals." At the end of the announcement, I provided the contact information such as the Web site, e-mail, and telephone number.

Smiling, Nick gave me the hand signal indicating "cut."

"You did a great job," Nick said.

"You think so? I was nervous."

"Couldn't tell. You ran through that like a pro. Have you done this before?"

"No." I shook my head. "It was my first time."

I followed Nick to a desk that had a couple of monitors and we reviewed the tape. It looked good, and I was pleased to have gotten it right the first time. After giving Nick the green light, I left and headed to the hospital to visit Ambrosia.

I walked down the long corridor to Ambrosia's room with my heels clicking on the shiny tile floor. The distinct sterile hospital smell engulfed my nostrils. Upon entering Ambrosia's room, I was greeted by her mother. Mrs. Wrey's eyes were red and puffy. Apparently she had been crying. Her faced seemed sullen.

"Hi, Mrs. Wrey," I said, giving her a hug. I hated seeing

Ambrosia lying in that hospital bed, unconscious. "I just stopped by to check on Ambrosia. How is she?"

"She's resting. According to the doctor, the coma is helping her body heal itself. I pray she's right. That's my baby lying there." She patted Ambrosia's hand. "Thanks for the plant. It's beautiful."

I noticed a prayer plant sitting on the window ledge and a massive floral arrangement sitting on the stand next to Ambrosia's bed. "You're welcome."

"Do you think she can hear us?"

"Based on everything I've studied about coma patients, they are able to hear. They're just unable to respond." I paused and continued, "How are Mateo and Destiny?"

"Fine. I told them that their mommy had to go away for a while. See," she said, pointing to some pictures drawn with crayons posted up on the wall with scotch tape. "They drew those."

"They're beautiful. What little artists they are."

She smiled and sighed deeply. "Yes, little artists . . ." Her voice trailed off.

"Mrs. Wrey, try and remain optimistic. Ambrosia loves her children more than anything else in this world. She'll pull through this if for no other reason than to see Mateo and Destiny's gorgeous faces again."

"You always know what to say."

No, I don't always know what to say. I just know how to pray and the Holy Spirit instructs me on what to say.

I felt my cell phone vibrating in my purse. Gabriella's number was displayed. I thought about letting the voice mail pick up and decided against it. Having to check the message and call Gabriella back was more of a commitment than I wanted to make. "Excuse me," I said to Mrs. Wrey as I stepped into the hallway. "Hello."

"I'm so glad you answered. I've got to see you right away." Her voice sounded frantic.

"You all right?"

"I'll tell you when I see you. Can I meet you at your house in thirty minutes?"

"Sure. I'm at the hospital visiting a patient, but I'll head out shortly."

"Thank you, Sky. I really appreciate it."

I hung up the phone and went back into the room. "Mrs. Wrey, I have to leave, but I'll call and check on Ambrosia." I handed her my card, which had my cell and office numbers. "If there's any change or you just need to talk, please don't hesitate to call me."

She studied the information. "Thanks." She looked away from the card and stared me in the eyes. "Dr. Little, Ambrosia thinks very highly of you. I know your being here means a lot to her."

"It means a lot to me, too. Ambrosia's important to me." We hugged, again, and I went home.

It was a good thing that traffic wasn't bad. I arrived a few minutes earlier than Gabriella. I used that opportunity to boil some water in my favorite cherry-red-colored tea kettle. I grabbed two cups with matching saucers from the cabinet and placed teabags in each one. When the kettle began to whistle, I removed it from the eye on the stove and poured water into the cups. I allowed the bags of Red Zinger tea to steep for a couple of minutes. That's when the doorbell rang.

"Hey," I said. "You're right on time. I made us some Red Zinger tea." We hugged and she followed me into the kitchen. "Sugar?"

"Yes. Two spoonfuls, please."

I discarded the bags and sweetened the hot drinks with sugar. We each grabbed a cup and saucer and went into the living room. I sipped my tea and asked, "What's going on?"

After setting her cup and saucer on the coffee table, she

pulled out an envelope from her purse and handed it to me. "Read this," she instructed.

I removed a letter from the envelope and began reading. "No, aloud," Gabriella said.

"Oh." I looked at Gabriella, wondering why she wanted me to read the letter aloud. She didn't say anything. She just looked back at me. So I began reading the letter:

Dear Gabriella,

You don't know me personally, but we are connected. I'm writing to you because I'm ill. I've been diagnosed with viral cardiomyopathy. I don't know whether I'll make it through this. Therefore, I must ensure that my children, Mateo and Destiny, are taken care of.

I stopped reading. My heart raced. As I held the letter in my hand, I looked at Gabriella. Tears were streaming down her cheeks.

"Go on," she encouraged.

"You sure?"

She nodded.

I continued.

By now you're probably wondering what any of this has to do with you. Well, I never meant for you to find out this way, but your husband, Kevin Laron James, is the father of my two children. Let me say that I never intended to get involved with a married man. When I met Laron, he didn't tell me he was married. I didn't find out until I was already pregnant with Mateo.

I'm truly sorry about getting involved with your husband. The only reason I stayed with him was because I thought that he and I were going to be a fam-

ily. I was naïve and stupid. When I realized he wasn't going to leave you, I broke it off.

I can understand that you're probably very confused right about now. This whole situation is messed up. As a mother, though, I'm pleading with you to please not blame my children. They're innocent. It's my prayer that you'll accept Mateo and Destiny and encourage Laron to remain an active part of their lives. Again, I'm so very sorry about all of this. I hope you can find it in your heart to forgive me and Laron. May God bless you and your family.

Sincerely,
Ambrosia Wrey

I folded the paper and placed it back inside the envelope. "Wow. Where did you get this?" was all I could say.

"It was in the mail." Her voice started off calm and became progressively more intense. "He has children with her. How could he? How could he do this to me and our family? I'll never forgive him for this. I hate him. You understand? I hate him."

I listened attentively, not knowing what else to say. Of course, clinically I knew what to say. But personally—woman to woman, friend to friend—I was at a loss for words. I didn't interrupt her as she continued to vent about Kevin's betrayal. Finally, she stopped talking and broke down crying. I sat next to her on the couch and hugged her, trying to console her. My heart ached for her. Even though this was all about Gabriella, I couldn't help but pray that I'd never have to experience anything like this with my own husband.

CHAPTER NINETEEN
Monday

Monday got off the phone with her mom, dreading Paige's upcoming visit.

"All she wants is money," Monday complained. "What's that about?" She sucked air through her teeth and said, "Whatever." She went into Alexis's room. "Alexis, get up. Your grandma is on her way over."

"Come on, Mom, I'm tired." Alexis pulled the sheets over her head.

"Girl, don't make me come over there. Get your butt out of the bed and help me straighten up the house."

Alexis responded with an exaggerated grunt.

"What?" Monday said. "I know I didn't hear you say something. Now meet me downstairs." She chuckled.

Monday was in the kitchen putting dishes in the dishwasher when Alexis joined her. "Look at you," Monday said. "You look tore down from the floor down. Rough night?"

"Yeah. I went to bed late," she said, picking at some lint on her PJs. "What you want me to do?"

"Here." Monday handed her a wet dishrag. "Wipe down

the countertops. And when you're finished, sweep the floor."

After filling the dishwasher, Monday started a load. Then she went into the living room and fluffed the pillows on the couch, dusted off the coffee table, and ran the vacuum cleaner over the carpet. "I'll be back," Monday said to Alexis. "I'm going to put on some clothes."

Alexis nodded and finished sweeping the floor. Not long afterward, Monday returned dressed in jeans and a pullover shirt. Her hair was pulled back at the nape of her neck into a ponytail. Alexis was sitting on the couch, eating a bowl of cereal.

"Get dressed after you finish eating your bowl of cereal," Monday instructed.

Alexis nodded and slurped some milk. The doorbell rang. Alexis took her bowl upstairs as Monday answered the door.

She greeted Paige and they went into the living room.

"Where's Lexi?" Paige asked.

"In her room. She's getting dressed." Monday sat on the couch and Paige sat on the love seat. "So how you doin'?"

"I'm doing all right." She sighed.

"You don't sound like it. What's wrong?"

"Everything. My money is funny and my change is strange. I'm tired of having more month than money."

"I can understand that. I've been there before, too."

"You're not there now, though. You got a good job and a new house." She rolled her eyes.

"Ma, my house costs money. And so does my teenage daughter."

"Monday, you've always been better at managing your money than me."

"That's because you gamble with your money. You'll take

your mortgage and go to the casino with it. You need to stop."

"Now you sound like your younger brother Malik. Y'all need to quit trying to tell me what to do. I'm a grown woman." She patted her chest. "I'm the momma."

"I know, but when you come up short, Malik and I are the ones who take up the slack."

"Children are supposed to take care of their parents."

"Yeah, if they're incapable of taking care of themselves. Look, Ma, you're only fifty years old and in excellent health. You have a full-time job as a nurse. We shouldn't have to take care of you."

"You're so ungrateful. After everything I've done for you . . ."

"Everything you've done for me? What? Raise me? I don't owe you for that. You chose to have me. I didn't ask to be born."

Alexis entered and interrupted their conversation. "Hey, Grandma."

"Hey, baby," Paige said as Alexis sat next to her and gave her a hug. "Did Malik tell you that your father has left Tennessee and moved back to Atlanta?" Paige asked Monday.

"No. He didn't tell me. I can't believe he's here. What does he want?"

"Apparently, he's a minister now. He's got a small church out in Douglasville. He contacted me and told me he wants to make amends with his family."

"Minister my behind. I don't trust him, and I'll never forget what he did to me. I'm not interested in having him as a part of my life."

"That's understandable, but don't let bitterness block your blessings," Paige cautioned.

"Whatever," Monday said. "I'm sure God knows my heart."

"Anyway, I gotta go pay my past-due light bill and phone bill before they get cut off."

"How much is it?" Monday inquired, regretting it before the words proceeded out of her mouth. Even though Paige got on her nerves, she could never feel good knowing her mother's basic needs weren't being met.

Paige gave a faint smile, more like a smirk. "The past-due amount of the light bill is $150 and the overdue phone bill is $125."

Monday grabbed her purse and handed her mother three c-notes.

"Thanks," Paige said, accepting the money. She leaned over and kissed Alexis on the cheek. "Love you."

"Love you too, Grandma."

Monday walked Paige to the door and locked it behind her. She rejoined Alexis in the living room. "Can you believe that?"

"What?"

"Stan has the nerve to call himself a preacher." She sucked air and twisted up her face. "I wish lightning would strike that peanut-head, wannabe Negro dead. What is the world coming to?"

Alexis stifled a laugh, and said seriously, "Mom, I'm sorry for what he did to you. Do you think it's possible he could've changed?"

She cut her eyes at Alexis. "Anything's possible, but I doubt it."

"Would you be mad if I told you I wanted to meet him?"

Monday stared at her daughter like she was crazy. "Why would you want to do that?"

"Because he's my grandfather," she explained, biting the corner of her lip. "I'm curious about him."

"I don't know, Alexis." She shook her head. "He's a pervert. What if he tries something with you? I'm not about to catch a case."

Alexis laughed. "I'm grown, Mom. I think I can handle a dirty old man."

"That is so not funny. You know I'd throw a brick in church about you. I don't think it's a good idea for you to let him into your life, but like you said, you're grown. If you want to see him, I can't stop you. But as for me, I don't care if I never see him again in life."

CHAPTER TWENTY
Gabriella

Emotionally, Gabriella was a wreck. After leaving Skyler, she called Giselle, her older sister, and asked her to pick up the kids from school, and watch them until Kevin came home. Her mind was on overload, and she needed time to think, clear her head. She checked into a hotel and spent the night. She didn't even bother to call Kevin because she couldn't bear to hear the sound of his voice. To make sure she wasn't tempted to speak with him, Gabriella turned off her cell phone.

Images of Kevin making love to a faceless woman haunted Gabriella throughout the night, causing her to wake up drenched in sweat. Even now, thinking about her husband sharing intimate moments with Ambrosia made her eyes well with tears. *That dirty, rotten scoundrel didn't just cheat, he lived a double life. Children. Plural.* In time, she probably could've forgiven Kevin for being unfaithful, but children with his mistress was incomprehensible. As far as Gabriella was concerned, that was like asking her to eat cow manure and pretend it was steak. She couldn't do it.

The next day, Gabriella checked out of the Four Seasons

Hotel in Buckhead and headed home. She missed her children and hoped that seeing them would make her feel better. As she pulled into the garage, she noticed that Kevin's car was parked on the left side. Suddenly, she felt anxious and her heart pounded so loudly she could hear it. It seemed as if it were going to beat right out of her chest. She fumbled with the keys at the front door, dreading the confrontation waiting for her on the other side. When she didn't see anyone in the kitchen or family room, she walked toward the stairs.

"Where you been?" Kevin asked as soon as Gabriella entered the foyer. "I was worried sick about you. Why didn't you call? And why weren't you answering your cell phone? I left you several messages. What if something had happened to the kids?"

Gabriella gave him a look that was more like a scowl. "How dare you interrogate me like that?" She reached inside of her purse, retrieved the letter, and threw it at him. The paper fell on the floor.

"What's that?"

"Read it!" she demanded.

Kevin kneeled down and picked the paper up off the ground. Unfolding the letter, he began to read it silently. Gabriella watched as his mouth flew open.

"Gabby, I . . ." He shook his head and rested the letter on the vanity in the foyer.

"You what? Huh? What?" she yelled, and Jr. and Imani came rushing down the stairs.

"Hey, Mommy. You all right?" Jr. asked.

"Hi, my babies. Come and give me a hug." She extended her arms, welcoming both of her children. Then she squeezed them. "You guys have the best hugs ever. What were you doing upstairs?"

"Watching *Shrek*," Imani said.

"Okay. Well, Mommy and Daddy are talking. Go on back upstairs, and I'll be up in a little while to check on you." They did as she requested. "Love you," she yelled behind them.

"Gabby, let's go in the living room so that we can have more privacy."

"We don't need any privacy. What do you have to say to me?"

"I'm sorry."

"Yeah, you're sorry all right." She stormed upstairs and into the master bedroom. Kevin followed, closing the door behind them.

"Come on, don't do that. We can work this out."

"Are you crazy?" She pulled the suitcase from the closet and placed it on the bed. Then she yanked open the dresser drawer, and started throwing clothes inside of the luggage. "I loved you. I trusted you. Now, I can't even look at you."

"Gabby, stop. Stop!" He reached for her hands, and she jerked away.

"Why did you do this to me, Kevin? I don't understand." She continued to remove his clothes from the dresser drawer and place them in the luggage.

"I never meant for this to happen. I never meant to hurt you."

"Yeah, right. You have two children with this woman. You're just like your father." Shaking her head, Gabriella tried unsuccessfully to fight back the tears. She plopped down on the edge of the bed and covered her face with her hands.

Kevin rested his arm on her shoulder and pulled her close to him. "I love you, baby. You're my world. I'm so sorry. Please forgive me."

"Why? Why did you do this?"

"It just happened. We started out as friends."

Gabriella wiped her face with the palm of her hand. "You're lying. Things like this don't just happen. You love her?"

Kevin didn't answer.

"Oh my God." Gabriella stood up and zipped the suitcase. She ran her hand through her hair.

"Gabby, I'm willing to do whatever it takes to make our marriage work. I don't want to be without you. I love you. We can go to counseling."

"No." She shook her head. "It's too late for that. It's over between us. You hear me? It's over!" she spewed.

He placed his hands on her shoulders.

"Don't touch me." She raised her hand in a dismissive gesture. She pulled the suitcase off of the bed.

"If you need time, I respect that. Just don't leave. The kids need you. You stay here. I'll go."

"You got that right. This bag is yours. Take your stuff and go. You can't stay here."

Kevin seemed surprised, but he picked up the suitcase and opened the bedroom door. "Jr., Imani, come here," he yelled down the hallway.

"Yes, Daddy," they said together.

He kneeled down, looked them in their faces and said, "Daddy's going away for a while." He hadn't realized just how much Jr. looked like him. People always said it, but now he could see it for himself. And his beautiful little girl had her mother's delicate features.

"No, Daddy, don't go," Imani begged. She hugged him tightly around the neck, causing him to fall slightly off balance.

As Kevin hugged his daughter back, his eyes became misty. "I love both of you." He released Imani and stood to his feet. "Take care of your mom and do what she says."

"Where are you going, Daddy?" Jr. asked.

"I'm not sure, yet. I'll call you, though."

"When will you be back?" Jr. said.

Kevin looked at Gabriella and said, "That's up to your mom." He picked up the suitcase and walked down the stairs.

Jr. and Imani stood on top of the stairs wailing. When Gabriella heard the garage door open, she cried, too. She embraced her children, trying to console them. She tried to hate Kevin for betraying her, but she couldn't. He was and always would be the father of her children. Even though she wasn't sure she would ever get over the hurt she was feeling, Gabriella didn't want Jr. and Imani to hate their father. Kevin was a good provider and devoted dad.

Gabriella wondered if her children would blame her for Kevin leaving. She didn't want that and wasn't prepared to deal with it either. She stood there in between her children wondering what she was going to do. How was she going to make it?

CHAPTER TWENTY-ONE
Kevin

Kevin drove along the interstate feeling confused. Destination unknown. He felt like he was on autopilot. Merely existing. His body was numb. He wondered how all of this had happened. *Was having an affair with Amber worth losing my wife and family?* He knew that if Gabriella ever found out about his infidelity, losing everything that mattered to him was a real possibility.

He'd never forget the disappointed look on Gabriella's face. That image of her crying because of something he'd done replayed over and over on the screen of his mind like a mini-movie. He would have given anything to take back the hurt and pain he caused her.

Gabby's a good woman, he thought. If Gabriella chose to divorce him, he'd understand. That's not what he wanted, but he would understand. Besides, if the shoe were on the other foot and Gabriella had let another brotha hit it, Kevin wouldn't be forgiving, forgetting, or understanding. She'd have to go. No two ways about it. He shook his head, thinking about the double standards between men and women. Then he shrugged it off and deduced that life wasn't fair. That's just the way it is. Society expects men to be promiscuous. But women, they're wives and mothers. They're supposed to be virtuous.

Kevin drove for about thirty minutes before pulling up in Donovan's driveway. He parked the car and rang the bell. He hoped that someone was at home. Inside the house, he heard a woman say, "Just a minute."

The door opened. "Hey, Sky," Kevin said.

"Hi, Kev. Come on in."

He followed her into the living room and took a seat on the couch.

"I didn't mean to come by without calling, but I didn't have any other place to go."

"Did something happen between you and Gabriella?"

"Yeah, she uh, found out about Amber and kicked me out the house. I need a place to crash."

"You know you're always welcome to stay here."

"Thanks, Sky. That means a lot. Especially after everything I've done."

"Just give her some time. Prayerfully she'll come around." Skyler went into the kitchen and opened the refrigerator. "Want something to drink?"

"Yeah, thanks. Whatever you got will be fine. Where's that husband of yours?"

"He's upstairs on the Internet. He should be down soon. You want me to get him?"

"Nah. No need to interrupt him." Skyler handed him a glass of ice-cold lemonade. He took a sip. "This is good." He smiled, setting the glass on top of a coaster on the end table.

Skyler said, "You all right?"

"Not really, but I'll make it."

"Feel like talking about it?"

"If you mean do I feel like being psychoanalyzed, no." They both laughed.

"What's so funny?" Donovan said as he entered the room.

"Dude," Kevin said. "I didn't even hear you come into the room. What are you? Casper the Friendly Ghost?"

Donovan chuckled. "Something like that. What brings you by?"

Kevin dropped his head. "Gabby kicked me out."

"She found out?" Donovan asked.

Kevin nodded. "Yeah. Amber mailed her some letter. Told her about the affair and the kids."

"That's deep, man. Sorry to hear that."

"Don't be. It's my own fault. I never should've tipped out on my wife anyway. Every time I think about it, I feel sick to my stomach."

"Well, if you need a place to stay, *mi casa es su casa,*" Donovan said.

Kevin nodded and gave a faint smile.

"Do you still love Gabriella?" Skyler asked of Kevin.

"Most definitely. She's my world. I can't even imagine my life without her." He took a sip of lemonade. They eyed him suspiciously. "Come on. Don't look at me like that."

"Like what?" Donovan and Skyler said in unison.

"You know. That 'why'd you do it?' look."

"Well, why did you do it?" Skyler delved.

Kevin told her the same thing he had confided in Donovan. He explained that after Jr. was born, his sex life became non-existent. Gabriella seemed to lose interest in having any relations. She stopped dressing up and wearing makeup. It was like she didn't care anymore. Whenever he made a move, she would reject him. Their relationship became all about the baby. Gabriella was no longer his best friend and lover. Every conversation centered around the baby. Things got so bad sexually that they were only making love once every couple of months. He was frustrated but committed to his marriage. By the time Imani came along, they were intimate only on special occasions.

Meeting Amber was a welcome change. She talked to

him, listened to what he had to say, and made him feel special. He didn't intend to get involved with her, but Kevin felt vulnerable. Amber was willing to do all of the things his wife wasn't. She had a way of making him feel valued, appreciated. And after Amber gave birth to Mateo, as soon as she was cleared by her doctor, they resumed their sex life. She always seemed to want him. For Kevin, that was hard to walk away from. He thought he loved Amber, but his loyalty to Gabriella kept him from filing for a divorce.

Kevin felt torn between two amazing women. Because of it, he developed high blood pressure and an ulcer. The guilt was killing him. He hated lying. Especially to the people he loved. On some level, he was relieved that everything was out in the open. Even if it cost him his marriage.

Skyler sat next to him on the couch and held his hand. "How's Gabriella holding up? I need to call her."

"She didn't come home last night."

"I'm aware," Skyler said. "She talked to me about the letter yesterday. I told her to check into a hotel. She needed time to think. Sort things out."

He released Skyler's hand. "Why didn't you call me? Warn me?"

"I couldn't do that. Gabriella asked me not to call you. I figured that if you called me looking for her, then I would tell you. I wasn't going lie, but I wasn't going to initiate the conversation either. Besides, even if I had told you, it wouldn't have changed anything."

"You're right. I'm trippin'." He gave Skyler a hug. Tears escaped from his eyes, landing on her shoulder. Kevin released her and wiped his eyes with the palms of his hands. "I don't want to lose Gabby," he lamented.

"I pray that doesn't happen. She loves you, and I believe you love her, too. I've counseled patients who have successfully overcome extramarital affairs. I can tell you that the road to recovery isn't easy. You have to be willing to give up your privacy. That can include giving Gabriella access to your email and cell phone. You must be accountable and reachable whenever you leave the house."

"I don't care," Kevin said. "I'm willing to do all that if she'd take me back."

"I hear you, but you need to understand something. Overcoming issues of the flesh like adultery, fornication, and pornography is serious. It's not something that most people can handle on their own. The Word states that 'the spirit is willing but the flesh is weak.' Unless you're willing to commit yourself to the Lord and allow your flesh to die daily, you'll find yourself right back in the same situation. That's why so many people end up going back to the person they cheated with. It's like an addiction. The Lord is the only one who can help you control desires of the flesh. Not you. Not your spouse. Not your children. Not your friends. Nobody. Only God can deliver you."

"Sky, you know me, and you know I've never been big on religion. I've been searching for a long time. I felt like something was missing in my life. I don't go to church, but it's important to me that my children do. Until now, I thought meditating and being a good person was enough. I see that it's not. I'm ready to make a change." He forced a smile.

Skyler embraced him with tears streaming down her cheeks. "I love you, and I'm so proud of you."

They prayed and Kevin repented for his sins. Then he accepted Jesus Christ as his Lord and Savior. His heart was so moved that he couldn't stop weeping.

"Father, forgive me." Kevin cried. "I'm so sorry."

CHAPTER TWENTY-TWO
Reggie

Reggie was asleep in his king-sized bed when he heard a door slam. He got out of bed, heart racing, and grabbed his stainless steel baseball bat. He walked down the hall of his condo wearing boxer shorts and a wife beater with his hands gripped tightly around the makeshift weapon, prepared to swing. When he rounded the corner to go into the kitchen, he saw someone standing there near the kitchen nook.

"What are you doing in here?" He tried to sound intimidating.

Flinching, Tatiana turned around. "You scared me."

"I scared you?" He lowered the bat. "You almost got yourself killed. How did you get in?"

She dangled a key in the air. "Remember when you went out of town? You gave me a key so that I could come over to feed Rufus and check your mail. Make the place look lived-in."

Speaking of Rufus, Reggie greeted his yellow-plumed parakeet, "Good morning."

"Good morning," Rufus repeated.

Reggie walked toward Tatiana and grabbed the key. "Thanks. Now what are you doing here uninvited and unannounced?"

"You weren't returning my calls, and I had to see you."

"Why did you have to see me?"

"Let's sit down and talk about it." She motioned toward the black leather sofa.

"No. Tell me now."

"Reggie, I'm pregnant."

"Reggie, I'm pregnant," Rufus mimicked.

Reggie laughed and said, "Congratulations."

"That's all you have to say?"

"Yeah, what you want me to say? It ain't got nothing to do with me."

"The baby's yours."

He let out a hearty laugh. "Yeah, right. Try again."

"I haven't been with anybody else. It's yours."

"No, ma'am. I always wear a jimmy hat." He opened the refrigerator door and grabbed a carton of orange juice. He thought about drinking from the container, but retrieved a glass from the cabinet instead.

"Condoms aren't one-hundred-percent effective. They've been known to break. It could've been outdated and leaked."

"Look, I'm not trying to be mean, but I don't have time for this. I'm not your baby's daddy. Accept it."

"If you think you can just sleep with me and discard me like the newspaper in the bottom of the freakin' bird's cage, you got another thing coming."

"See, that's why I don't call you. You crazy. Now get from up outta here."

Tatiana gave him a scathing look and bit her lip so hard she drew blood.

"Here." He handed her a damp paper towel.

She snatched it out of his hand and stormed out the door. Reggie still couldn't believe what happened with Tatiana. He knew she was a trip, but this was some *Fatal Attraction* mess.

The first time he met Tatiana was at Vegas Nights nightclub in Marietta, a suburb of Atlanta. Something told him to leave her alone. She pushed up on him and bought him a drink. A Black Russian. He remembered that she wore a tight-fitting ebony dress that made her look like Cindy Herron Braggs, a member of EnVogue, the all-girl singing group.

Tatiana seemed different than most of the women Reggie had encountered in Atlanta. The sisters in the ATL wanted a man with means, and it didn't necessarily have to be a brother. All they cared about was money. Not Tatiana. She had a good job and could afford her own luxuries. She didn't need and wasn't looking for a man to support her. Good company and fun was what Tatiana said she wanted. And he had no reason to doubt her because they went home together the same night they met.

They hooked up a few more times until Tatiana started showing signs of jealousy and possessiveness. She'd ask him who he was with, drop by without phoning, and call late at night to see if he had company. Once he saw that she had stalker potential, Reggie bounced. He stopped returning her calls. He was glad that he only gave out his cell phone number. That way, if a woman started to trip, he could screen the calls or turn off the phone at night.

Reggie pulled his truck into Dr. Little's driveway and began to unload his equipment. Today, he was prepared to work on pruning her hedges and pulling weeds from her flowerbed. He hoped that she was at home, because he really needed to talk. He thought that Dr. Little was a great listener and gave helpful advice.

Not long after he started removing weeds, the front door opened. It was Dr. Little. Reggie was relieved.

"Good morning, Reggie. I heard you when you drove up,

and saw your truck from my bedroom window. How are you?"

"I'm good. And you?" He continued pulling weeds and placing them in a large brown Home Depot lawn bag.

"Fine. I just put on a fresh pot of coffee. And I baked some cinnamon rolls. Fresh from the oven. Want some?"

"How can I refuse cinnamon rolls? Thanks, Dr. Little."

Reggie left his tools on the ground and followed Dr. Little into the kitchen. The sweet smells of cinnamon and the sugary glaze filled the air, making Reggie's mouth water. "May I use your bathroom? I need to wash my hands."

"Sure." She opened the door to a half bathroom and flicked on the light switch.

When Reggie returned, Dr. Little poured two cups of coffee and handed one to him. He sat down on a bar stool next to the island.

"Thanks."

The smell of freshly brewed coffee engulfed his nostrils. A crystal sugar bowl filled with sugar cubes was in the center of the island.

"Creamer?" Dr. Little asked.

"Yeah, thanks."

Dr. Little had an assortment of creamers: hazelnut, vanilla, Irish cream, and original from which to choose. Reggie selected hazelnut to flavor his coffee and two cubes of sugar. Dr. Little removed the cinnamon buns from the oven and set them on the stove. The delicious smell was making Reggie hungry. His stomach grumbled.

"Hungry?"

"Skipped breakfast," Reggie explained, slightly embarrassed.

While waiting for the sweet treats to cool, Dr. Little said, "So, how are things going, Reggie?"

"Whew." He exhaled and chuckled. "Crazy."

"What do you mean?"

"Dr. Little, remember when I told you about the two women I was seeing?"

"Yes." She took a sip of coffee.

"Well, one of them you know."

She tilted her head with curiosity. "I do?"

"Yeah, Monday. Monday Jackson. I referred her to you."

"Oh, Monday's your friend."

"Yep. Anyway, we hooked up recently and she told me she wants a relationship."

"By 'hooked up' I take it you mean you had sex."

He dropped his head. "Yeah."

"Go on. I'm listening." She grabbed a spatula and scraped a roll from the pan. After placing it on a saucer, she set it in front of him. She removed a couple of forks and butter knives from the kitchen drawer, and handed one of each to Reggie. Then she placed another roll on a saucer for herself.

"Monday's a good person, and I could see myself kickin' it with her. It's just that she needs to work through her issues first. She's got a lot going on with her daughter dropping out of high school, her inability to tell her mother 'no,' and unresolved issues from being molested by her father. I don't want to complicate her life any more than it already is."

"That's commendable." Dr. Little stuffed a piece of cinnamon roll into her mouth.

"Then there's Tatiana. That heifer is crazy. I met her at a club and we hooked up a few times. Then she started acting like a stalker. This morning, I woke up and she was in my house. Had the nerve to tell me she's pregnant and the baby is mine."

"Whoa. She sounds dangerous. How did she get into your home?"

"I forgot that I gave her a key when I went out of town. I

had asked her to stop by and feed my bird. When I got back, I forgot to ask for it back." He bit into the roll.

"You should probably have your locks changed. Most likely she made a copy of the key. Do you have an alarm system?"

"I do, but I don't always turn it on."

"Did you give her the code when you went out of town?"

"Aw, snap, I sure did."

"You definitely need to change that, too. Seems like you put a lot of trust into that woman. Why?"

"She seemed cool at first. She owns her own catering company. Makes her own money. I didn't think she was whacked."

"And what about the baby? Do you think it's yours?"

"Not at all, Dr. Little. I used protection every time we were together. Quiet as it's kept, I don't think she's pregnant."

"If she is pregnant and it's yours, what will you do?"

Reggie shook his head. "I don't even know."

"Let me tell you something. When I was little, my parents encouraged me to wait until I was married before having sex. But my mom told me that if I couldn't wait, I should never go to bed with someone I wouldn't want to marry, because unplanned pregnancies happen all the time. I don't mean to sound like a prude, because I'm not." She laughed. "I hear people talk about casual sex all the time, but in actuality, there's no such thing. Why do you think the talk shows are filled with so many people regretting those so-called 'one night stands' and casual flings? Once someone starts catching feelings, the relationship becomes anything but casual. And heaven forbid if a child results from two people who can't stand each other, or the woman doesn't know who fathered her child, it can be a nightmare."

"You're right. All I can do is hope and pray that Tatiana is not pregnant with my child." He finished his last piece of sweet roll.

"Be careful. I don't get a good feeling about this Tatiana person. She sounds mentally unstable to me."

"Maybe I need to refer her to you." They both laughed.

"Here's a little piece of trivia for you. Do you know why polygamy isn't acceptable for women even in the countries where the practice is permitted?"

He shook his head. "No."

"For lineage purposes. If a man has more than one wife and his wives are only intimately involved with him, when the women conceive, he's the father. If a woman has more than one husband and becomes pregnant, she can't be certain about the paternity of her child."

"That's wild, Dr. Little. I never heard that before. Makes you think twice about that whole polygamy thing."

Mr. Little walked into the kitchen and peck-kissed Dr. Little on the lips. He then turned to their guest and said, "Morning, Reggie."

"Good morning," Reggie replied.

"Those rolls smell good, baby. I better get some before Kevin gets up and eats them all. You know that brotha can eat."

Reggie stood up. "Thanks for the talk, Dr. Little. The coffee and cinnamon roll were delicious. I need to go finish pulling up the weeds before it heats up outside."

"You're welcome. Let me know how things turn out."

"Will do. Have a good one, Mr. Little." Reggie waved.

"You too, man." He gave a heads up gesture. "And you can call me Donovan. It's cool."

"Thanks, Donovan."

Reggie continued working in the flowerbed. Sweat spilled down his forehead and onto his nose. He wiped the moisture from his brow. As he discarded weeds and dried leaves into a lawn bag, he noticed a candy-apple-red-colored Corvette driving down the street. He panicked because Tatiana drove a car just like that one. Since he couldn't get a clear view of the driver, he dismissed the thought, chalking it up to paranoia.

CHAPTER TWENTY-THREE
Tatiana

"I knew he was cheating on me," Tatiana seethed with frustration as she thought about Reggie.

She whipped her Corvette into the garage of her three-bedroom, Tudor-style home. Slamming the door behind her as she entered the house, she flung her keys on the plush red chair. Briskly pacing the hardwood floor, she contemplated her revenge.

"How dare he?" she hissed to no one in particular. "I don't know who he thinks he is, but I'm Tatiana Strawberry. Don't nobody do this to me. Told him I was pregnant and he go running to some woman's house. Out there doing her lawn. He ain't never even cut my grass." She wrung her hands. "That's all right, though. I got something for him."

Tatiana thought about the first time she saw Reggie. He looked handsome dressed in a white linen shirt with matching pants. His bald head made him look sexy like Michael Jordan. Reggie exuded confidence, and Tatiana liked that quality in a man. He walked around the club like he owned it. That's why she bought him a drink. In a room filled with beautiful women, she wanted to do something to set herself apart from the rest.

Tatiana realized there was a possibility that Reggie would think she was aggressive or too forward, but she was willing to take that chance. She wanted him. Initially, Tatiana didn't intend to jump into bed with Reggie the first night. Having had too much to drink contributed to her lapse in judgment.

Ever since her nasty break-up with Darnell five years earlier, Tatiana hadn't seriously dated anyone. They were engaged to be married and living together. She considered her split from Darnell to be "nasty" because she caught him with another woman and flipped out. She ended up stabbing Darnell with a pair of scissors and killing him. A jury called it a "crime of passion" as a result of temporary insanity. She was acquitted. That's when she moved from Dallas to Atlanta. Admittedly, it was difficult to find a man willing to date a woman who had killed another man in cold blood. So, she stopped telling people about her past. That's what it was: the past. She had gone to the court-ordered therapy, moved to a new city, and started a successful catering company.

Deep down inside, Tatiana wanted to be happy. She couldn't figure out why she kept attracting unfaithful men. *What's wrong with me?* She stopped pacing the floor and sat down on the steps separating the kitchen from the sunken family room.

"What to do, what to do?" She sighed deeply.

Tatiana could feel herself obsessing, so she got up and turned on the TV. She didn't like her negative train of thought and decided she needed a distraction. As she flipped through the channels, a beautiful lady talking about The Sky's the Limit Foundation caught her attention. She couldn't take her eyes off the plasma screen TV.

"That's her!" she exclaimed. "That's the woman messing with Reggie."

CHAPTER TWENTY-FOUR
Gabriella

It took a concerted effort for Gabriella to get out of bed in the morning. One week had passed since Kevin moved out. Depression consumed her. She tried to put on a brave facade for her children, but deep down inside, she felt as if her heart had been shattered by a sledgehammer. It was especially difficult when the children questioned her about why she made Daddy leave. Gabriella hadn't told Jr. and Imani the truth about why their father was no longer living in the house with them. She considered telling them about Kevin's extramarital affair and his illegitimate children, but changed her mind. Several things stopped her. Even though she couldn't stand to be in the same room with Kevin, he was still Jr. and Imani's father. No matter what, she didn't want her children to hate their dad. There was something inside of her that wouldn't allow her to break her children's hearts that way. She loved them too much. If it meant looking like the "bad guy" so that Jr. and Imani would continue to have a wholesome image of their father, so be it. She wasn't trying to be a martyr, just a good mother. So, she told her children, "Mommy and Daddy are dealing with some adult issues right now. It has nothing to do with you. We both love you very, very much. Don't worry, we'll work it out."

Apparently, telling the children not to worry was easier said than done. Gabriella had to meet with Jr.'s teacher, Mrs. Crabapple, because his grades were slipping. Thinking about Mrs. Crabapple made Gabriella chuckle. Mrs. Crabapple looked about as old as Jane Pittman. Her hair was silver; she had a mustache and a large, black mole above her lip. Her name was fitting.

All of Jr.'s life, he had been an honor-roll student and respectful. Now, he wasn't paying attention in class, and he wasn't turning in his assignments. Gabriella explained to Mrs. Crabapple that she was recently separated from her husband, and Jr. was taking it hard. She assured Mrs. Crabapple that she'd talk to Jr. and help him through it.

And then there was Imani. She seemed to blame Gabriella for running Kevin away. Imani appeared to be emotionally detached from Gabriella and deeply angry. Every time Gabriella tried to hug or kiss Imani, Imani pulled away, causing her mother greater pain.

Gabriella desperately wanted to be there for her children. She felt as if she were on psychological overload. She wished that Kevin was there to help her, but she wasn't ready to face him. Thoughts about her failed marriage gnawed at her like a flesh-eating disease. Washing her hair, brushing her teeth, and even bathing seemed like a chore to Gabriella. She didn't know what to do with herself. Life without Kevin seemed miserable, yet the possibility of taking him back seemed unconscionable.

The ringing of the cell phone snapped Gabriella out of her zombie-like state.

"Hello," she said into the receiver.

"Hey, Gabriella. It's Caleb. How are you doing?"

"I've been better."

"I hadn't seen you around at the gym. I was worried about you. You all right?"

"Actually, Caleb, I'm not all right."

"What's wrong?"

"Everything." She began sobbing into the phone.

"Gabriella, please calm down. I hate for a woman to cry. Tell me what's wrong."

"Kevin and I separated."

"Sorry to hear that," consoled Caleb. "Sounds like you need a friend. Want me to come over?"

"I don't think that's a good idea."

"Why? Are your children at home?"

"No, they're at school. It's just that I don't feel like I'd make very good company right now." She grabbed a tissue from the nightstand next to her bed and blew her nose.

"I don't need to be entertained. I'm simply coming over as a friend."

Gabriella hesitated for a moment before saying, "I guess that'll be all right." She gave him directions from the gym to her house.

After hanging up the phone, Gabriella showered and washed her hair. Rather than blow-drying her hair, she slicked it back into a long ponytail. She applied a little makeup to her face so that she wouldn't look as horrid as she felt. Then she put on a pair of jeans and fitted T-shirt.

Gabriella figured Caleb must've left the gym as soon as they got off the phone, because he was knocking at her door within twenty minutes. Her heart raced as she felt a bit nervous. Her stomach fluttered. It was Caleb's first time visiting her home, and she felt guilty, as if she was disrespecting Kevin. She rubbed her hands on her thighs, removing the sweat from her palms. She exhaled, trying to gain her composure.

You can do this, she reasoned. *Kevin's the one who had*

the affair, not you. You don't have anything to feel guilty about.

Gabriella placed her hand on the handle and opened the door. A faint smile appeared across her face. His perfectly round, bald head reminded her of a scoop of ice cream. "Hi, Caleb."

Caleb entered through the front door and smiled. He had on a nylon sweat suit. "Hey, Gabriella. It's good to see you."

She closed the door behind him and led him into the living room, which was decorated with a couple of short pillars with bust statues atop each. There were decorative scented candles throughout the room. Gabriella had lit a few of the candles because the dim light relaxed her. "Want something to drink?" Gabriella said.

"No, thanks." He sat on the plush, lavender-colored couch. "Tell me what's going on."

Taking a seat in the rocking chair, Gabriella slowly rocked back and forth. She contemplated whether she should tell him the truth and get him involved in such a personal matter. After searching his face and seeing the sincere look in his eyes, she was no longer reluctant. "I recently found out that Kevin has been having an affair."

"Wow. You don't say."

"Yeah. And as if it's not bad enough he cheated on me, he has two children with that woman."

"No! I can't believe that! Not Kevin!"

"Yes, it's true. Her name is Ambrosia. She wrote me a letter telling me all about the affair and the children."

"What did Kevin have to say for himself?"

"What could he say? It was all true."

"Did he at least try to explain?"

"You think I want to hear anything he has to say? There's nothing he can say that would make any difference."

"True. How are you holding up?"

"It's hard, you know? I feel like Jr. and Imani blame me for their dad not being here. I wish things could be different, because the children really love Kevin. They don't understand why he moved out. I feel like I'm responsible for them not having a father."

"They have a father. You shouldn't blame yourself for any of this because it's not your fault. Kids are resilient. They'll be all right."

"I hope you're right."

Caleb kneeled next to the rocking chair and held Gabriella's hand. "You're a beautiful, desirable woman. Any man would be lucky to have you. Kevin's a fool for letting you get away."

A tear slid down Gabriella's cheek. She felt vulnerable. Her heart had belonged to Kevin, yet he tossed her to the side like yesterday's video game cartridge. Kevin had been her best friend. She had trusted him, and he had betrayed her. No one had ever hurt her so deeply. The fact that she was still Kevin's wife, and he was still her husband, meant something to her. Kevin may have disregarded his wedding vows, but she couldn't. Marriage was still an honorable institution. Until she was divorced, Gabriella was married. Married to Kevin. *And what about the children? Jr. and Imani adore Kevin. He adores them, too.* She would never want her children to be raised without their father. Gabriella desperately needed to make a decision. Should she stay with Kevin for the sake of the children?

Caleb leaned in closer to Gabriella. He was only inches away from her face, staring at her lips. She could tell that he wanted to kiss her.

"Caleb, I can't." She released his hand. "You're a great guy, but I'm not ready."

He stood up. "I understand. No pressure. I should probably get going anyway."

"Wait." Gabriella stood up, too. "I hope I didn't hurt your feelings. I didn't mean to."

"It's okay. I'm not upset."

"Are you sure?"

"I'm sure." He kissed her on the cheek. "It's all good." They walked to the door. "You still going to go to the gym, right?"

"I need to. Help me release some of this stress." She laughed nervously.

"Keep your head up. Call if you need me."

She nodded. "Thanks. I appreciate you coming over."

"No problem."

She closed the door behind him. *What am I doing?*

CHAPTER TWENTY-FIVE

Kevin

Rather than taking a leave of absence from work, Kevin spoke with his boss, and they agreed that Kevin could work from home. Kevin felt relieved because working from home gave him more flexibility.

I've got to see my kids. All of them. I miss them too much. Kevin picked up the phone and dialed Gabriella's cell number. His heart rate increased. He hadn't spoken with her since he moved out of their home. Not speaking with her was difficult for him. He missed her terribly. There were several times every day that he was tempted to call her, but he didn't follow through. He felt as if he had done enough damage and didn't want to do anything else to alienate her.

Gabriella answered the phone and Kevin couldn't speak. "Hello, hello. Is anybody there?" said Gabriella as she checked for a number on the display screen.

Kevin cleared his throat and said, "Baby, it's me."

Gabriella sighed. "What do you want, Kevin?"

"I want to see Jr. and Imani." There was an uncomfortable silence. He wondered whether she had hung up on him, so he asked, "You still there?"

She breathed heavily into the receiver and said, "Fine."

He wasn't expecting her to be so amiable. He expected a fight. "When would be the best time for me to come over?"

"No. Aren't you staying with Sky and Donovan?"

"Yeah."

"Then I'll stop by after dinner. You can spend some alone time with the kids. I need to talk to Sky."

"Thanks, Gabby. I really appreciate this."

"Okay. Bye."

They hung up. Hearing Gabriella's voice fueled the longing that was already in his heart. He wanted to be with her. To be the husband she deserved. He realized that he had violated the integrity of their relationship, and he was sorry. There was nothing he wouldn't do to get his wife back. He loved her.

Kevin was determined to fix the mess he had made. He went to the hospital to visit Amber. This was one of the few times Mrs. Wrey wasn't holding vigil in Amber's room. Having this time alone with Amber was something he relished. There was a lot on his mind; he needed to share it with her. Even with tubes protruding from her body, Amber looked so peaceful, so angelic.

He sat down next to the bed and held Amber's hand. "Amber, I don't know what to say. We've been through so much together." Tears welled in his eyes. "I can't lie. When I first found out about the letter you sent to Gabby, I was angry. I couldn't believe you dropped a dime on me. That was before I found the Lord. I've been praying, reading the Bible, and going to church. I realize now that I never should've been angry with you. I'm the one who did this. I cheated on my wife. I lied to you. I was wrong, and I accept that. If you can hear me, please accept my apology. I'm sorry for lying to you. You're a good woman. You deserve better. I pray that you get up out of here and find someone who'll be good to you.

"I know you were worried about Mateo and Destiny. Don't. I'm going to talk to your mom and arrange for me to get custody should anything, God forbid, happen to you. I love them, and I love you for giving them to me. They are an important part of my life and it's time everyone knows it. I'm ready to take responsibility for my actions. I hope that makes you happy."

Just then, Amber's heart monitor began to beep. "What's going on? Amber?" Kevin ran into the hall yelling, "Nurse. Somebody get in here. Something's wrong with Amber."

The robust nurse hurried past him. When she saw Amber's body convulsing, she called for back-up. "You can't be in here!" she barked at Kevin.

He stood outside of the door wondering what was happening. He prayed that God wouldn't call Amber home just yet. When the door opened, Kevin could tell by the solemn look on the doctor's face that the news wasn't good. He braced himself and prepared for the worst. Having heard the words, "I'm sorry. We did everything we could. She went into cardiac arrest, and we couldn't save her," Kevin broke down crying.

"God, no. Not Amber." He turned and punched the wall. He felt as if life wasn't fair. *What about Mateo and Destiny? How am I going to explain this to them?*

Kevin phoned Mrs. Wrey and told her that he was on his way over. By the time he arrived at Mrs. Wrey's ranch-style, three-bedroom house, he had popped several antacid tablets to alleviate the pain in his stomach.

Mrs. Wrey greeted him at the door. "Hi, Laron. What's wrong? You look like you've been crying."

He searched her face, dreading the news he had to deliver. He walked into the living room and took a seat on the plaid couch. Pictures of Amber, Mateo, Destiny, and other family members were displayed on a wooden table. He swallowed the lump in his throat and said, "Mrs. Wrey, there's no easy way to tell you this." He started crying, again. "But Amber died today."

Mrs. Wrey's knees buckled and she collapsed to the floor. Kevin rushed to her side. She began sobbing uncontrollably. "No, no, no. Not my baby."

Kevin placed his arm around her shoulder as she moaned and rocked slowly. He felt as if he should've been the one dead, not Amber.

The rest of the day Kevin functioned in a dazed state. He could hardly keep his thoughts together. He stayed with Mrs. Wrey until Anastasia came over to comfort her. Mateo and Destiny were at daycare, so Kevin picked them up earlier than usual. They were happy to see him. He hugged them very tightly. He didn't want to let them go. He took the children to get vanilla ice cream with rainbow sprinkles, and tried to explain the best way he could that Amber was in heaven. Neither one of the children understood the concept of death, but Kevin tried to break it down in a manner that they could comprehend. He explained that Mommy had fallen asleep. God had realized that He was missing an angel and called Mommy home. Even though they wouldn't be able to see Mommy anymore, she was in heaven watching over them. He pulled out a worn photograph of Amber from his wallet and told them that Amber would always live in their hearts.

Mateo and Destiny both started asking for their mommy. Kevin felt as though he were having an emotional meltdown. *Why didn't I let Skyler help me break the news to the children?* He tried unsuccessfully to console his children. It seemed like the harder he tried, the more they whined and cried. Finally, he broke down crying, too, and admitted that he didn't understand why Mommy wasn't coming back to them. The three of them hugged and cried together until Kevin took them home to their grandmother.

When Kevin arrived with Mateo and Destiny, Mrs. Wrey was in her bedroom resting. Anastasia let them in and told Kevin that she had had to call Mrs. Wrey's doctor. Dr. Anniston had given Mrs. Wrey a sedative because she became hysterical after Kevin left. Kevin felt as if an apocalyptic cloud was looming over his head.

Anastasia took Mateo and Destiny into one of the guest bedrooms and played a *Dora the Explorer* DVD to distract them. Kevin remembered that Gabriella was supposed to be bringing Jr. and Imani over for a visit, and he considered canceling. Canceling would only postpone his troubles, so he dismissed that idea.

"Anastasia, I have some things I need to take care of," Kevin said when she reentered the living room. "Will you be all right with your mom and the kids for a while?"

"You go ahead. Spending time with my niece and nephew is exactly what I need right now. Besides, I left Christopher a message at his office and he'll be over here as soon as he gets out of court."

Christopher was Anastasia's husband of two years. He was a high-powered attorney and enjoyed a jet-setting lifestyle. He didn't mind providing Anastasia with the luxuries of life; in return, she agreed not to have any children. According to Christopher, he didn't want the responsibility of being a parent. Judging by the way Anastasia doted on Mateo and Destiny, Kevin thought she would make a great mother. He couldn't understand why a woman would give up motherhood in exchange for material possessions. He felt sorry for her. She had no idea that a loving family makes you rich. If he didn't realize that before, he certainly realized it now.

Since neither Skyler nor Donovan were at home yet,

Kevin used the spare key Donovan gave him to let himself in. The house seemed overly quiet. He couldn't get Amber off his mind. He thought about her warm smile. Her laughter echoed in his mind. It was as if she were standing right there with him, laughing. He thought about the first time they met; Mateo's birth; Destiny's birth; and all of the special little things Amber did for him. Amber was so thoughtful. She used to write him love letters and cook his favorite meal: jambalaya. She learned how to make it especially for him. Then there were the oatmeal raisin cookies she used to make from scratch. To say the homemade treats were delicious was an understatement. They were so good he encouraged her to start a business and sell the cookies to the masses.

A faint smile appeared across his face. His spirit was simply broken. He had cried so much that his tear ducts were dry. Even though his stomach grumbled, he didn't feel like eating. He wondered if Skyler knew that Amber was . . . that Amber had . . . He couldn't say it. Transitioned. That's it. That's the word he would use. The "D" word seemed so sad, permanent.

Kevin called Skyler's office phone, and Yahkie answered.

"Hey, Yahkie. This is Kevin. Is Sky available?" He tried to sound upbeat.

"You're in luck. She's in. Let me patch you through."

"Thanks."

There was brief silence on the line before Skyler answered. "This is Sky."

"Hey. It's Kevin." He swallowed hard.

"How are you?"

"What time are you coming home?"

"I'm done seeing clients for the rest of the day. I was working on a case study. Is something the matter?"

"Sky, Amber. She, she . . ." He became silent.

"Oh my God, has something happened to Ambrosia?"

He nodded his head, pinched the bridge of his nose, and mouthed the word, "Yes."

"Where are you?"

"At your house."

"Don't go anywhere. I'm on my way." She hung up the phone.

Kevin sat silently in the living room waiting for Skyler to come home.

CHAPTER TWENTY-SIX

Skyler

I can't believe that Ambrosia is dead! This doesn't make any sense. I thought the medically-induced coma was supposed to improve Ambrosia's chances of survival. I wonder what happened. And what about those two beautiful children of hers? I hope Kevin assumes his responsibility and takes care of them.

So many thoughts were wandering in my mind that they were canceling each other out. I knew I wouldn't be able to concentrate on work. *I have to get out of here.* After packing up my laptop, locking up my desk drawers, and grabbing my purse, I said to Yahkie, "An emergency has come up. Ambrosia died. I'm leaving for the rest of the day and probably tomorrow, too."

Yahkie gasped. His mouth dropped open. "What happened?"

"I don't have any of the details yet. All Kevin told me was that she died."

"That's shocking, and so sad. Her poor kids."

I headed toward the door and yelled over my shoulder, "If anything comes up, call my cell or PDA."

"Will do."

In my car, I phoned Donovan at work.

"Honey, I'm on my way home. Kevin called and told me that Ambrosia died."

"What?" He sounded shocked. "What happened?"

I rolled my eyes upward and fought back tears. "Not sure. Just wanted to let you know what was going on."

"You all right, baby?"

I swallowed the lump forming in my throat. "I'm hanging in there even though I'm feeling a bit jittery. This seems surreal."

"What about Kevin? How did he sound?"

"Not so good, but that's to be expected. That's why I left work. I didn't think he should be alone."

"I have a meeting in thirty minutes," he explained. "As soon as it's over, I'll be on my way home. Okay?"

"Sure, sweetie. I love you."

"Love you, too. Do you need anything?"

"Just you." I smiled.

I parked my car in the garage and checked my face in the rearview mirror. Just as I thought, my eyes were red from crying. I took a deep breath and tried to regain my composure. I wanted to be strong for Kevin. The only thing I grabbed from the car was my purse. My laptop would have to wait. Besides, the way I was feeling, I wouldn't be able to get any work done anyway.

I entered the living room and saw Kevin slumped on the couch. "You all right?" I asked as I set my purse on the table.

He stared at me blankly. I took a seat next to him on the couch and wrapped my arm around his shoulder.

"She's gone, Sky," he managed to choke out.

"I know. You feel like talking about what happened?"

"I went to see her at the hospital. Told her I was going to raise Mateo and Destiny. I basically let her know she didn't have to worry about the kids, because I was going to man up. Next thing I know, the monitor starts going off like crazy. Beeping all over the place. The nurse rushed in and kicked me out of the room. It all happened so fast."

"Where are Mateo and Destiny now?"

"They're with Amber's sister, Anastasia. After I told Mrs. Wrey what happened, she needed to be medicated."

"I see."

"Gabby's bringing Jr. and Destiny over this evening. I have no idea how that's going to work out."

"Let me break the news to Gabriella," I said.

"Why?"

"Because if she hears it from you, she'll take it as another act of betrayal. Seeing you grieving for your lost love will undoubtedly make her resent you even more. It may make her feel hopeless."

"I don't get it. Why would she take it like that?"

"It's hard to explain. It's like she could convince herself that maybe your relationship with Ambrosia was physical; maybe you didn't love her. If she sees you visibly upset, grieving, she'll know that you actually loved this woman. That would hurt her even more because she may feel as if you didn't save anything for her: not your love, not your body, not your children. If Gabriella can't find something to hold on to, she may give up and ask for a divorce."

"Well, a divorce is the last thing I want." He sounded somber and pressed a balled fist to his mouth. "I'll let you tell her."

I removed my arm from his shoulder and looked him in the eyes. "You've got to be strong for your children. They're depending on you to get them through this."

He nodded his head. I could tell by the worn expression on his face that he was having a difficult time accepting Ambrosia's death. For that matter, so was I.

A few hours later, Gabriella arrived with Jr. and Imani.

When the children saw their dad, they leapt into his arms like dancers in the Alvin Ailey Dance Company. It was obvious that Kevin missed them as much as they missed him. Surprisingly, Gabriella was cordial toward Kevin. They exchanged pleasantries before parting ways.

Kevin took the children into our finished basement where he was staying. The basement was like separate living quarters; complete with bedroom, kitchen, bathroom, and game room. Donovan had gotten home from his meeting. He was upstairs in his office working, so Gabriella and I sat in the family room drinking cups of Red Zinger tea.

"Gabriella, how have you been?"

"I have good days and bad, you know?"

"What about the kids? How are they handling the separation?"

"They don't understand. Jr. is acting out in school. And Imani, she's rebelling. It's hard on all of us right now." She took a sip of tea and looked around the room. Apparently she wanted to ensure we were alone. "I want to tell you something."

"Sure."

"There's this guy at the gym named Caleb who has become a good friend to me."

"Oh really?"

"It's not like that. We're just friends. Kevin knows him."

"And?"

"Well, he came over to see how I was doing. We talked, and I felt comfortable talking to him." She looked around as if she were making sure were still alone. "It's just that . . . he wanted to kiss me."

"What did you do?" I scratched my head.

"I didn't. He's nice and very attractive, you know?" She laughed. "But I couldn't do it. I don't know why I couldn't. I just couldn't."

"What stopped you?"

"You're the shrink, you tell me." She looked at me with questioning eyes.

"In a nutshell, you aren't ready. You aren't ready to move on from your marriage because you still have feelings for Kevin."

"That's true, but Kevin hurt me. I don't know if I'll ever get over it." She blinked rapidly.

I cleared my throat. There was no easy way to say what I had to say. "Well, something tragic happened today." I set down my cup before looking her in the eye. "Ambrosia died."

She gasped and covered her mouth with her hand. "What?"

"You already knew she was in the hospital for viral cardiomyopathy."

Gabriella nodded her head.

"She went into cardiac arrest," I explained.

"I can't believe it. This keeps getting worse and worse. I mean, I'm at a loss for words."

"This must be awkward for you, I'm sure." Her hand was resting on her thigh, so I patted it. "As a mother, you probably feel sorry for the kids. As the scorned wife, you may feel a bit relieved. But you're a decent person. Even though you weren't a fan of Ambrosia's, you wouldn't have wished this on her, I'm sure."

"No." She shook her head vehemently. "I would never have wanted this to happen to her. I admit I was angry when I found out about the affair. At first I probably wanted to strangle her and Kevin with my bare hands. Once I calmed down, the violent thoughts went away. Of course, I didn't want them to be together and live happily ever after either, but I never could've imagined something like this." Her voice trailed off, and she stared at a speck of dirt on the floor.

I picked up my cup and sipped some tea. The smell of

raspberry entertained my nostrils. "Gabriella, Kevin really needs you now. He's got a lot resting on his shoulders."

She shook her head. "Please don't ask me to take him back. He cheated on me." Her eyes pleaded for understanding. "Do you understand how hard this is for me?" I nodded and she continued. "I loved Kevin with all my heart. I could've forgiven him for being unfaithful, because it's just sex. I'm not the jealous type. You know me. I'm real laid back and easy going. I give Kevin freedom. It's the fact that he lied. Trust is important to me. Without trust, we have nothing. Lying for me was the deal-breaker."

"I'm not asking you to take him back. That's your decision and your decision alone. What I am asking is for you to pray before you make a decision that's going to affect you and your children for the rest of your lives. Yes, Kevin made a mistake, a big one. I'm not negating that fact. Even if you did agree to work things out with Kevin, you would still have a long road ahead of you. I realize that. You can either focus on your anger and hatred for Kevin or you can focus on the love. I want you to dig deep in your heart and pull out the love for Kevin. If you do, then no matter what happens, the two of you will always act in the best interests of your children. Besides, anger and hostility benefit no one. Do you think you can do that?"

"I hear you, and I'll think about what you said." She sniffled and wiped the corners of her mouth with her hand.

"Please do. And while you're at it, think about how you're going to tell Jr. and Imani about their brother and sister."

"Oh, God." She placed her cup on the saucer and pressed her back against the sofa. "Is this ever going to end?" She threw her hands in the air.

"Everything in life is temporary." I stroked the back of her head. "This too shall pass." I gave her an encouraging smile.

"Why do I have to tell Jr. and Imani about Kevin's kids? He's the one who messed up; let him tell them."

"I understand that you're hurt. You and Kevin should tell your children together. The two of you need to present a united front. Your reaction could mean the difference between Jr. and Imani hating their father and refusing to accept their siblings, as opposed to forgiving Kevin and being willing to accept his other children."

"I don't want them to hate him," she admitted.

"I'm glad to hear that. I know this is a troublesome time for you; I'm here to help you through it. You need to be aware, though, that Kevin wants to raise Mateo and Destiny."

"I'm not surprised." She closed her eyes for a moment; then opened them and looked at me. "I mean with their mother being dead and all."

"If the two of you reconciled, would you be willing to accept them and love them as your own?" I rested my hands on my lap, fingers intertwined.

She shook her head. "I can't even wrap my mind around something like that, you know? It's hard." She sounded frustrated.

"You don't have to decide on anything right now. I just wanted to let you know what's going on."

"I appreciate that. I don't know what I'd do without you."

I smiled. "Hey, if you want Jr. and Imani to spend the night, I'd be glad to have them. It's been a minute since we've had a sleepover."

"I can't ask you to do that. Besides, it's a school night."

"What are you talking about? Did you forget who I am? I'm Aunty Sky," I reminded her. "Tomorrow is Friday, and Yahkie isn't expecting me in the office anyway. I can get up and get the kids ready. No problem."

"You really don't mind?"

"Of course not."

"But I didn't bring them anything."

"They have extra clothes, pajamas, and their own tooth-brushes upstairs in the guest bedroom."

"You're right. I forgot about that. In that case, I guess it's a done deal." She stood up. "I'm going to go. I'm feeling a little tired."

"Sure." I gave her a hug and said, "It'll be all right."

She grabbed her purse off of the couch and yelled down-stairs into the basement, "Jr.! Imani! Mommy's about to go. Come upstairs please and give me a hug."

Jr. and Imani raced up the carpeted stairs. They wrapped their arms around Gabriella's waist. Gabriella kneeled down and kissed them both on the forehead. "I love you," she said. "I'm going to let you spend the night here with Daddy and Aunty Sky."

"Thank you, Mommy," they said in unison. Their eyes lit up like lights on a pinball machine.

"You be good," Gabriella instructed before leaving.

I was glad to have the children in the house. I enjoyed spending time with them. They were good kids, and spend-ing time with Kevin was exactly what they needed. Not to mention that loving on Jr. and Imani would also be thera-peutic for Kevin. Right then, he needed all the love and sup-port he could get.

CHAPTER TWENTY-SEVEN

Monday

Dressed in a clingy, low-cut top, dress pants, and heels, Monday entered the lobby at Twelve in Atlantic Station and took a seat at the bar. There were mostly men at the bar, conversing and laughing with each other. Judging by the mannerisms and closeness of the two men sitting next to her, Monday deduced that they were on a date. The bartender, thin, blond-haired, and baby-blue-eyed, introduced himself as Tim. Monday ordered an individual lobster pizza and diet soda as she waited for Larry to arrive.

She hadn't seen Larry in years, but felt that the upcoming conversation was worthy of a face-to-face meeting. Feeling a bit self-conscious, she wondered how Larry would feel about her weight gain. The last time he saw her, Alexis was in junior high school, and Monday was fifty pounds lighter.

It wasn't long before the bartender served Monday a piping hot pizza and an ice-cold, fizzing drink. She sipped her cola before devouring the tasty thin-crust pie. After dabbing the crumbs from her mouth, she pulled a mirrored compact from her purse and reapplied her lip gloss.

"Sorry I'm late," apologized Larry. His head looked bigger

than Monday remembered. She felt like calling him "Meat-loaf." The thought caused her to chuckle. He was dressed in a polo shirt, jeans, and dress shoes.

Monday closed her compact and placed it, along with the gloss, back in her purse. She pressed her lips together before placing a stick of gum in her mouth. She said "Hello" and offered Larry a piece, which he accepted. Larry took a seat on the vacant stool next to her. Tim asked if he could get something for Larry, and Larry replied, "No, thanks." Tim removed Monday's clean plate and empty glass.

"You're looking good. What's going on?" Larry asked.

"Thanks." Monday blushed. "I didn't want to get into this over the phone. It's about Alexis. She dropped out of high school."

"What?!" He stood up.

Noticing that people were looking at them, Monday instructed Larry to sit back down. He did as she requested.

"The reason I didn't tell you this before was because I was trying to handle the situation myself prior to involving you. Anyway, long story short, Alexis is going to Job Corps."

"Job Corps? Why?"

"What do you mean, 'why'? Why what?" Monday repeated sarcastically.

"You still haven't told me why Alexis quit school in the first place."

"It's a lot of stuff. The kids were picking on her about her weight and skin problems. Then she wasn't doing well in her classes. Plain and simple, she hated going to school. She told me that she felt dumb because her classes were too hard. She just wasn't getting it. I told her she had to do something, because she wasn't going to be a high school dropout. We checked into some alternative schools, and we both agreed that Job Corps was the best bet."

"You want me to talk to her?" he said sternly.

"For what? Job Corps has a good program. I checked it

out. She'll still be able to finish high school, and she can learn a trade."

"Will she be living in their housing?"

"Yes. I'm comfortable with it because they closely supervise those kids. Besides, it'll teach Alexis how to be more responsible. At least she'll finish something she started."

"Well, it sounds like you've got everything under control. You really didn't need me for anything." He sighed.

Monday felt like saying, "You're right. You haven't been here all this time. We really don't need you for anything." Instead she said, "You're her father, Larry. I wanted you to know what was going on with your daughter."

"All right." He clasped his hands together. "So what else is going on?"

"Not too much. That was the biggie right there."

"I wish you would've talked to me about this before it got to this point."

"Talk to you? You trippin'. It's not like Alexis and I had a discussion. We didn't just sit down and mutually agree that she needed to quit school. It wasn't like that. Alexis came to me after the fact. I didn't even know things had gotten so bad for her."

"I'm sorry. It's not your fault."

"Thank you." She pursed her lips.

Tim placed the tab on the counter and Larry picked it up. He pulled his wallet out of his back pocket and paid the bill.

"Look at you," Monday teased. "That's so sweet." She tapped him on the arm. They both laughed.

"I got a job," he announced.

"Congratulations. Doing what?"

"The company I worked for paid me to go to school, so I got a degree in communications. I've been working at a radio station as a programmer for the past two years."

"Good for you." Monday was genuinely pleased. For

most of the time she had known Larry, he had a difficult time holding down a job. That's the main reason she didn't go after him for child support. It was a waste of time and money. A long time ago, she accepted the fact that Larry lacked ambition, yet she allowed Alexis to spend time with him whenever he wanted.

"I didn't tell you or Alexis because I wanted it to be a surprise. I wanted to be sure I was going to finish school and be able to get a job."

"Hey, I understand." *Two years, huh? That's a record*, Monday thought.

He stood up and said, "Keep me in the loop, okay?"

"Okay."

He leaned over and kissed Monday on the cheek. "Ready?"

"Yeah, I guess."

They walked out together and waited for the valet to bring their cars. Monday was glad that she and Larry were getting along so well. She finally felt as if they were on one accord when it came to Alexis. Granted, it had taken eighteen years. Better late than never.

Before Larry got into his silver Mercedes coupe, he placed a bank-certified check in the amount of $2500 in Monday's palm.

"What's this?" Monday said with a perplexed expression on her face.

"It's a little something for Alexis. You've been carrying the load by yourself for too long. Now that I'm able to help, I will. I know I can't make up for lost time, but I'm serious about being a constant part of Alexis's life."

"I don't know what to say." Monday was smiling so hard she looked like someone had handed her a check for a million dollars. Hugging him, she whispered in his ear, "Thank you so much."

He kissed her on the cheek and said, "I'll be in touch." Larry got in his car while Monday stood there with her mouth agape.

When Monday arrived at her home, she was content, like a baby after being spoon-fed dinner and given a warm bath. She kicked off her high heels and propped her feet on the couch. She couldn't believe that Larry had given her $2500. The thought gave her goose bumps. She couldn't wait to tell Alexis.

After taking a thirty-minute nap, Monday felt so good that she decided to fix spaghetti with meatballs and garlic cheesebread for dinner; it was Alexis's favorite dish. Having removed the ground chuck from the freezer, Monday placed the meat in a copper pot filled with hot water to help it thaw faster and set the container in the sink.

The meat would take a while to thaw, so Monday poured herself a glass of chilled blackberry wine. She went back into the family room and watched a Lifetime movie. Near the end of the flick, Alexis walked in.

"Hi, Mom. Surprised to see you. What are you doing here?"

"Hello to you too, Miss Lady." Monday chuckled. "Last time I checked, I lived here."

Alexis joined her mom on the couch. "How was your day?" Alexis asked.

"Actually, today was a good day."

"Really?"

"Yes. I met with Larry."

"My dad?"

Monday nodded. "We had lunch. More like I had lunch. He paid the bill," she clarified. "Anyway, I told him what was going on with you and school."

Alexis held her head down.

"No, honey. It wasn't bad. You're not in trouble. I figured he'd be asking about your high school graduation and wanting invitations soon, so I told him about you going to Job Corps."

"What did he say?"

"Nothing really. After I got done explaining it to him, there wasn't really much to say." She reached inside of her purse and pulled out the certified check. "Here."

"Is this real?" Alexis examined the bank tender, smiling.

Monday laughed. "It's from your dad. He told me that he got a job at a radio station as a programmer."

"For real?"

"That's what he said. Oh yeah, he also went to college and got a degree in communications. He looked like he was doing well."

Alexis rested her head on her mom's shoulder and said, "I'm happy for him."

"You don't sound like it."

Sitting upright, Alexis leaned forward to place the check on the coffee table. She looked Monday in the eye and said, "I am happy that he's doing well. It's just that . . . you and I have been through so much together. Even though you haven't said it, I know it's been rough on you raising me all by yourself. I may not act like it all the time, but I think you're a good mother. And I love you, Mom."

Monday's eyes welled with tears. "Awww, I love you too."

"Mom, I want you to be happy."

"What makes you think I'm not happy?"

"I can tell. I wish you'd find a good man to spend the rest of your life with. Someone who'll love you for you and provide for your every need. You've been so busy taking care of me that you've sacrificed yourself."

"Listen to you," Monday joked. "Trying to sound all grown up." She dabbed the corners of her eyes with her right ring finger. Even though she tried to put on a brave front, Monday knew that she wanted to get married.

When Alexis was little, Monday devoted herself to providing for her child. Due to Larry's inconsistent involvement in Alexis's life, Monday tried to overcompensate by taking on the role of both mother and father for Alexis. Although she dated, she used Alexis as an excuse for not getting too close to any man. There was a protective shield that Monday had built around her heart that wouldn't allow her to fall too deeply for anyone.

Because she had been molested by her father and disappointed by Larry, Monday had trust issues. She expected men to hurt her; in turn, she developed an "I don't care" attitude. Now that Monday recognized her "areas for improvement," as she preferred to call them, and was seeking help, she felt ready for a committed relationship.

"You want to help me make spaghetti for dinner?" Monday asked.

"What do you want me to do?"

"Oh my goodness," Monday teased. "You mean you're actually going to help me cook? Wow! Okay. Who are you and what did you do with my daughter?"

"Very funny, Mom."

They went into the kitchen that was designed with maple wood cabinets and black countertops. Monday drained the water from the ground chuck and began seasoning the meat. Alexis removed a head of lettuce from the black refrigerator and rinsed off the debris. She chopped the leaves and placed them in a large wooden bowl. Then she washed and diced tomatoes and cucumbers, adding them to the salad. She topped the vegetables with shredded cheddar cheese.

"Good job, Alexis," Monday commented while browning the beef on the stove.

"Thanks. The meat smells good."

Monday smiled. She enjoyed spending time with Alexis. "Fill up the stock pot with water and place it on the stove, please."

Alexis did as she was asked. Since the water was for the spaghetti noodles, Alexis added some olive oil, like she had seen her mother do on countless occasions, and turned the stove on high to bring the water to a boil. When bubbles formed, she added the pasta.

After adding sauce to the meat, Monday preheated the oven and placed the bread inside. As they waited for the noodles to cook and bread to bake, Monday and Alexis stood around the island talking about what they were going to do with the money Larry had given his daughter. Alexis wanted to buy clothes, but Monday nixed that idea. Monday explained that Alexis had plenty of clothes, so Monday suggested they save the money or use some of it to buy a new computer. Their current computer was outdated and slow. It didn't have a whole lot of memory. They both agreed that a new computer was a good idea.

The smell of garlic and cheese teased Monday's nostrils. She licked her lips and opened the oven door. "Looks good." She grabbed an oven mitt so that she could remove the pan containing the bread.

"Smells good," Alexis said.

Monday set the pan on top of the stove and turned off both the oven and the stove. Alexis grabbed the colander from one of the cabinets and placed it in the sink. She took the pot off the stove and drained the contents into the colander, being careful not to splash the scalding water.

They each fixed a plate and went into the dining room to eat. The phone rang and startled Monday. She excused herself from the table and went into the kitchen to answer it.

"Hello."

"May I speak to Monday?"

"This is Monday. Who's this?"

There was a pause. "It's your father, Stan."

Her heart raced. "Why are you calling me?" she snapped, tempted to hang up the phone.

"I'm probably the last person you want to hear from, but I need to see you."

"You don't need to see me." She felt her neck roll.

"There's so much I want to tell you. I'm sorry for hurting you."

"So what you want? My forgiveness?"

"Someday, I pray. For right now, I want to see you again."

"I don't think so."

"Monday, please. I wouldn't ask if it wasn't important."

"Let me think about it." She hung up the phone and went back into the dining room.

"You all right?" Alexis asked, noticing that her mother was shaken.

"No, I'm not all right. That was Stan." Monday took a seat.

"What did he want?"

"How about that old pervert wants to see me?"

"Are you going to see him?"

"I sure am. As soon as I'm a size zero," Monday said sarcastically. She took a bite of cheese bread. "I wonder how he got my number anyway."

"I think I know," Alexis volunteered. Monday stopped chewing and looked at her as if to say, "Go on."

Alexis continued. "Mom, don't be mad. I called Stan, but he wasn't there. So I left a message with our home telephone number. I wanted to meet him. I guess he wanted to check with you first."

"Unbelievable!" She threw her hands in the air, exasperated. "What were you thinking?"

"I told you before that I was curious about him. I wasn't trying to hurt you."

After seeing the sincere look on Alexis's face, Monday calmed down. "I know you weren't trying to hurt me." She got up and hugged her daughter.

So many thoughts ran through Monday's mind. Hearing Stan's voice after so many years caused her to panic. She couldn't believe how fearful she felt just by the sound of his voice. The thought of Stan made her cringe. It brought terror to her soul. Until now, she hadn't realized how much she detested Stan. Thinking about him fondling her and stealing her innocence caused her to hyperventilate. How could she ever forgive her father for violating her? She wondered whether she was wrong for harboring a grudge against him. *And what if I forgive him and he hurts Alexis?* She'd never be able to forgive herself. Trusting Stan wasn't an option. Monday needed to talk. She couldn't wait for her next appointment with Skyler.

CHAPTER TWENTY-EIGHT

Skyler

"Dr. Little's office. This is Yahkie. How may I help you?" Yahkie spoke into the speaker phone as he continued filing folders in the drawer. The door to my office was open, so I could hear his conversation and the file cabinet drawers closing.

"Did you say your name was Yuckie?"

"No, I said Yah-key." He sounded slightly annoyed and picked up the receiver, taking the caller off of speaker.

I walked into the doorway to be sure everything was all right. I continued standing there until he got off the phone. "What's going on?" I asked.

"Oh, hey, boss lady. That was some woman named . . ." He looked at a piece of paper with a name and number scribbled on it. "Anna. She said she saw your PSA for the Sky's the Limit Foundation. I gave her the number to the foundation, but she insisted that she speak with you. I told her I'd pass along the message and have someone call her back."

"Did she at least say what it was regarding?"

He shook his head.

"Sure, I'll call her back." He handed me the paper, and I looked at it. "I heard her call you Yuckie. I thought you were going to reach through the phone and choke her or something."

We both laughed.

"I felt like it. That's why I took her off speaker phone. No telling what I would've blurted out in the heat of the moment."

I was about to go back to my office when Yahkie said, "Boss lady, how you holding up? You feel up to meeting with Monday today?"

"I have to. She sounded upset, like she really needed me. Besides, work keeps my mind off of Ambrosia."

"I hear you." His wrist was limp. "That whole situation was bananas."

I couldn't help but laugh. Yahkie had a way of making the most serious situations seem funny.

"Well, I have no idea how any of this will pan out. Tomorrow is Ambrosia's funeral. Will you be attending?"

"Oh no." Yahkie threw his hands in the air. He made a face as if he had smelled a foul stench. "I don't do funerals. As a matter of fact, I think I'll skip my own." He smiled.

I squeezed the bridge of my nose; then released my hand by my side. There was a wilted leaf in the plant by the door, so I removed it and tossed it in the trash. "After the funeral, I'm supposed to help my friends deliver some disturbing news to their children."

"I don't envy you on that one. I don't know the situation, but hopefully the kids won't be confused and devastated."

I walked over and stared out at the picturesque vision behind Yahkie's desk. It was a clear view of downtown Atlanta. The buildings looked huge and the streets seemed busy. I thought about what Yahkie said and realized he was right. Jr. and Imani would be confused now. Once they understood the full scope of the situation, they'd be devastated. I hoped and prayed that all of the children would accept and, one day, love one another.

My thoughts drifted to the frailty of life. We aren't promised another day. Death doesn't discriminate. It doesn't matter whether you're young, old, rich, poor, or healthy for that matter. When it's your time, it's your time. I wasn't morbid, but after Ambrosia's death, my own mortality kicked in. I had been thinking more and more about having children.

I walked in front of Yahkie's desk and said, "Yahkie, do you think I'd make a good mother?"

His face lit up like the sky during Fourth of July fireworks. "You got something to tell me?"

"No, no," I assured him, dismissing his hints of pregnancy. "I was just wondering. That's all."

"Oh." He sounded disappointed. "Of course, I think you'd make a terrific mom. Any child would be lucky to have you."

I smiled. "Thank you."

"Now, I know women are having babies later and later, but don't you do that. You have a good husband and a prosperous career. Have a baby while you still have good eggs left. You don't want people thinking your baby is your grandchild."

"I know that's right." I chuckled. I noticed from my peripheral vision that someone had walked into the office. I turned around. "Hi, Monday. How are you?"

"I'm okay," she replied. "Hey, Yahkie." She waved.

"Hey," Yahkie replied.

We walked into my office, and I closed the door behind us. She took a seat on the couch, and I sat across from her in a chair. We prayed before beginning our session.

"What's going on?" I inquired.

"Ooh, Sky." She exhaled. "What's not going on?"

I listened attentively.

"I have good news and bad news. Which do you want to hear first?"

"Whichever you feel like telling me."

She rubbed her hands together. "Okay. I'll start with the good news. Alexis is going to Job Corps. Hooray!" She raised her arms in the air, palms facing upward.

I grinned so hard, my cheeks hurt. "That's wonderful news."

She put her arms down. "There's more. I met with Alexis's dad, Larry. He has a steady job, and he seems to be doing well. You ready for this?"

I nodded.

"He gave me $2,500 to give to Alexis."

"What?"

"Mm hmm. He sure did. I was shocked."

"How do you feel about Larry now?"

"That's a good question, Sky. I thought about that. For a long time I couldn't stand Larry. I resented him for not being a more responsible parent. We were both young, and he used that as an excuse for not taking care of Alexis. I was angry with him because I gave up my youth to raise my child. Don't get me wrong—I love Alexis's dirty drawers. That's my baby and I wouldn't trade her for anything. But for a long time I was hurt and very bitter. I didn't feel like it was fair for everything to fall on my shoulders while Larry got off scot free.

"I'm glad Larry finally got his life together, but I'm not impressed. He had eighteen years to party, go to school, and get a life. It's about time. He was free to do whatever he wanted. I'm more happy for Alexis's sake. Maybe now she can have a real relationship with her father."

"How does Alexis feel about Larry's grand gesture?"

"Are you kidding me? She was happy to get that money." She laughed. "Seriously, though, Alexis loves her dad, but she's cautious. He's disappointed her too many times in the past. He'd say he was coming over and wouldn't. He'd promise to send money or gifts in the mail and never followed through. Once, he promised to send Alexis some CDs for her birthday. I knew he wasn't going to. I didn't want to see the disappointed look on Alexis's face, so I bought and mailed the CDs to her myself and put his name on the package. She treasured those CDs. And just as sure as I'm sitting here, Larry never sent any CDs."

I nodded. Judging by her tone, I could tell this was still a sensitive issue for her. "Are you concerned that Larry will disappoint Alexis again?"

"Not really. I used to worry about that a lot when she was younger. Now that Alexis is an adult, she can make her own decisions. She knows about her past with her father. He was inconsistent when she was growing up, but he seems to be making a sincere effort now. I don't think he'll hurt her."

"I agree. The fact that Larry met with you to discuss the well-being of your daughter speaks volumes. It shows he cares. Not only was he willing to get involved, he put his money where his mouth is. He wasn't under any court order to pay you any money. He did that out of his own moral obligation. In his own way, he was admitting his fault and trying to be accountable for his actions." I moved a strand of hair off my forehead. "Is Larry married?"

"Not that I'm aware of. He hasn't said anything to me, and when I saw him, he wasn't wearing a wedding band."

"Any other children?"

"I don't think so."

I nodded. "Interesting."

"Why? What are you thinking, Sky?" She placed the tip of her thumbnail in her mouth.

"Nothing. I'll reserve my opinion for another time." I paused and continued, "Any more good news or are we on to the not-so-good news?"

"I heard from Stan." She sounded serious.

"Your father?" I put down my pen.

"Yes." She sighed. "He called me."

"What did he want?"

"To meet with me."

I was surprised to hear that. I wondered what was going on in Stan's life that prompted him to reach out to his daughter. "Why now?" I said.

"I found out that Alexis contacted him. She wants to get to know him."

"Does Alexis know what he did to you when you were a little girl?"

"She knows. I think her curiosity was piqued when my mom told us he was a minister living in Atlanta. According to my mom, Stan has a church in Douglasville."

"You don't say?"

"Yup, it surprised me too. Black people are some of the most forgiving people in the world. Go to our churches and our ministers have backgrounds as colorful as the United Nations. Here's Stan, a convicted child molester—pastor of a church. I went to a church where the pastor was having an affair with a married woman. The woman's husband caught them in bed together, and the pastor killed him. How 'bout his church got him off? He's still preaching. I left that church."

"That's not just a problem in the black churches. Many powerful leaders are being brought down in shameful ways. It's not a black or white issue. It's two things that will bring a man down." I held up my pointer and middle fingers. "Money and temptations of the flesh. I think that people in general should know more about their pastors, period. We do more research on cars and computers than we do on the things that directly impact our lives like daycares, churches, and politics. We have missed the mark when it comes to our religious leaders. It's almost taboo to question a man of

God. But it's not if it's done in a respectful manner. If you ask the average layman, they don't know whether their pastor has a degree in theology or who ordained him. We don't even know whether our minister has a criminal background. Nothing. That's why so many people become disillusioned by churches.

"Most people go to church seeking spiritual guidance, acceptance, and help. A lot of people don't know the Lord for themselves. They trust the pastor to interpret the Word for them. If the pastor isn't truly a man of God, he will eventually be revealed, leaving those babes in Christ feeling confused and abandoned. People need to stop and read the Word for themselves and develop a consistent prayer life. The Bible is clear about putting your trust in the Lord, because man will forsake you."

"You're right, Sky. What do you think I should do about Stan?"

"I can't tell you what to do. You have to follow your heart. If you want closure, maybe you should meet with him. Even if you don't have a relationship with him, at least you can forgive him and move on."

"True, true." She nodded her head in agreement.

"Then there's Alexis. You may need to meet with Stan anyway just to cover some ground rules. You need to let him know that you'll be watching him, and if you think there's any impropriety between him and Alexis, he's going down." I smiled.

"You got that right."

We ended our session with prayer, and I went home. I felt tension in my neck and shoulders. It had been a while since I had had a massage. I made a mental note to call and schedule an appointment at Spa Sydell.

Donovan's home early, I thought as I pulled into the garage and saw his car parked on the other side. When I walked in I was greeted by the sweet smell of vanilla. The room was filled with lit candles.

"Hey, baby," Donovan said and kissed me on the cheek.

I placed my briefcase and laptop case on the floor. Wrapping my arms around his waist, I hugged him tightly, resting my head on his chest. "What's all this?"

His hands rubbed up and down my back. He said, "Baby, you've been stressed lately. I want to help you relieve it. Now go upstairs and get out of those clothes. I have a milk bath waiting for you."

I smiled. Donovan always had a way of making me feel so loved, so appreciated. Milk baths were one of my favorites. I couldn't wait to go upstairs and soak away my cares. At least for a while. I kicked off my heels and hurried up the stairs. The bedroom was also filled with lit candles. *How romantic!* The bronze-colored comforter was pulled neatly back, waiting for us to get in. There was a terry-cloth bathrobe on the bed, too. I took off my clothes and placed them on the edge of the sofa.

The bath was warm and relaxing. My eyes were closed. I hardly noticed Donovan when he walked in. I felt the tips of his fingers gently massaging my shoulder.

"You coming to join me?" I asked.

"Not this time." He sat on the tiny step next to the Jacuzzi, squeezed vanilla-sugar body wash onto a loofah pad, and washed my back. It felt so good. After I finished bathing, Donovan wrapped me up in the robe that was on the bed. I felt like a queen for the day.

"Take off the robe and lay on the bed," Donovan instructed.

I did as he requested. I loved for Donovan to take charge. He was so confident.

"Beautiful." He admired my body, making me feel sexy. "Now turn over."

I lay on my stomach. I felt Donovan's strong hands, covered in warm oil, rub my back. He gave me an incredible massage. The lyrics from the EnVogue song featuring Salt 'N Pepa kept playing in my head, *What a man, what a man, what a man, what a mighty good man.* My body was so relaxed, I fell asleep thinking about how much I truly loved my man.

CHAPTER TWENTY-NINE
Tatiana

*W*hat *kind of name is Yah-key?* Tatiana wondered. *I knew Yuckie wasn't going to give that lady my message. I've got to find another way to get next to her.*

Tatiana got in her car and went to Reggie's condo. She knocked on the door several times. When no one answered, she used the extra key she had made to get in. She was relieved that Reggie hadn't changed the lock or turned on the alarm. The place was dark, so she turned on a lamp in the living room.

"Hello," Rufus chirped, startling her.

"Hi, Rufus."

She walked into Reggie's bedroom and sprawled out on his bed. She sniffed his pillow, inhaling the lingering scent of his aftershave cologne. Then she searched his drawers, looking for something to connect him to another woman, mainly Dr. Little. Her search for incriminating evidence was futile. There weren't any feminine items lying around the condo. Not even a letter or card. She refused to leave empty-handed, so she stuffed a couple of pairs of silk boxers from Reggie's underwear drawer into her oversized purse. She needed something to make her feel closer to him since he had stopped communicating with her.

Just as she was about to leave, she heard, "Psycho."

"What did you say?" she said to Rufus.

"Psycho."

Tatiana became enraged and told Rufus to shut up. But he wouldn't. He continued to call her psycho. All she could think about was silencing that bird. She felt as if he were deliberately taunting her. She saw red before she snapped Rufus's neck like a brittle piece of tinder.

"Bet you'll shut up now," Tatiana said as she wrapped Rufus's lifeless body in the newspaper lining his cage. She stuffed him in her purse, turned out the light in the living room, and locked the door behind her.

"Reggie's going to kill me," she said as she drove frantically away from his condo. She regretted killing the bird, but felt that she really didn't have a choice. She had to shut him up.

She drove until she arrived in front of Dr. Little's house. Reggie's truck wasn't there. Tatiana took a deep breath and removed Rufus's corpse from her purse. Walking briskly to Dr. Little's front doorstep, she left Rufus's remains there. She sprinted back to her car and drove off without her headlights on. She waited until she was farther up the street before turning her lights back on. Beads of sweat formed on her forehead as she contemplated her next move. She wondered if Reggie would call her now.

CHAPTER THIRTY

Skyler

I woke up in the morning feeling refreshed. A delicious smell wafted up from downstairs. *Donovan must've gotten up and fixed breakfast.* I appreciated him for letting me sleep in later than usual. Especially since today was Ambrosia's funeral. My body needed the rest.

I got out of bed and went into the bathroom to wash my face and brush my teeth. I put on a wife beater T-shirt and a pair of Juicy Couture sweatpants before going downstairs.

"Morning, love," Donovan said with a wide smile.

"Good morning, sweetheart." I planted a warm kiss on his lips. "Something smells good." I noticed that he had prepared an authentic Jamaican-style breakfast of bammy (cassava bread), boiled green bananas, roasted breadfruit, cornmeal porridge, yams, and herring. "I'll fix the tea."

"Dude," Kevin said as he entered the room. "That's you in here burning like that? I thought it was Sky."

"Yah, mon!" Donovan gave him a daps handshake.

"Morning, Kevin. How you feeling?" I asked.

"Not too bad. I tossed and turned most of the night

thinking 'bout Amber. But you know what? I'm at peace with the whole situation. Amber's in a better place."

"She certainly is," I said. "You riding to the services with me and Donovan?"

"Mrs. Wrey asked me to ride in the limo with her and the family, but I don't feel right doing that. I'd like to ride with you guys, if you don't mind." Kevin poured himself a glass of orange juice.

"Of course not." I retrieved three plates from the cabinet and lined them up on the counter. We each fixed a plate. The smell of cinnamon leaf tea permeated the air. "Kevin, you want a cup of tea?" I asked.

"No, thanks. I'm straight."

I filled two mugs with tea. "Here." I handed a cup to Donovan.

"Thanks, baby."

We went into the dining room to eat. We said our grace before devouring the scrumptious meal.

I got dressed for the funeral. I chose a black Donna Karan dress with a large pearl necklace and earrings. Donovan wore a black Armani suit with a gold tie. While waiting for Kevin to come downstairs and join us, I intended to go outside to get the *Wall Street Journal*. When I opened the door, I noticed that the sky had a slight overcast. It was a good thing that I looked down before stepping out the door. *What in the world? A dead bird on my doorstep!* I felt so bad. *The poor thing must've been flying and crashed into the door. What a shame.* I shook my head.

"Donovan, come here, please."

He came to the door. "What's up?"

"Look," I said, pointing at the yellow bird.

"What is a dead bird doing at our doorstep? That can't be a good sign."

"Since when did you become superstitious?"

"I'm not," Donovan clarified. "I'm just saying . . ." He knelt down to take a closer look. "Looks like his neck is broken."

"He must've crashed into the door pretty hard. Did you hear anything last night that might've sounded like a thud?"

"No." He examined the body closer. "This bird didn't crash into the door. This is a parakeet. It's a pet. Someone put him here."

"What? How can you be sure? Why would someone do that?" The questions rolled off my tongue like warm butter.

"Do what?" Kevin interrupted. He was wearing a black, double-breasted suit and black tie.

"There's a dead bird on the doorstep," I said.

"For real?" Kevin said, moving closer to catch a glimpse of the bird.

Donovan stood up and ushered us back inside. He closed the door and said, "I'm going to call Animal Control to come pick up the bird. But I'm telling you." He looked me in the eyes and reiterated, "Somebody put that bird on the doorstep."

"Dude, who'd do something crazy like that? You got a stalker?"

"Stop playing, Kevin," I said, tapping him on the arm. An animated tremor came over me.

Donovan went into the kitchen to place the call to have the bird's remains picked up. He was concerned about avian flu. I went outside and gathered the paper and the mail. As I sorted through the mail, I noticed a card-style envelope and a letter addressed to me. *Curious.* Neither of them had return addresses. I didn't have time to read the parcels, so I placed them on the counter, intending to read them later.

We arrived at the funeral about twenty minutes early. There were a few cars in the parking lot, including the limo for Ambrosia's family. The entranceway of the church displayed an eleven-by-sixteen photo of Ambrosia dressed in an off-white-colored pantsuit. She looked like a beautiful angel.

A heavyset white woman with an enormous bosom greeted us with hugs and kisses on our cheeks. She handed each of us a program before we entered the sanctuary. Inside of the sanctuary, people were sprinkled throughout. The mourners all had lugubrious expressions on their faces as they offered their sympathies to the family. Ambrosia's white, open casket was at the front of the room. A spectacular display of red roses finished in Ti Leaves and Dagger Fern covered half of the casket. Next to the coffin were wreaths, a spray of snapdragons, white carnations, and daisies, and a cross made of traditional white mums and red roses with lemon leaf bender.

"I'm so glad you could make it," Mrs. Wrey said to me, giving me a big hug.

I offered her a warm but sad smile. Then she hugged and kissed Kevin.

"Mrs. Wrey, this is my husband, Donovan," I introduced.

"Nice to meet you. Will you all be sitting up front with the rest of the family?"

Donovan and I both deferred to Kevin, waiting for a response.

"No, we'll sit back here." He gestured toward the pews on the right side, near the back.

"You sure? You know you're like part of the family," Mrs. Wrey said.

"Thanks, Mrs. Wrey. I'm sure." Kevin searched the room. "Excuse me; I'm going to talk to Anastasia." She was standing near the coffin.

Donovan and I took our seats as Mrs. Wrey mingled with the other people in the room. Even though Kevin's back was to us, I noticed Kevin touch Ambrosia's hand. I felt tears forming in my eyes when Kevin bent over and kissed Ambrosia's lifeless lips.

"You all right, baby?" Donovan asked, wrapping his arm around my shoulders.

"I'm okay. Be glad when this is over." I sighed.

"Me, too." He pulled me closer to him.

"Sweetheart, I've been thinking."

"Baby, you're a psychoanalyst. You know no man likes to hear his woman say, 'I've been thinking.'"

He was right. I chuckled. "Let me rephrase that. The thought of us having a baby has been weighing heavily on my mind. If you're ready, I'm ready to have a little bambino."

"You serious?" He removed his arm from my shoulders and looked at me incredulously.

"You know I wouldn't kid around about something like that."

A huge grin appeared across Donovan's face. He tried to contain his excitement, but it was obvious. He kissed me on the forehead and said, "I can't wait to get started."

The services were about to begin. Kevin took his seat next to me.

"How are you holding up?" I asked Kevin.

"I'm cool." He patted my hand.

The minister began and ended services with prayer. After leaving the funeral, we followed the processional to the burial site, where I bid Ambrosia a final farewell. She was dressed in a lilac-colored dress. Her makeup looked good, not caked on or pale like other corpses I had seen.

I said, "Ambrosia, I pray you're at peace. You'll be sorely missed. Don't worry about your beautiful little angels. Kevin is going to take care of them, and I promise to be involved in their lives, too. Until we meet again, my friend . . . I love you. You'll be in my heart forever."

CHAPTER THIRTY-ONE

Monday

Monday was pleasantly surprised to receive a delivery of a dozen pink roses from Larry. After reading the enclosed card thanking her for meeting him, she called him. He answered on the second ring.

"Hi, Larry. This is Monday."

"Hey, I was hoping to hear from you."

"Is that right?" She laughed.

"Did you get the delivery?"

"I sure did. The roses are beautiful." She took a whiff of the arrangement sitting on her kitchen counter. "Thank you so much."

"You're welcome. Hey, I was wondering. If you don't already have plans for dinner, would you like to join me tonight?"

"What? Are you serious?" She smiled.

"Yes."

"I don't know." She bit the corner of her lip nervously.

"I'm sorry. I wasn't trying to offend you. Do you have a man?"

"It's not that." She chuckled. "I don't know if we should,

you know . . ." She was hesitant because she didn't want to get her or Alexis's hopes up and end up disappointed.

"What? Date?"

"Yeah, that."

"You don't have to call it a date. We have a child together. We're two old friends trying to get reacquainted."

"You can save all that 'old' stuff. I'm not hardly old," she joked.

He laughed. "I feel you. So what do you say?"

She took a deep breath and blew into the receiver. "I guess it couldn't hurt."

"Great! I'll pick you up at your house at seven o'clock."

Monday gave him directions since he had never been to her home. She hung up the phone smiling. *I can't believe I'm going on a date with Larry!* She decided not to tell Alexis because she didn't want to give Alexis any false hopes. Even though Alexis had never mentioned to Monday that she wanted her parents to get back together, Monday knew that all children wanted their parents to live as a family. She was relieved when Alexis called to ask if she could spend the night with Grandma Paige. Monday quickly agreed.

Monday wore a sexy, semi-sheer gold blouse with rhine-stone cuff links, navy blue pin-striped slacks and dark blue, leather sling-back three-inch pumps. When Larry arrived, he looked stylish in an ecru dress shirt, tan trousers, and brown shoes.

"You look gorgeous," he said, handing her a bottle of sparkling apple cider.

"Thank you." She grabbed the bottle and kissed him on the cheek.

"I hope you don't mind," he said, referring to the non-alcoholic beverage. "I don't drink."

Monday looked at the bottle and read the label. "Why would I mind? Alexis and I drink sparkling drinks all the time. I'm not a big drinker either, but I do like wine."

They went into the kitchen, and Monday placed the bottle in the refrigerator.

"Where's Alexis?" Larry asked, smiling.

"Oh, she's spending the night with my mother."

His smile faded. "Sorry I didn't get to see her. Did you tell her we were going out tonight?"

Monday could tell that he was disappointed. "No, I didn't. You know how kids are. I didn't want to get her hopes up."

He grimaced. "No problem. I understand." He looked around and said, "You have a nice home."

Smiling, she replied, "Thank you. Where are we going?"

"Copeland's in Buckhead."

"Sounds good. I'll get my purse."

They rode in Larry's Mercedes.

"This is a nice car," Monday complimented.

"Thanks. A friend of mine, Darius, owns a dealership and gave me a good deal on it. Let me know if you're in the market for a new car, and I'll put you in contact with him. Speaking of cars, does Alexis have one?"

"No. She catches the bus everywhere she needs to go."

"We're going to have to do something about that."

Monday smiled. For the rest of the ride, Monday told stories about Alexis's childhood. When they arrived at the restaurant, Larry parked in the parking deck. Once inside of the restaurant, the waitress seated them in a booth and handed them each a menu. The waitress took their drink order; Monday ordered sweet iced tea, and Larry, a Coke. They perused the selections. The waitress returned with their drinks and took their food order. Monday ordered the crawfish étouffé, and Larry ordered shrimp creole.

"So, Larry, have you ever been married? Any other children?" Monday asked, taking a sip of tea.

"No and no." He laughed.

"Why did you laugh?"

"It's just that I always thought I'd end up marrying you!"

"Excuse me?"

"I've always thought highly of you, Monday. I admire your strength. You're a real go-getter. When we got together all those years ago, I was still a boy. Immature and not ready for any real responsibility. I didn't know how to be a man, let alone a father. I'm not trying to make excuses—I'm being real. It took me a long time to get my act together. I never felt like I was good enough for you. I promised myself that one day I'd become the man you and Alexis need me to be."

"I had no idea."

"How could you? I never shared that with you." He took a sip of Coke. "There's something else you should know."

"What?"

"Not long before I decided to go back to school, I got saved. I gave my life to Christ."

"That's great." Monday smiled.

"Thanks. I've been praying that the Lord would bring us back together. I want us to be a family."

"Whoa!" Monday halted her hand. "Slow your roll." She laughed nervously. "You're laying a lot on me right now. I wasn't expecting any of this."

"I'm sorry. I wasn't trying to scare you off. We have so much history; I thought I could talk truthfully to you."

"You can."

He looked her in the eyes and said, "I love you. Always have. I'll do whatever it takes to gain your trust."

The waitress returned with their food. The plates were hot. They closed their eyes, and Larry blessed the food. "Lord, thank You so much for the food we're about to receive for the nourishment of our bodies. In Jesus' name, we pray. Amen."

Monday loved spicy food, and the étouffé was seasoned to perfection.

"How's your food?" Larry asked.

"Delicious. Yours?" Monday ate a piece of biscuit to counteract some of the heat forming in her mouth. Then she sipped more tea. Spicy foods tended to make her sweat if she didn't drink plenty of liquids after nearly every bite.

"It's good. How do you feel about what I told you?" Larry inquired.

"Fine. I mean, I've spent a lot of years resenting you. It wasn't until recently that I actually forgave you. My bishop preached about forgiveness. The message really hit home for me. I realized that I was holding on to a lot of baggage from my past. Not just you, but my father, too."

"Really? I suppose I should be thankful for your forgiveness. Where do you go to church?"

Monday told him the name of the church she attended in Lithonia, a suburb of Atlanta, and was surprised to learn that Larry was a member of the same congregation, but they attended different service times.

"It's destiny," Larry said. "I don't believe it's a coincidence that we belong to the same church."

Monday didn't respond. She continued to eat her spicy dish.

"You mentioned you had issues with your father," Larry said. "What's that about?"

Monday shifted uncomfortably in her seat. "When I was five years old, my father molested me."

Larry gasped. "What?"

"Yeah. I hate to even call him my father. We don't have a relationship, and he went to jail for what he did to me."

"I'm so sorry. I never knew that. Is he still incarcerated?"

"No." She chuckled. "He's out and living in Georgia. Get this: He's a minister."

"Come on. You're kidding, right?"

"I wish I were. The worst part is that Alexis contacted him. She wants to get to know him."

"Kids." He shook his head.

"Stan—that's my father—he called, wanting to meet with me."

"For what?"

"From what Alexis told me, he wants me to give him permission to meet Alexis."

"What are you going to do?"

"At first, I wasn't trying to hear it. He would've had a better chance of winning the lottery. After speaking with Sky, I'm going to meet with Stan so that I can get closure."

"Sky?"

"That's my psychoanalyst. She's been helping me sort through my issues."

He nodded his head. The waitress returned and removed their empty plates. They each ordered a slice of strawberry cheesecake for dessert.

"Do you want me to go with you when you see Stan?" Larry offered.

"You're sweet, but no. I have to do this by myself."

After having dessert, Larry paid the tab and left a twenty percent tip. Monday was impressed. She didn't like cheap, stingy men. He drove her home and walked her to the door. She invited him in, but he declined. He said he had an early meeting and needed to rest. Monday understood.

"I had a wonderful time tonight," Larry said.

"Me, too." She batted her eyes a couple of times, flirting with him.

"I'll call you so that we can arrange to do this again."

"I'd like that."

He leaned over and kissed Monday on the cheek.

"Good night," Monday said as she placed her key in the lock.

"Night." Larry waited until Monday locked the screen door before heading to his car.

Once inside, Monday peeled off her heels and went upstairs to her bedroom. She checked her phone and noticed a stuttering dial tone, indicating that she had a message. It was from Alexis. She dialed Alexis's cell phone because she didn't feel like talking to Paige.

"Hey, Mom," Alexis said. "Where you been?"

Monday didn't want to lie to Alexis. She prided herself on keeping the lines of communication open with her daughter. The date with Larry had gone very well, and she was confident that they'd be seeing a lot more of each other. Larry seemed much more secure, stable, and spiritually attuned than she remembered. Even though she had reservations earlier, Larry put her concerns to rest. And since Alexis asked her outright where she had been, she decided to tell her the truth. "On a date."

"On a date with who?" She sounded surprised.

"Your dad."

"What? You and dad? How come you didn't tell me?"

"Because there wasn't anything to tell. He asked me to go out to dinner with him, so I went."

"Uh huh," Alexis said suspiciously.

"Anyway, I miss you. Are you having a good time?"

"Of course, Grandma and I have been watching movies and playing Uno."

"Sounds like fun." She yawned. "Well, I'm about to get ready for bed. I just wanted to say good night. I love you."

"Love you, too, Mom. Did you have a good time tonight?"

"I did." She laughed, thinking about how charming Larry had been. "We went to Copeland's."

"Okay." Alexis sounded upbeat. "See you later. Good night."

They disconnected the call, and Monday took a quick shower before putting on her nightgown. She brushed her teeth. Then she went into her bedroom and wrote an entry in her diary.

Today Larry sent me a dozen beautiful, pink roses. We ended up going to Copeland's for dinner. I couldn't believe it when he told me that he loved me. Wow! I've never been one to believe in soul mates, but Larry is making me reconsider my position on the subject. He was really nice and a perfect gentleman. I never in a million years thought Larry and I could be together. If he continues behaving all loving and attentive, I may have to give him a chance. He told me that he had been praying for us to come back together. I didn't want to tell him that I, too, had been praying for the Lord to send me the man He had for me. Could Larry be that man?

CHAPTER THIRTY-TWO

Reggie

"Calm down, Reggie," Dr. Little said.

"No, Dr. Little, I'm sorry. Tatiana's gone too far this time. She killed Rufus! How you gon' kill a man's bird? She knew what Rufus meant to me." He paced back and forth in Dr. Little's living room.

After coming home and finding Rufus's empty bird cage, Reggie suspected foul play. He lost sleep thinking about Rufus and what could have happened to him. Before confronting Tatiana in an infuriated state, he contacted Dr. Little the following day. He had hoped that she'd help him calm down. Dr. Little explained that she couldn't meet with him the day he called because she had a funeral to attend. However, she was available the day after.

When Dr. Little described the bird left on her doorstep, Reggie was livid. He wanted to strangle Tatiana with his bare hands.

"I feel like knocking Tatiana out," Reggie confessed. His eyes were bulging out.

"Don't you dare!" Dr. Little warned. "Stay away from her."

"What am I supposed to do?" Reggie wanted to know.

"Get a restraining order and change the locks to your house."

Reggie took a deep breath. He was so angry; he felt like punching something. "She's the one who's crazy. Why do I have to go through all these changes?"

"Listen. You need to be careful. Tatiana seems to be mentally unstable. She's already showing signs of being obsessive and a possible stalker. I'm not trying to make you paranoid. I want you to start paying attention to your surroundings. I can't express it enough. . . . Be careful."

"I will. I need to get going. I have a lot to do between getting locks changed and filing police reports. Thanks for your help."

"Anytime, Reggie." Reggie was about to leave when Dr. Little stopped him. "Wait, let's pray." They stood in the living room and prayed. Dr. Little said, "Lord, You said in Your Word where two or more are gathered, You are there in the midst. We come humbly before You asking for Your protection and divine intervention. Lord, we're asking that You protect Reggie by Your power. Give him wisdom and knowledge. Make his enemies his footstool. Your Word states that no weapon formed against us shall prosper. Keep him safe from all evils and harm. We thank You for Your angels that have charge over Reggie, and pray that no harm come his way. In Jesus' name, we pray. Amen."

Reggie hugged Dr. Little. "Thanks. I really appreciate that." Then he left.

While driving, Reggie found himself checking his rearview mirror repeatedly. He couldn't shake the feeling that someone was following him. After pulling into a gas station to fill his tank, he spotted Tatiana's Corvette. Seeing her outraged him. He was tempted to run over to her. He felt like snatching her out of the car. Instead, he pumped his gas and drove off.

He called Tatiana's cell phone, and she answered. Trying not to sound angry, he invited her over to his house to talk about the baby. She happily agreed. He drove home.

Tatiana arrived at the condo ten minutes after Reggie.

"Come on in," Reggie welcomed her.

Tatiana seemed cautious. She entered slowly and kept looking around. Reggie closed the door behind her.

"Have a seat." He led her to the couch and sat down.

She sat on the opposite end of sofa. "What's up?" Tatiana asked.

"You tell me."

"Tell you what?"

Reggie couldn't take it any longer. He had to confront her. "Why did you kill Rufus?"

"I don't know what you're talking about."

"Look, don't play me for stupid. I know you've been sneaking in here when I'm not at home. Tell me why you killed my bird and dropped him off at Dr. Little's house."

"It was an accident," she confessed.

Reggie balled his fists. "I've never hit a woman before in my life, but you . . . you make a brother want to lose it."

"Go ahead. If it'll make you feel like a big man, go ahead. Hit me," she baited.

"I'm not going to hit you. But I am going to tell you to leave me alone. You better get out of my house and out of my life! Don't you *ever* come around here again, or I'll have you arrested. And stay away from Dr. Little. She doesn't have anything to do with this. Do you understand?"

Tatiana's eyes became misty. "Why are you treating me like this?"

Reggie stood up and walked toward the door. Tatiana followed and pleaded with him to give her another chance. He opened the door and roared, "Leave!"

She touched his chest with both hands, and he pushed

her away. Her face became wet from crying. "Reggie, I love you. You can't leave me. What about the baby?"

"Stop it! You're not pregnant. Even if you are, there's no way the baby's mine. Now leave me alone." He shoved her out the door and locked it.

Tatiana banged on the door. "Reggie! Reggie! Open this door. You can't do this to me."

"Step away from the door, Tatiana. Don't make me call the police," he threatened.

She stopped knocking. Reggie looked through the peephole and Tatiana wasn't there. He breathed a sigh of relief. He felt like calling Monday since they hadn't spoken in a while. Then he realized that Monday hadn't called him either. He decided against it. *She probably has another guy,* he thought. Even though he really liked Monday, he didn't want to drag her into the middle of his drama. He immediately placed a call to a locksmith.

CHAPTER THIRTY-THREE

Kevin

Kevin invited Mrs. Wrey and Anastasia over to Skyler's house for dinner. He had discussed it with Skyler, and they had agreed that they would tell Mrs. Wrey and Anastasia together that Kevin was married. They also planned to discuss custody of Mateo and Destiny. He was thankful to have Skyler to lean on. He hadn't realized how much he missed having her as a confidant until he went through this crisis. Now it was like they were best friends again. She was a great listener and had an eloquent way of expressing herself. He felt comfortable having her around. In fact, he preferred it.

"Kevin," Skyler began. "Have you thought about what you're going to say to Ambrosia's family?"

"Have I? I haven't been able to think about anything else."

Skyler continued cleaning the house. It wasn't dirty, but Skyler wanted to make it extra immaculate for a favorable impression. She mopped the kitchen floor, dusted, and vacuumed. When she finished, she prepared shrimp alfredo for dinner.

Mrs. Wrey and Anastasia arrived on time. They were both dressed in dark clothing.

"Come on in," Kevin greeted, kissing them both on the cheek.

Mrs. Wrey looked around and said, "This is a beautiful home."

Skyler came out of the kitchen and into the foyer. "Thank you. It's nice to see you both again." She shook their hands and smiled pleasantly. "Follow me."

They walked into the living room. Mrs. Wrey and Anastasia sat next to each other on the sofa.

"Donovan will be downstairs shortly," Skyler explained. "He's on the computer, as usual. Would either of you like something to drink?"

"Yes," they said in unison.

"Let me help you," Kevin volunteered, following Skyler.

From the kitchen, Skyler rambled off a list of drinks ranging from juice to tea to coffee to soda. She ended up pouring them each glasses of cranberry-apple juice. She and Kevin carried the drinks back into the living room. They talked about how much Mateo and Destiny had grown and how quickly the years had passed. When Donovan came downstairs, they all went into the formal dining room and ate.

"Mrs. Wrey, I wanted to talk to you about custody of Mateo and Destiny," Kevin said.

"Yes?" Mrs. Wrey asked, placing a shrimp in her mouth.

"I want full custody. You're their grandmother, and you can see them anytime you want. I'd never do anything to come between you and the kids."

"I expected that. You're their father. Why wouldn't you want custody of your children? I don't have a problem with that."

Kevin seemed relieved. "I'm glad to hear it. There's more."

Mrs. Wrey set her fork down and looked intently at Kevin.

"Mateo and Destiny aren't my only children," Kevin admitted.

"I . . . I don't understand," Mrs. Wrey said.

"Well, when Amber and I met, I was already married. I have two children from my marriage."

Pushing her chair back from the table, Mrs. Wrey stood up. "What are you saying? Are you still married?"

"Yes."

"I can't believe this! You used my daughter. How dare you!"

"Mom, calm down," Anastasia admonished. "Hear him out."

"Hear him out? What else is there to hear? He's a liar! He used your sister." Mrs. Wrey looked at Anastasia and continued. "You don't seem surprised by this."

"I'm not," Anastasia confessed. "Amber told me. She made me promise not to tell you."

"What? You agreed to that?" Mrs. Wrey let out a loud sigh. "Take me home," she demanded, walking toward the door.

Kevin got up from the table and followed her. "Mrs. Wrey," Kevin said, grabbing her arm. "Wait a minute. Please!"

"Get your filthy hands off me," Mrs. Wrey yelled, snatching her arm back. Kevin stepped backward. Everyone else joined them in the foyer. "My daughter was raised with morals and values," she spewed. "You tainted her with your black self. I told Ambrosia that you'd end up hurting her. I warned her not to get involved with a black man, and I was right. You have many wives and many children."

Kevin was speechless.

"Just a minute," Skyler interjected. "With all due respect, Mrs. Wrey, you're out of line. I realize that you've just received some shocking news in addition to having to cope with your grief. Even so, I won't allow you to disrespect black men. Especially not in my home. No doubt, Kevin was wrong to get involved with Ambrosia because he was married. He acknowledges that. But affairs are not exclusive to any one race. Infidelity affects everyone. And as far as your view of black men having many wives and many babies, that's a racist stereotype. Kevin is educated and has only been married once. He takes care of his wife and children. My own husband," she pointed to Donovan and continued, "only has one wife and no children. I resent your slander. I can name numerous black men, including my own father, who love and cherish their wives and provide for their families."

"Mom, she's right," Anastasia said. "Amber loved Kevin; even after she found out he was married. She told me that Kevin treated her better than any other man she had ever been with. He spent quality time with Mateo and Destiny. Not only did he pay child support regularly, he bought them gifts and made sure their needs were met. He's not a dead-beat."

Mrs. Wrey seemed to calm down a bit. "I'm sorry," she said to Kevin.

"Me, too," Kevin replied. "I never meant to hurt your daughter. I loved her. And I love Mateo and Destiny with all my heart. As long as there's breath in my body, I'll be here for them. I hope you will be, too."

Mrs. Wrey's face was wet from tears. "You know I will."

Kevin gave Mrs. Wrey a hug.

She broke the embrace and said, "Sky, thanks for everything. I'm sorry about what I said. Please forgive me."

Skyler nodded her head in the affirmative and smiled. She reached out and gave Mrs. Wrey a hug. "Grief can cloud our judgment and cause us to say all sorts of things we wouldn't ordinarily say. I'll charge it to your head and not your heart."

"Thank you," Mrs. Wrey whispered. She released Skyler so that she could wipe away the tears streaming down her face. "Good night."

"Hey," Kevin said, causing Mrs. Wrey and Anastasia to turn around and face him. "Let me know if you need my help packing up Amber's apartment. I'm sure it will be very emotional for you. I'd be glad to help, and I'll call you this week to let you know when I'll be by to pick up Mateo and Destiny."

"Okay," Anastasia answered.

After Mrs. Wrey and Anastasia left, Donovan, Skyler, and Kevin didn't finish eating. They sat in the living room talking about the evening.

"That went well," Kevin joked.

"Man, Mrs. Wrey don't play," Donovan teased. "She was about to jack you up about her daughter." Donovan laughed.

"Yeah, but dude. Sky . . . Man, Sky was on her like funk on day-old collard greens."

They all laughed.

"You're so silly," Skyler said.

"Seriously, though," Kevin said. "Do you think all white people are racist?"

"Come on now," Donovan said. "You can't take the actions of a few people and categorize an entire race. No, I don't think all white people are racist any more than I think all black people eat chicken and are lazy."

"You got that right," Skyler said. "Every race has stereotypes. It doesn't make it right, but that's reality. I can tell you this, though: regardless of all the -isms, everybody has problems. No family is perfect, and every individual has flaws."

"So you don't think Mrs. Wrey will have a negative impact on Mateo and Destiny?" Kevin asked.

"Absolutely not. She loves them. She was spewing venom because she was angry with you," Skyler explained.

"All right. I won't make a big issue out of her comments," Kevin said. "Anyway, I'm going upstairs to call Gabby. Wish me luck."

CHAPTER THIRTY-FOUR

Gabriella

Jr. and Imani were fast asleep in their beds when Caleb came over to watch movies with Gabriella.

"I made us some cappuccino," Gabriella said, handing Caleb a warm mug. She sat next to him on the couch.

"Thanks." He took a sip. "This is as good as Starbucks."

"Yeah, right." She laughed.

They placed their cups on the coffee table.

"I've really enjoyed the time we've spent together lately," Caleb confessed.

"It's been nice."

He placed his arm around her shoulder. She seemed uncomfortable.

"Caleb, I've already told you. You've been a wonderful friend, and I really like you."

"But . . ." He leaned toward her.

"But I'm not ready to get involved in another relationship. I'm still married, and I have a lot of decisions to make. I don't know whether my marriage can be saved. Honestly, I don't know whether I want it to be. I just know that bringing you into this messed-up situation wouldn't be fair to you."

"I'm a big boy. I can handle it."

The phone rang. "Excuse me." Gabriella picked up the cordless phone and pressed the "talk" button. "Hello."

"Hey, Gabby. It's me. You busy?" Kevin said.

"Sort of." She coiled a strand of hair on her finger.

"Are Jr. and Imani still awake?"

"No," she said, walking into the kitchen for more privacy. "They're asleep."

"Oh. Well, I wanted to know if I could meet with you tomorrow."

"For what?"

"We need to talk."

"I'm tired of talking."

"Baby, I love you. We have some major decisions to make. We can't stay in a state of flux indefinitely. If we're going to work on our marriage, then I need to move back home. We don't stand a chance if we're living apart."

"And if I don't want to work on it?"

"Then, we need to deal with that, too. Either way, we've got to do something. What time is good for you?"

"Where are your napkins?" Caleb interrupted. "I spilled some coffee on my jeans."

Panicking, Gabriella covered the mouthpiece with her hand and pointed to the roll of paper towels sitting on the counter. She realized that she hadn't covered the phone fast enough, but she hoped there was a chance Kevin hadn't heard Caleb talking to her.

"Gabby!" Kevin yelled into the phone. "Who's that?"

Gabriella felt flustered. "I'll call you later and let you know what time we can meet." Then she hung up the phone.

"Sorry about that," Caleb said, wiping the damp spot on his pants.

"Don't worry about it."

They went back into the living room. Kevin called back a couple more times. Neither time did Gabriella answer. She let the voice mail pick up.

"Everything all right?" Caleb asked.

"That was Kevin. He heard you in the background and got upset. I think it's best if you leave. Knowing Kevin, he's probably on his way over here."

"I'm not going to leave you alone to deal with his rage."

"It's not like that. Kevin isn't the violent type. More than anything, he hates being disrespected. To him, having another guy over here is the epitome of disrespect."

"Are you sure you don't want me to stay?"

"I'm sure." She stared at a skewed fiber in the carpet. "Maybe we should cool it for a while. At least until I'm divorced, if that's the way it goes."

"It's not fair." Caleb shook his head. "Some brothers get all the luck. They have beautiful, devoted, faithful women at home, and they still want to cheat. I don't get it. If you were my lady . . . Never mind." Caleb stood up. "I'll respect your wishes." He bent over and kissed her on the cheek.

"Caleb, I don't want to lose your friendship."

"You won't."

He left, leaving Gabriella confused. She wondered whether she was doing the right thing by letting Caleb go. Her mind kept telling her to get revenge. She wanted to hurt Kevin as badly as he had hurt her. Somehow her heart wouldn't agree. No matter how hard she tried to deny it, she was still very much in love with Kevin. Now that Ambrosia was permanently out of the picture, they could start again. Or could they?

CHAPTER THIRTY-FIVE
Tatiana

Tatiana thrashed fitfully in bed. When she awoke, her body was cold and wet. Her nightgown clung to her body. She sat straight up, her pulse pounding a melody of fright. "That was awful," she said, remembering the nightmare she'd had about her pregnancy. The details of the dream were so vivid. It was as if she was reliving the day she removed Reggie's condom from the trash can and injected the contents into her body with a turkey baster. She had lain on her back with her legs propped up so that the "little swimmers" would charge upstream and attach themselves to her uterus. In the dream, Reggie found out about her deception and beat her senseless.

She had a busy day ahead. Tatiana got out of bed and took a shower. She had a meeting with a potential client about catering a birthday party. Dressed in fitted Baby Phat jeans, an olive Baby Phat shirt with the gold logo on front, gold accessories, and olive mules, she drove to the South DeKalb Business Incubator. Since she didn't have a storefront location or restaurant, Tatiana rented a space at an incubator. It was a huge white building without any signage.

Unless you were looking for it, you wouldn't notice it. Several other businesses shared the facility with Tatiana.

She phoned her business partner, Jasmine. She and Jasmine met during a cake decorating class they had enrolled in. They conversed and quickly discovered that they had a lot in common, like the fact that neither one of them had ever been married nor had any children. They both wanted to start a catering company. Jasmine's strengths included being a wonderful cook and a background in accounting. With Tatiana's excellent interpersonal skills and marketing degree, they decided to go into business together. It seemed to be an excellent fit.

"Hello."

"Hi, Jazz. It's Tee."

"Hey, girl. What's going on?"

"I'm headed to the incubator. Wanted to know if you were coming in this morning. I have a meeting with a potential client about a birthday party."

"I'm walking out the door right now. See you in a few."

Tatiana hung up and listened to Jamie Foxx's CD. She sang along to "Unpredictable." When she arrived at the facility, Jasmine pulled up behind her. They parked next to one another and walked inside of the building together. The facility housed a commercial kitchen, which consisted of stainless steel appliances, sinks, and countertops. Oversized pots and pans hung overhead.

After discussing a few of their popular food choices for the customer to sample, Jasmine put on her white chef's hat and white cooking jacket before going to prepare the selections. Not long afterward, the intercom buzzed. With a questionnaire, clipboard, and pen in hand, Tatiana went to the front of the building and pressed the button. The door unlocked, and a handsome man with neatly styled dreadlocks walked through the glass door. Tatiana was taken aback by how good he looked. He was tall with a smooth, chocolate complexion. His teeth were pearly white, and his smile mesmerized her.

"Hi, I'm Tee Strawberry." She extended her hand to him.

"Nice to meet you. I'm Donovan Little." He gave her a firm handshake.

His voice sounds even sexier in person than it did over the phone. "My partner, Jasmine, is in the back cooking up some samples for you to try. We can discuss the particulars of your event out here in the lobby. It's much more comfortable."

"Okay."

Tatiana sat in a comfy, green chair and crossed her feet at the ankles. Donovan sat on a matching loveseat. She confirmed the date and time of the event prior to reviewing the questionnaire with him.

"Who's the party for?" She smiled.

"It's for my wife, Skyler."

Tatiana's smile faded. *You've got to be kidding me. This fine man is married to the same woman messing around with Reggie? She doesn't deserve him.* "Oh, congratulations." She faked a smile. "She's lucky to have you." She scribbled Skyler's name on the sheet and circled it.

"Thanks," he said modestly.

"Do you have a theme for the party?"

"Not really. Sky's real classy and elegant. Whatever we do, it's got to be upscale."

"I understand. Do you have any food preferences?"

"Well, I'm Jamaican. I prefer Jamaican dishes; however, Sky loves seafood. Shrimp, lobster, crab . . . she likes it all." He chuckled.

Tatiana made a note of that. "Did you want hors d'oeuvres, like at a cocktail party? Or something more formal like a sit-down dinner? Or perhaps a buffet?"

Donovan rubbed his chin as he mused. "A buffet."

"How many people will be attending the event?"

He furrowed his brow. "About one hundred."

"That's a nice number to work with." She jotted that down. "Does your wife know about the party?"

He laughed. "I want it to be a surprise, but who knows . . . Sky notices everything. She's a psychoanalyst, so it's hard to get anything past her."

"Is that right? A psychoanalyst?"

"Yes." He nodded. "So please make sure you only call me in the office or on my cell."

"Will do."

Jasmine joined them, carrying a tray with barbecue meatballs, meatballs with mint yogurt sauce, barbecue chicken wings, lemon pepper wings, and crab cakes.

"This is Jasmine," Tatiana introduced.

"Nice to meet you." Jasmine set the silver serving tray on the wooden coffee table. "Please, help yourself."

"Thank you."

Jasmine went back into their working quarters. Donovan tasted the samples.

"What do you think?" Tatiana queried.

Donovan waited until he finished chewing and said, "Delicious. I definitely made the right choice for a caterer."

"I forgot to ask," Tatiana added. "Who referred you to me?"

"Jack Briscoll. We work together. He highly recommended your company."

Tatiana smiled and wrote down Jack's name on the paper. She regularly sent thank you notes to her customers whenever they referred someone to her. Donovan finished eating the tasty treats.

"I know Jack. I'll have to send him a note of thanks."

Jack had been her loyal customer ever since she started the catering company. He was always throwing parties for birthdays, anniversaries, and holidays. Tatiana stood up. "I think I have enough to get started. I'll put together some selections for you to choose from and get back with you."

"Sounds good." Donovan stood up, too. He shook her hand and left.

Tatiana stared admiringly at him as he walked away. "That's a fine brother," she said to no one in particular. *He deserves better than the conniving wife he's got.*

CHAPTER THIRTY-SIX

Kevin

Kevin slept in irregular spurts thinking about Gabriella. The thought of another man touching her nearly drove him insane. His first impulse was to go over there and confront them. *What good would that do?* He cried, sulked, and blamed himself. He felt as if he had lost her, his punishment for being unfaithful. All he could do was pray. He pleaded with God to heal his marriage. A divorce was the last thing he wanted. Kevin promised God that if Gabriella came back to him, he'd never commit adultery again. He realized that making such a vow to God was serious, and he had every intention of honoring it.

He waited until Donovan and Skyler left before he went downstairs. He didn't want to tell them about his phone call to Gabriella. *Another man? Who was it?* He closed his eyes and balled his fist. Tears welled in his eyes. He didn't have much of an appetite. He fixed himself a bowl of cereal for breakfast. After slurping down the last bit, he got dressed and ran some errands, including a trip to the jeweler, before going to his and Gabriella's house.

By the time Gabriella came home from work with Jr. and

Imani in tow, Kevin had done some handiwork around the house. He took out the trash, replaced burned-out light bulbs, oiled squeaky door hinges, and fixed a clogged drain in the bathroom sink. He even left an expensive gift for Gabriella in the nightstand drawer next to the bed. For dinner, he made steaks for himself and Gabriella, and hamburgers for Jr. and Imani, on the family-sized George Foreman grill. A large salad sat on the countertop.

"Daddy!" Jr. and Imani said automatically.

Kevin hugged them. Then he picked Imani up and twirled her in the air. She loved it when he did that. He enjoyed seeing her smile and hearing her giggles. He put her down and said, "You guys go upstairs and get washed up for dinner."

"Okay, Daddy," they said and did as they were told.

"What's all this?" Gabriella asked.

"I wanted to spend some time with my family. I miss you guys."

"I thought I was supposed to call you first."

"Look. Enough's enough." He checked the meat. "I've been away long enough. I still love you, and I believe you love me, too. Yes, I messed up. I've repented and apologized. Again, I'm sincerely sorry for hurting you. But Gabriella, we can't lose what we have together. We love each other, and that's not something you find every day. Nobody said that love or marriage was easy. We've been through a storm, but baby, our love is worth fighting for. We owe it to ourselves and those two beautiful children upstairs to fight for what we have."

"I'm scared. I don't know if I can trust you, Kevin. You hurt me."

"Baby,"—he held her hand—"it's going to take time. I realize that." He wrapped his arms around her waist and kissed her on the lips. Initially, she tried to resist. He pulled her closer to him, and they shared a passionate kiss. "I love you, baby."

With tears streaming down her face, Gabriella admitted, "I love you, too." Then she paused with a quizzical expression. "What do you mean you've repented? Have you found religion?"

"You could say that, but I think I'm more spiritual than religious."

"How long is that going to last?" She sounded skeptical.

"Baby, this is not a fad. I promise you that I've changed. You'll just have to see for yourself."

"I want you to come back home," she admitted with tears streaming down her cheeks.

Kevin wiped away her tears with his thumb and nodded his head. "Thank you." Then he took the meat off the grill, and Gabriella fixed the plates.

Kevin yelled upstairs, "Time to get your grub on. Come on."

After dinner, Kevin helped Jr. and Imani with their homework. When it was time for them to retire for the evening, Kevin read them a bedtime story and tucked them in. He was elated to have his family back. He loved them so much.

Kevin and Gabriella waited until Jr. and Imani were asleep before going upstairs into their bedroom. They showered together in the master bathroom and enjoyed being close to one another. Kevin felt so good, he wanted to shout. Shout to the world that he had his family back. Inside, he thanked God the entire time.

As they lay in each other's arms, Kevin said, "Let's renew our wedding vows."

"Are you serious?"

Kevin removed a small, blue box from the nightstand. "Here."

Gabriella sat upright and opened the box. "Oh my God. It's beautiful." She held the three-carat princess-cut diamond ring in her hand. She leaned over and kissed him.

225 DIVORCING THE DEVIL

"You like it?" Kevin asked.

She took off her wedding ring and slipped the impressive new jewel on her ring finger. She smiled as she admired the diamonds set in platinum. "You didn't have to."

"Hey, if you want me to take it back . . ." Kevin teased.

"Not on your life. I earned this ring." She laughed.

"So, does that mean you want to renew our vows?"

"Yes. And Kevin, promise me you'll never do anything like this ever again. I don't think I could survive it if you did."

He caressed her face with his hand. Looking her directly in the eyes, he said, "Never, ever again. I promise you that."

"Tell me about Ambrosia's funeral," Gabriella said.

"You sure you want to hear about that? Especially now. We just got back together."

"Yes." She nestled her head on his chest. "I want to hear it."

"Well, the church was full. There were lots of flowers. It was just like any other funeral." He cleared his throat.

"You loved this woman. I want you to feel like you can talk to me about anything."

"I appreciate that. I really don't feel like talking about this, though."

"Okay." She rubbed his chest. "How are Mateo and Destiny doing?"

He cleared his throat again. "They're all right. They don't fully understand everything that's going on."

She stopped rubbing his chest and slightly raised her head. "Are you going to raise them?" She sounded serious.

"Is that a problem for you?" He furrowed his brows.

"You're not supposed to answer a question with a question, silly." She lightly tapped his chest before resting her head back on his chest. "Anyway, they're a part of you. If we're going to be together, I have to accept them. I admit that I had a hard time with it. I didn't think I could do it. Now, I realize that I love you enough to accept them into our family."

Kevin didn't even realize he was crying until he felt a tear roll into his ear. "Baby, I don't know what I ever did to deserve you, but I thank God for you."

In the back of his mind, Kevin wondered about the mystery man who had been at the house with Gabriella. Things were going so well between him and Gabriella that he didn't want to ruin it with jealousy. Even if she had cheated, in all fairness, he couldn't blame her. It would hurt, and he'd be angry. He silently prayed that Gabriella hadn't stepped out on him. He decided to trust her. What other choice did he have?

CHAPTER THIRTY-SEVEN
Skyler

It was my first day back in the office since Ambrosia's funeral. Yahkie left a small vase with a delicate forget-me-not on my desk when I got in to work. *How sweet of Donovan.*

"How's it going, boss lady?" Yahkie asked.

"Much better. Things seem to be looking up."

"What do you mean?"

"Well, Kevin and Gabriella got back together."

"Get out of here! I guess it's true what they say about white women." He laughed.

"I know you didn't just go there," I scolded.

"I'm just playing. I'm glad they worked things out. Especially since they have kids."

"Sure." I gave him an incredulous look. "Anything new on the horizon?"

"Not really." He paused and tapped his fingers on his mahogany desk. "I almost forgot. That Anna person called you again."

"I meant to call her back, but I haven't had a chance."

"Save your breath. She doesn't need to speak with you

now. She explained the nature of her call, and it was regarding mentoring. I referred her to the foundation."

I breathed a sigh of relief. I was usually very good about calling people back. "Thanks, Yahkie. You're the best."

"That's why you pay me the big bucks."

I smiled and went into my office to get caught up on some paperwork. An hour later, Monday arrived for our scheduled appointment.

"Hi, Monday. You look nice today," I complimented her. She had her hair slightly curled at the ends, hanging past her shoulders.

"Thank you."

We prayed. At the conclusion of our prayer, I said, "Tell me what's been going on."

"Sky," she beamed. "Remember when you asked me whether Larry was married or has other children?"

"Yes, I remember."

"Well," she said, unable to stop smiling, "Larry's single. He doesn't have any other children. And Sky, you aren't going to believe this: We went on a date."

That made me smile. "Oh, really?"

"Yes. He took me to dinner at Copeland's, and we talked and talked. It was great. He even sent me roses."

"That sounds wonderful. How did it make you feel?"

"Special. I've never had a man treat me like that before. And you know what?"

I shook my head.

"We both go to the same mega church, but at different times. I'm beginning to think this is fate."

"That's certainly a plus."

"At first I was like, take it slow. Don't get your hopes up. Then I thought about it: Larry and I have waited eighteen long years. Neither one of us got married. We're both more mature and stable now. I'm going to go for it. If I don't take a chance, I'll always wonder what could've been."

"I'm happy for you. What about Reggie?"

"What about him?" she asked sarcastically, leaning back on the couch. "I mean, I'm not worried about him. I haven't called him, and he hasn't called me."

"Are you done with him?"

"Pretty much. We can be friends. That's about it."

I could tell that something positive was happening with Monday. She seemed more confident and self-assured. *A new love can do that for a woman. Or should I say an old flame rekindled? My instincts tell me that Larry is going to be around for a while. And that's a good thing. Especially since he is the father of Monday's daughter.*

"All right then." We both laughed. "Anything else you want to discuss?"

"Not discuss, but I need prayer."

I raised a brow and crossed my right leg over the left.

"I'm going to see Stan," Monday said. "I'm a bit nervous about it. I'll let you know how it goes."

"Certainly." The timer went off. "As a matter of fact," I continued, "we can pray about that right now." We closed our eyes and I said, "Heavenly Father, we ask that You be with Monday. Tell her the right things to say. Order her steps and direct her path. Protect her by Your power. Reveal to her what she needs to know. Bless her meeting with Stan. Thy will be done. In Jesus' name, we pray. Amen."

Monday stood up and said, "I need a hug."

We embraced and she left. I checked my watch and realized that I needed to leave if I was going to be on time for my lunch date with Gabriella. I grabbed my purse.

Yahkie was typing busily. "Hey," I said, waiting to get Yahkie's attention. "I'm going to Mick's for a lunch meeting with Gabriella. Want me to bring you anything back?"

"Ooh, that's my spot." He retrieved a ten-dollar bill from his wallet and said, "Bring me back an Oreo cheesecake, please."

I took the money and left. I hated driving on Peachtree Street. Unless you were driving in the middle lane, you were in the wrong lane. The right lane was usually filled with buses that stopped frequently, and the far left lane always seemed to have cars turning.

When I arrived at Mick's, Gabriella was already waiting for me. We exchanged pleasantries and hugged before being seated at our table. I didn't need to look at the menu; I knew exactly what I wanted: a fried-chicken salad and a vanilla Coke. Gabriella ordered a turkey sandwich and lemonade.

I noticed that Gabriella seemed to be glowing. "You look happy."

"I am," Gabriella confirmed. "I never thought things could be so good between me and Kevin. He's so loving and attentive."

"He wasn't before?"

"He was, but it's different now. It's like he realizes how much his family means to him."

"That's good. I'm happy for you guys."

"You know we're having a recommitment ceremony. I want you to help me plan it."

"I'd be happy to. What did you have in mind?"

"I want something simple. Maybe twenty-five people."

"An intimate ceremony."

"Yeah, that's it. Intimate. You know I still don't know all the English words." She laughed.

The waitress returned with our drinks. I sipped the sweet-tasting cola.

"Have you thought about where you're going to have it?"

"Not yet. Any suggestions?"

"What about Stone Mountain? Lake Lanier? Or Chateau Elan?"

"I'll check on all of those. Thanks." She sipped her ade. "Mateo and Destiny are going to be living with us."

"Good. They need a stable home life. Have you told Jr. and Imani yet?"

Gabriella stared out the window, looking at the cars drive by. "We did."

"How did it go?"

"They had a lot of questions. They were happy about Kevin moving back home. When we told them they had a brother and sister who were coming to live with us, they didn't understand. Jr. asked, 'Mom, when did you have a baby?' Kevin did the best he could to explain that *I* wasn't Mateo and Destiny's mommy. It was awkward. I felt like crying, but I waited until I was alone. It was tough, but we made it seem like a good thing. And, in all honestly, it *is* a good thing. Jr. and Imani are excited about meeting their little brother and sister. It'll work out."

"I'm sure it will."

The waitress returned with our food, and I ordered Yahkie's Oreo cheesecake slice to go. We ate and talked about color schemes, music for the reception, and wedding dresses. I noticed a lady staring at me.

"You see that?" I asked Gabriella, referring to the lady sitting a couple of tables away from us.

"What?"

I shifted my eyes toward the left and said, "That woman keeps staring at me."

Gabriella looked and noticed that the woman wearing a charcoal gray pantsuit was indeed staring. "How rude!"

The waitress delivered Yahkie's dessert and our tab. As we got up to walk to the register, Miss "Why-don't-you-take-a-picture-it'll-last-longer" got up and headed toward me.

"Excuse me," she said. "I didn't mean to be rude. Please forgive me for staring at you. It's just that you look like someone I know. I apologize."

The woman made me feel uneasy. There was something about her that vexed my spirit. I smiled politely and said, "I

understand." Gabriella and I paid our bills. We walked outside to our cars. A shiny, candy-apple-red Corvette was
parked next to my car.

"That was weird," Gabriella commented.

"You're telling me," I concurred. I was about to get in my
car when I immediately noticed that my back tire was flat.
How can that be? I didn't remember driving over anything.
And I certainly didn't notice it earlier. "I don't believe this.
My tire is flat."

"Did you notice it being low earlier?" Gabriella asked.

"No."

Since I didn't know how to change a tire, I pulled out my
cell phone and called Triple A.

"I'll wait with you," Gabriella said.

"Thanks."

Then I called Donovan to thank him for the thoughtful
gift and tell him about my tire.

"Hi, sweetie," I said. "Thanks for my gift. I loved it."

"What gift?" he said.

"You didn't have a vase delivered to my office?"

"No. It wasn't me."

"Oh, I assumed it was from you. Must've been one of my
clients. Anyway, Gabriella and I are waiting for someone
from Triple A to come and change my tire. I got a flat."

"That's not good. Do you need me to come out there?"

"No. We're fine. Thanks, though. I'll talk to you later. Love
you."

"Right back at ya."

I flipped the phone and placed it back in my purse. I inspected the tire more closely and noticed a shiny, metal ob-
ject embedded in the tread. It looked as if someone had
deliberately flattened my tire. *Why would someone do that?*

CHAPTER THIRTY-EIGHT
Tatiana

Tatiana had finally come face-to-face with Dr. Little, her arch nemesis. At least that's how Tatiana viewed her. Curiosity had gotten the best of her. She had to see Dr. Little, up close and vulnerable. Although she had seen her on TV and from a distance, Dr. Little was even prettier in person. That irked Tatiana even more! The encounter at Mick's threw Tatiana for a loop. She hadn't intended to speak to Skyler. She enjoyed watching from afar. It was just that she became captivated by the way Dr. Little carried herself. She was gorgeous and perfect. Tatiana could tell just by looking that Dr. Little was articulate and even-keeled—everything Tatiana wanted to be.

Tatiana expected Dr. Little to explode when she discovered that the tire on her luxury car was flattened. After all, that was the whole reason Tatiana punctured the tire in the first place. Even then, Dr. Little acted with class. Nothing seemed to rattle her.

Tatiana's thoughts shifted to the life growing inside of her. She placed her hand on her stomach. Since she was only a few weeks pregnant, she couldn't feel any movements from the baby. The thought of being a single parent didn't appeal to her. Somehow she thought that if Reggie knew she was pregnant, he'd be there for her; they'd get married and live happily ever after. *How foolish,* she admitted silently. She remembered hearing Jasmine say, "If a guy doesn't want you when your stomach's flat, what makes you think he's going to want you when your belly is as big as a basketball?"

Her thoughts shifted to her former fiancé, Darnell. She had loved Darnell with all her heart. He seemed to be everything she ever wanted in a man. He opened doors for her to enter and exit, took her to upscale dining establishments, bought her expensive gifts, and took her on exotic vacations. The relationship seemed perfect, until she got pregnant. Even though they were engaged to be married, Darnell wasn't happy about the baby. She thought that perhaps he was feeling insecure and possibly jealous about sharing her with someone else. She hoped his disposition would change.

Tatiana remembered the fateful day that changed her life forever. She had been out shopping for items for the baby. When she arrived at the three-bedroom home she shared with Darnell, she yelled for him to come downstairs and see what she had bought. But he didn't answer. She checked the rooms downstairs and didn't see him. So she walked upstairs, still calling out his name. No response. She found it strange that the door to the master bedroom was closed, and she remembered hesitating before opening it. When she did turn the knob and push the door open, she saw Darnell in a compromising position with a woman she had never seen before. She felt like screaming, but no sounds escaped past the lump stuck in her throat. A pair of scissors was sitting on the edge of the dresser. She picked up the shears and used them to stab Darnell through the side of his neck. He emitted one shrill cry and then was silent. The scissors were lodged in Darnell's neck as he attempted to remove them. The other woman, who Tatiana later discovered was Shantasia, Darnell's co-worker, screamed and pushed Darnell off of her. Shantasia had blood splattered on her face and body. Tatiana went into shock and after four months of pregnancy, suffered a miscarriage.

The district attorney asked that Tatiana be arraigned immediately. The months around the murder trial wreaked havoc on Tatiana emotionally, spiritually, and physically. In addition to feeling remorse for killing Darnell, Tatiana was grieving the loss of a baby that she desperately wanted. Her life seemed to have no purpose. She wanted to die. If it weren't for the loving support of her maternal grandmother, who had raised Tatiana after her mother died, Tatiana didn't think she could've gone on.

After being exonerated of the murder charges, Tatiana wanted to start a new life. Shortly after the acquittal, Tatiana's grandmother died of a stroke, which devastated Tatiana. Without her grandmother, Tatiana didn't feel she had any reason to stay in Dallas.

Thinking about her grandmother caused Tatiana to sob. She missed her so much. Suddenly, there was an unbearable cramping feeling in Tatiana's abdomen. It caused her to double over in excruciating pain. It hurt so badly, she shrieked. Throbbing pains shot through the right side of her abdomen, crippling her. Unable to walk, she crawled to the telephone in her bedroom, and dialed 911.

The operator answered the phone and asked Tatiana the nature of her emergency.

"I'm pregnant, and my stomach is cramping really badly," Tatiana said, sobbing.

"Are you bleeding?" the 911 operator asked.

Tatiana didn't feel any wetness in her pants. "No."

"Do you think you're having a miscarriage?"

"I don't know. Maybe"

Tatiana provided the operator with her address and waited for the ambulance. Fifteen minutes later, the paramedics arrived and transported Tatiana to the hospital.

At the hospital, the doctor administered a vaginal exam, determining that Tatiana had an ectopic pregnancy. Tatiana was in stable condition and the embryo was extremely small. Due to the abdominal pain Tatiana was experiencing, the doctor decided that rather than administer methotrexate, laparoscopic surgery needed to be performed. Tatiana was given general anesthesia before the OB-GYN examined Tatiana's fallopian tubes with a tiny camera inserted through a small incision in her navel. The doctor successfully removed the embryo while preserving Tatiana's tube.

While Tatiana was resting in her private room, the doctor came in to check on her.

"I'm sorry about your loss," Dr. Cook offered. "How are you feeling?"

"How did this happen?" Tatiana asked, blaming herself.

"Not to sound like a textbook, but after conception, the fertilized egg travels down your fallopian tube on its way to your uterus. If the tube is damaged or blocked and fails to propel the egg toward your womb, the egg may become implanted in the tube and continue to develop there. Because almost all ectopic pregnancies occur in one of the fallopian tubes, they're often called tubal pregnancies. If an ectopic pregnancy isn't recognized and treated, the embryo will grow until the fallopian tube ruptures, resulting in severe abdominal pain and bleeding similar to what you experienced. It can cause permanent damage to the tube or loss of the tube. If it involves very heavy internal bleeding and is not treated promptly, it can even lead to death. Fortunately, the vast majority of ectopic pregnancies are caught in time."

"Doctor," Tatiana said, "Will I be able to have more children?"

"Yes. The earlier you end an ectopic pregnancy, the less

damage you'll have in that tube and the greater your chances will be of carrying another baby to term."

"Okay," Tatiana said. "How long will I have to stay in the hospital?"

"As long as you remain in stable condition, you'll be able to go home tomorrow. The recuperation period is one week. You'll need to take it easy. No heavy lifting! Let me know if you need anything," Dr. Cook said as he left the room.

"Thanks."

Tatiana was disappointed about losing yet another baby. *If it weren't for bad luck, I wouldn't have any luck at all,* Tatiana thought. She picked up the phone and called Jasmine.

"Hello," Jasmine answered on the second ring.

"Hey, girl. It's Tee." She sounded sad. She was on the verge of tears.

"You don't sound so good. What's up?" Tatiana could tell by the sound of her voice that she was concerned.

"I'm in the hospital. I lost the baby," she explained.

"Oh, no." She gasped. "I'm so sorry to hear that. How'd it happen?"

"It was an ectopic pregnancy."

"That's terrible! I heard those things can kill you."

"That's what the doctor told me."

"Well, I'm on my way to see you."

"No. As much as I'd love to have you here, I could really use some rest. I'm so tired. I'll be released tomorrow. Would you come pick me up?"

"Of course I will."

Tatiana gave Jasmine the name of the hospital and the telephone and room numbers.

"Do you want me to call anybody for you?" Jasmine asked.

Tatiana's first thought was *no*. She didn't have anyone, other than Jasmine, who really cared about her. Then at second thought she considered Reggie. *He was the baby's father, so he should know.*

"Would you call Reggie?" Tatiana requested. "He *was* the baby's father."

"Of course."

Tatiana provided Jasmine with Reggie's number, and Jasmine called him on a three-way conference call. His voice mail answered, "Hey, this is Reggie. I'm unable to take your call at the moment. When you hear the beep, you know what to do."

After the beep, Jasmine said, "Hi, Reggie. This is Jasmine Tiles. I'm Tatiana Strawberry's business partner and friend. I was calling to let you know that Tatiana is in the hospital. She lost the baby. Thought you should know." At the end of the message, Jasmine left the telephone number to Tatiana's room and disengaged Reggie's line from the call.

"Thank you," Tatiana said, feeling herself getting choked up.

"Anything for you. Make sure you get plenty of rest. I'll see you tomorrow."

"Will do. Good night."

Tatiana felt lonely and afraid. She wondered whether she was being punished by a higher power. She was convinced that God didn't like her. Why else would He have taken her mother away from her when she was only six years old? And what about the terrible miscarriage she suffered previously. *Will anything ever be easy for me?*

CHAPTER THIRTY-NINE
Reggie

Reggie came home tired. Having worked on several lawns, he couldn't wait to take a hot shower to ease the aching in his back and shoulders. His business was thriving, and soon, he'd need to hire additional staff. He picked up his phone and noticed the staggering dial tone, indicating that he had messages. He dialed the number to his voice mail and input his four-digit code. His only message was from Jasmine.

"What?" he said aloud.

He hung up the phone without saving or deleting the message. He had never met Jasmine, but figured she had to be just as wacky as Tatiana. *Birds of a feather* . . . Rufus. He missed him terribly. Seeing that empty cage every day was disturbing. He considered getting a new pet, but felt it was too soon. Besides, another pet couldn't fill the void left in his heart by Rufus.

"I can't believe Tatiana!" He shook his head. "Yes, I can. How convenient? She lost the baby. Yeah, right! How can you lose a baby without being pregnant?" he asked skeptically. *That broad must think I'm stupid.*

He was relieved that Tatiana had given up on the delu-
sion of trying to convince him she was pregnant with his
baby. Maybe now Tatiana would move on to the next guy.
He was glad that he had taken Dr. Little's advice and gotten
the locks and the security code for his alarm system
changed. He hoped that he could finally put that whole Tatiana episode behind him.

Reggie took off his dirty work clothes and took a shower.
He slipped into a pair of silk boxer shorts and a wife beater
T-shirt, then he called Monday. He was so glad to hear her
voice.

"Hey, Monday. It's Reggie."

"Hey. How you doing?"

She didn't sound as excited to hear from him as he had
hoped.

"I'm all right," he said. "What's been up?"

"Not too much. You?"

"Been busy. I've been thinking about you, though. How's
Alexis?"

"She's fine. Thanks for asking." There was a brief pause.
"I really need to get going. I was about to go out. It was nice
hearing from you."

"Monday," Reggie interrupted.

"Yes?"

"Can I see you?"

"I don't think that's a good idea."

Reggie was disappointed. He realized that he had taken
Monday's affections for granted.

"Why?" Reggie asked.

She sighed into the receiver. "I'm sort of seeing someone."

"Oh, I see. Sorry I bothered you. Take it easy." He didn't
know what else to say, so he hung up the phone.

Reggie felt like calling Monday back and expressing his
adoration for her, but his pride wouldn't let him. He tried to

figure out what went wrong between him and Monday. Monday was a good woman, and he had let her go. *How could I have been so stupid?*

He realized that he had lost several decent women because of his own insecurities. Reggie had a problem with commitment. Since no one in his immediate circle was happily wed, he had given up on the institution of marriage without ever giving it a chance. His parents got divorced when he was a teenager, and it broke his heart. After that, friends and family members seemed to be getting divorced left and right, further reinforcing Reggie's stance on remaining single.

Through the years, Reggie became a certified "player." He was a good looking guy, nice dresser, and entrepreneur, so finding a woman wasn't a problem for him. He wasn't cocky or arrogant and that added to his appeal. Reggie convinced himself that monogamy wasn't natural. He didn't believe that a man was intended to love only one woman.

He hadn't admitted to anyone that his feelings for Monday had turned into what he imagined love would be. It scared him. He took a macho stance with Monday because he didn't want her to think he was "soft." He had seen the way women run all over nice guys, and he wasn't having it. That was one of the things he didn't like about women. They always wanted the opposite of what they had. Never satisfied. If they had a bad boy, they wanted a nice guy. If they had a nice guy, he was too wimpy; they wanted a player. If they had a rich guy, they complained that he didn't spend enough time with them. So, they fooled around with the broke guy. If they had a financially-challenged guy, they craved the finer things in life and desired a rich guy to take care of them. And on and on and on.

Reggie hated to admit that Monday had gotten to him. It wasn't supposed to happen. Especially not to him. His feelings for Monday were genuine. She had a way of making him laugh. Even when Monday allowed herself to be vulnerable, she was still strong. That quality appealed to him. Admittedly, he would miss her. He considered fighting for Monday, but decided against it. He cared enough about Monday to want her to be happy. If another guy was better suited for her, so be it. Like the ancient Chinese proverb says, "If you love something, set it free. If it comes back to you, it's yours. If it doesn't, it never was." *I have. It was never meant to be.*

CHAPTER FORTY
Monday

In anticipation of the upcoming meeting with Stan, Monday changed her outfit three times. She didn't want to show any skin, and certainly didn't want to wear anything that could be remotely construed as sexy or provocative. She finally decided on a gray, striped, ruffle shirt, a pair of charcoal-gray-colored dress slacks, and black high heels.

Monday arrived at the white church building that reminded her of a wedding chapel and felt anxious. Beads of sweat formed on the top of her lip even though the inside of her car was cool. *What am I doing here?* She hadn't seen Stan since she was a child. *Maybe I should've let Larry come here with me.* She dabbed the perspiration from her lip with the back of her hand. She said a silent prayer before entering the church.

Once inside, Monday made her way into the pastor's study where Stan was waiting for her. She had blocked the image of Stan's face out of her mind. When she saw him, there was no denying that he was her father. They had the same nose and mouth. Stan was approximately six feet tall with an athletic build. His hairline was receding.

"Monday, I'm so glad you made it," Stan said with a wide smile across his face. He extended his hand to her.

Monday felt as if she was five years old again. She looked at Stan's hand and refused to shake it. Those were the same hands that had molested her all those years ago. Suddenly, Stan's presence intimidated her. Her hands began to tremble. She could hardly speak.

When he saw that Monday wasn't interested in shaking hands, Stan said, "Please, have a seat."

The room held a mahogany desk, a bookshelf lined with spiritual and motivational books, a few Cordovan-colored leather chairs, and a framed copy of "The Lord's Prayer" hanging on the wall. Monday took a seat on the chair nearest to the door. Stan attempted to close the door, and Monday flinched.

"No!" she demanded. "Leave it open."

"I'm sorry. I didn't mean any harm. I was just trying to give us some privacy. No problem. We can leave it open." He walked behind the desk and sat down. "Let me start by saying that I'm truly sorry for what I did to you. I wasn't well back then. You were my sweet, little girl. It was my job to protect you. Instead, I hurt you. There hasn't been a day that's gone by that I don't regret what happened. It wasn't your fault. It was all on me. I'll have to live with that guilt for the rest of my life. I pray you'll forgive me, one day." His voice cracked, and his eyes became teary. He grabbed a couple of tissues from the box on the corner of his desk.

Monday wasn't moved by his words or the outpouring of emotions. She had years of hurt, and she doubted very seriously that this one encounter would be enough for her to reconcile with Stan. Point blank, she didn't trust him. Not around young girls. If he were perverted enough to molest his own flesh and blood, how could she ever believe that any other child would be safe in his presence?

In regard to forgiveness, she had prayed and asked God

to cleanse her heart. She believed that she had forgiven Stan. Forgiving and forgetting were different, though. She could forgive him because that's what she's supposed to do. As far as forgetting, this wasn't *Men in Black,* and there were no "Neuralizers," pen-like devices that erased the memory of anyone who gazed into their flashes. It wasn't that easy.

Monday asked the question that had been gnawing at her ever since she found out Stan started a church.

"How did you become a minister?"

"Good question. A lot of people don't believe a person can change. I'm here to tell you that they can. I'm living proof. While I was in jail, I read the entire Bible four times. I began to study and take courses. I was on a spiritual journey. That's the only thing that kept me alive. God had a plan for my life. You know how much people in prison hate child molesters? Most molesters don't survive because the other prisoners rape them, beat them, kill them, or torture them to the point they commit suicide. Well, one day, the Lord called me to preach. I was skeptical at first. How could a sinner like me be used for the up-building of the kingdom? But it's true. I was called and not answering would be disobedience. By the time I got out of prison, I had a degree in theology. I went to a local Bible school and got a master's degree in divinity.

"I didn't intend to open up a church. I started a program to help pedophiles get treatment. We offered counseling services and weekly meetings, like AA. We even worked to ensure convicted child molesters registered with the police department. From that, the ministry grew."

"Don't tell me your members are all child molesters?"

"No, no. Of course not. We're a regular church. The members know about my past. I don't keep it a secret. It's just that we still have the original program as one of our outreach ministries."

"Oh."

"I must say, I was surprised to hear from Alexis."

"I'll bet you were."

"I didn't know whether she was for real or playing a cruel joke. Does she know what happened to you when you were a little girl?"

"You mean does she know what *you* did to me when I was a little girl? The answer is yes. She does."

"I'd love to meet her. I told my wife, Loretta, about her, and she's excited about the possibility of us getting to know Alexis."

"You're remarried?"

"Yes. We've been married going on four years now." He handed her a photo sitting on the edge of his desk of him and Loretta. "She's a terrific lady with a loving spirit. I'm blessed to have her."

Monday smirked. *What kind of woman marries a convicted child molester?* She studied the picture, hoping to see something in Loretta's eyes that would reveal that she was just as evil as her perverted husband. Monday was surprised to see that Loretta looked completely normal. She wore a "church lady" suit, and her eyes seemed to twinkle.

"How did the two of you meet?" Monday asked, setting the picture back on the desk.

"She was a part of the prison ministry at her church. It started out with her writing me encouraging letters. Eventually, she came to visit me. We hit it off and became really good friends. She knew about my past, and she helped me understand the true meaning of unconditional love and forgiveness."

"Does she have children?"

"Her children are grown. They don't live with us. She also has two grandchildren."

"Stan, the fact that you have a wife is all fine, well, and good. But being a pedophile is like being an alcoholic or drug addict. It's a sickness. You can receive treatment, but you have to change your lifestyle. You wouldn't offer an alcoholic a drink, so why would anyone in her right mind allow a convicted child molester to be around children?"

"I understand what you're saying. Let me explain something to you. I don't put myself in the situation to be tempted or tested. I'm *never* alone with any child. I won't even let a kid sit on my lap. I've changed. I've been delivered. I don't have those tendencies anymore."

"I wish I could believe you."

"I don't blame you for not trusting me. If I were in your shoes, I wouldn't trust me either." He sighed. "You're my only daughter, and I love you. I wish things were different, but I can't change the past. If you give me a chance to be a part of your and Alexis's life, I promise, I won't let you down."

A lump formed in Monday's throat as she tried to choke it down. She blinked several times, trying to stop the tears. Her eyes burned. This reminded her of Bishop T.D. Jakes' movie, *Woman Thou Art Loosed*. She was at a fork in the road. She could either forgive Stan and release herself from emotional and spiritual bondage, or hold on to the anger and let it destroy her.

"All right, Stan. I'm having a small gathering at my house for Alexis. She's going to Job Corps, and we're having a family dinner. I'd like for you to join us and bring your wife."

Stan was speechless. Tears streamed down his cheeks. Monday grabbed a pen and piece of paper off of his desk and wrote down the details.

"See you later," Monday said as she clutched her purse and left.

Still unable to speak, Stan waved good-bye. Once at her car, Monday exhaled. She felt as if she had made the right decision, because she realized that she wasn't in control of this situation. God was in control. She had prayed and released it. She was operating out of faith and obedience.

CHAPTER FORTY-ONE

Gabriella

Finished with her yoga class, Gabriella headed to the shower room. She wanted to hit the sauna before going home.

"Hey, long time, no see," Caleb said, startling her.

"Hi, Caleb. It's been a while. Nice to see you."

"How have you been?"

"Good." She nodded her head, wondering whether she should tell him that she and Kevin had reconciled.

"How are things going with you and Kevin?"

She bit the corner of her lip. She didn't want to hurt his feelings, but she didn't feel right about leading him on either. "We got back together."

"Is that right?"

"Yes."

"That's cool. Congratulations. I'm glad you guys were able to work things out." He gave a faint smile.

"Thank you. I wish I could talk more, but . . ."

"Hey, I understand. It's all good. Take care." He kissed her on the cheek and left.

Gabriella could see the disappointment on Caleb's face.

Breaking his heart was the last thing she wanted to do. *Caleb's such a good guy.* Maybe if they had met under different circumstances . . . Gabriella shook it off. She was in love with her husband and that was that. No sense in dwelling on things that could never be.

She changed out of her clothes and wrapped a white towel around her body. She tried to relax in the sauna, but her mind wouldn't slow down. Thoughts about the laundry list of things she had to do kept canceling each other out. Planning the vow renewal ceremony. Cooking dinner. Making sure Mateo and Destiny were adjusting. Even though she had a lot to do, she enjoyed every minute of it.

Thinking about Mateo and Destiny brought a smile to her face. She thought about the day she and Kevin took all of the children to Chuck E. Cheese's to make the big announcement that their family would be expanding. Mateo and Destiny handled the news very well. They were excited to have a big brother and big sister. Imani cried, because she wasn't her daddy's only little girl anymore. Jr. was upset because he didn't think they were his real siblings. Kevin had to explain to him that Mateo and Destiny had a different mother, but he was their father as well. However, Mateo and Destiny were so sweet that it didn't take long before Jr. and Imani warmed up to them. It was such a relief to both her and Kevin. She felt fortunate.

Gabriella showered and put on her street clothes. She stopped off at the grocery store to pick up a bag of Caesar salad and a family-size pack of chicken breasts for dinner. It was her turn to pick up Mateo and Destiny from daycare, so she did that before picking up Jr. and Imani from after-school care and going home. She was amazed at how much she loved Mateo and Destiny. They were both well-behaved and smart. They also looked a lot like Jr. and Imani when they were that age.

Once at home, Gabriella gave each of the children two

cookies and a glass of milk. Jr. and Imani completed their homework at the kitchen table, while Mateo colored in his coloring book, and Destiny watched a *Dora the Explorer* DVD in the family room.

Gabriella was in the kitchen preparing dinner when the phone rang. She checked the caller ID, and it was Skyler's telephone number.

"Hey," Gabriella answered.

"Hey, Gabby," Donovan said.

"Donovan? I thought you were Sky."

"Don't sound so happy," he teased.

"It's all right. Kevin hasn't come home yet. I'll tell him to call you when he gets in."

"I wasn't calling to speak to Kevin. I actually need to talk to you."

"Oh. Is everything all right?"

"Yes. Everything is fine. Sky's birthday is coming up, and I want to throw her a surprise party."

"That's nice. What can I do to help?"

"Glad you asked. I've already booked a banquet hall in Buckhead and a caterer. I need your help with the decorations and keeping Sky off the trail."

She laughed. "Come on, this is Sky we're talking about. She's very . . . what's the word? You know, when people sense things."

"Intuitive."

"Yes. She's very intuitive. I'll do what I can to keep her from getting suspicious."

"Thanks. I knew I could count on you. How are the kids?"

"They're fine. Jr. and Imani are doing homework. Mateo and Destiny are in the other room watching Dora exploring."

"Okay. Hopefully, Sky and I will be joining the parent club sooner rather than later."

"That would be great. You'll enjoy it. I'm telling you, children change everything. They give you a reason to get out of bed in the morning. And once you have them, you can't imagine your life without them. There's a love for your children that's greater than any love you could ever have for another human being. You know how much you love your parents, right?"

"Yes."

"It's like, if your mother and your child were both drowning, and you could only save one of them, without hesitation, you would save your child."

"That's deep."

"It is," Gabriella concurred.

"I haven't had a chance to tell you, but I'm glad you and Kevin got back together."

"I know you are. Thank you for saying it. Anyway, I'm making dinner, so I'll talk to you later."

"All right. Have a good one."

Gabriella pressed the "off" button on the phone and finished cooking. She heard the garage door open and Kevin parking his car inside. He entered carrying a bouquet of pink roses.

"For me?" Gabriella said, smiling. She was so excited. It had been a while since Kevin had given her flowers. "What's the occasion?"

"Just because . . ." He kissed her on the cheek. "I love you."

"You're so sweet. Thank you, honey. I love you, too."

"Dinner smells good," Kevin said as he walked toward Jr. and Imani. "Come on over here and give your daddy a hug."

Jr. and Imani both rushed into his arms.

"I'm glad you're home," Jr. said.

"Me, too," Imani added. "I missed you."

"I missed you guys, too." He kissed them each on the tops of their heads. "Where's Mateo and Destiny?"

"They're in the family room watching TV," Gabriella answered, as she placed the elaborate bouquet in a crystal vase filled with water.

Kevin went into the other room and said, "Hello. Daddy's home."

"Hi, Daddy!" Mateo said excitedly.

Kevin kneeled down and gave him a big hug. He picked Destiny up and carried her into the kitchen. Mateo followed.

"Dinner's ready," Gabriella announced. "I need for everyone to wash their hands."

Jr., Imani, and Mateo each took turns washing their hands in the pedestal-style sink in the half bath downstairs. Kevin washed his and Destiny's hands in the kitchen sink.

"How was your day?" Gabriella asked Kevin.

"Nothing exciting. Work is work." Kevin dried his and Destiny's hands with a paper towel.

"Donovan called. He's planning a surprise birthday party for Sky."

"Sounds like fun."

They sat at the dinner table and Kevin led the family in prayer. "Lord, thank You for my family. Thank You for this food. Bless this meal. In Jesus' name, we pray. Amen."

In the two weeks that Kevin had been back, Gabriella noticed a change in him. He was praying not just at dinner, but in the morning and at night. He was even reading the Bible. Every Sunday, he insisted on taking the family to church. In fact, they joined a small Baptist church ten minutes away from their house. Afterwards, they would go to brunch. That was their new Sunday routine. Gabriella was happy that the children were all getting along and that Kevin was truly acting as the head of their household.

After dinner, Kevin loaded the dishwasher, and Gabriella got Imani and Destiny ready for bed. Afterward, Kevin supervised Jr. and Mateo's joint bath. Once the children were bathed and in their pajamas, Gabriella read them a bedtime story. At the end of the story, they all got on their knees and prayed aloud.

Since Jr. was the oldest, he went first. "God bless Mommy and Daddy and my brother and sisters. And God bless me, too. Amen."

Then Imani. "God, thank You for my family. Thank You for my friends. Thank You for giving me good grades in school. Thank You for my teachers. God bless us. Amen."

Mateo was next. "God bless Aunty Sky and Aunty Stasia and my mommy in heaven and Daddy and Destiny. God bless my brother and my sisters. God bless my grandma. Thank You, Lord. Amen."

Jr. corrected him. "You forgot to ask God to bless our mommy, too."

Mateo closed his eyes and pressed his hands together. "And God bless Ma Gabby. Amen."

Gabriella smiled and tucked Jr. and Mateo in their bunk beds. She walked Imani and Destiny down the hall into their princess-themed room and tucked them in. She went back into her bedroom.

"Everyone down for the count?" Kevin asked.

"Yes."

She thanked him again for the flowers before going to take a shower. When she finished, Kevin was fast asleep. She slipped into a nightgown and nestled next to him in a spooning position. He draped his arm over her waist and said, "Night, baby. Love you."

She felt truly blessed. Her marriage was back on track and seemingly stronger than ever. Not only did she have her own children, she inherited two more wonderful kids. Mrs. Wrey and Anastasia seemed to have accepted her and the situation. Gabriella was happier than she had been in a long time.

She wondered how she could use her experience to help other women dealing with marital infidelity. Since she and

Kevin started going to church as a family, she thought about volunteering for the couples' ministry. She remembered reading something in Joel Osteen's book, *Your Best Life Now: 7 Steps to Living at Your Full Potential,* regarding sowing seeds into the lives of others. Gabriella was convinced that she didn't go through all of the pain and suffering for nothing. Someone out there needed to hear her story. If her testimony could help one family stay together and rebuild their marriage, then it would've all been worth it.

CHAPTER FORTY-TWO
Tatiana

It had been one week and a day since Tatiana's emergency surgery, and she was ready to get back to work. During the time off, she blocked her number and called Donovan's cell phone several times late at night. Whenever Donovan answered, she gave a legitimate business reason for calling. She knew full well Donovan was in an awkward position and couldn't talk freely. She didn't care. She wanted to make his wife suspicious. A few times his wife answered, and Tatiana hung up. She was convinced that she had achieved her goal of making Dr. Little feel insecure about her relationship.

She had scheduled an appointment with Donovan to go over the menu and was looking forward to seeing him. They planned to meet at the incubator. Prior to the meeting, Tatiana and Jasmine met for breakfast at IHOP. They waited about twenty minutes before being seated at a booth. The waitress handed them each menus and took their drink orders. They ordered a carafe of orange juice.

"You're looking much better," Jasmine observed. "How are you feeling?"

"Better. I'm still sad about losing the baby."

"That's understandable. While I was married to my ex-husband, I had a miscarriage. It's a difficult process, but you will get over it. It takes time."

"I wonder if I'll ever be able to carry a baby to term."

"I thought the doctor was able to save your tube."

"He did. I was just thinking out loud. I tend to do that sometimes," Tatiana explained.

"You should be thankful that the doctor was able to save your tube. That's a blessing all by itself. Not to mention the fact that if your tube had ruptured, you wouldn't be sitting here today."

The waitress returned with two glasses filled with ice and water, two empty glasses, a carafe of orange juice and four straws. She placed the items on the table and took their food orders. Jasmine ordered the Rooty Tooty Fresh 'n Fruity, and Tatiana ordered Pigs in Blankets.

"Thanks," Jasmine said to the waitress. She took their menus and went to place their orders. "Anyway," Jasmine continued. "Don't start feeling sorry for yourself. Everything happens for a reason. We may not always understand it, but God has a plan for us."

"If you say so. I don't necessarily believe that there's a purpose for my life."

Jasmine raised a brow. "What? How can you say that?"

"Easy. My mom died when I was just a kid."

"As sad as that is—and believe me, it's sad—God still has a plan. You told me that your grandmother raised you. The way you described her, she was an incredible woman. Thank God for that. So many people are orphans, living in foster care and never even knew their parents. Be thankful that wasn't you." She unwrapped a straw and placed it in a glass of water.

"Do you ever see the negative of a situation?" Tatiana inquired.

"Of course, but I choose not to dwell on it. My dad was a stone-cold Jimi Hendrix fan. One day my dad and I were talking and he told me, 'The next time you think about complaining about the type of shoes you're wearing, look at the man with no feet.' I'm paraphrasing the lyrics to the song and my dad, but you get the gist. That stuck with me because it's so true. He also told me, 'If you have a problem that money can fix, you don't have a problem.' I figure, as long as I have my health, and I'm in my right mind, I'm okay. I may not have every material thing I want, but I'm far better off than a lot of people."

Tatiana looked away from Jasmine and noticed a woman, who appeared to be in her early twenties, sitting in a wheelchair. The woman didn't have any limbs, and was sitting with a group of people. The guy sitting next to her was feeding her, yet she seemed happy, laughing and conversing with everyone at the table.

Tatiana diverted her eyes back to Jasmine, who was sipping some water. "I see what you mean," Tatiana said, unable to figure out why she felt so empty inside.

"You seem like something else is going on with you. What's up?" Jasmine probed.

"A lot of stuff."

"We're girls. If you can't tell me, who can you tell?"

Tatiana smiled. Even though she and Jasmine were close, Tatiana wasn't sure she could confide everything in her. Especially not all the devilment she had been getting herself into lately. Impregnating herself with a turkey baster. Playing immature games with Dr. Little. She decided to tell Jasmine about Darnell. If Jasmine could handle that, their friendship could survive anything.

The waitress set their plates in front of them.

"Can I get you anything else?" the waitress asked.

Tatiana shook her head, and Jasmine said, "No, thanks. The food looks good."

They began to eat their breakfast, and Tatiana went on to explain her relationship with Darnell. She told Jasmine about their engagement, the baby, miscarriage, murder, trial, and acquittal.

"You've been through a lot," Jasmine said. "You may not realize it now, but God has a calling on your life. There's a reason why you went through what you went through. You need to pray and ask God to reveal His purpose for your life."

She's certainly consistent, Tatiana thought about Jasmine's response. Nothing seemed to surprise Jasmine. *She doesn't just talk the talk; she actually walks the walk.* They finished eating breakfast and paid the bill.

Tatiana trailed Jasmine to the incubator. Once there, they began preparing food for an upcoming event. Not long afterward, the buzzer rang, indicating that Tatiana's appointment had arrived. She went to the waiting area and pressed the button to unlock the door. To her surprise, a slender white woman was standing on the other side.

"Hi, I'm Gabriella," the woman said, extending her hand to Tatiana. "Donovan had a scheduling conflict and asked me to go over the menu with you instead. I hope that's all right."

Tatiana was upset, but she tried not to show it. *The nerve of Donovan not to come himself. Was he upset about me calling late at night?* "That's fine. I'm Tee. Nice to meet you." She offered a weak smile. They shook hands. Tatiana motioned her hand toward the couch and said, "Please, have a seat."

Wearing the chef's hat outside of the kitchen seemed unnecessary, so Tatiana removed it and placed it on the wooden coffee table. She noticed Gabriella looking at her sideways.

"I've seen you somewhere before," Gabriella proclaimed.

Tatiana recognized her, too. She was the woman dining

with Dr. Little at Mick's. "Not sure. People tell me I have one of those faces that look like a lot of people." She chuckled.

"No," Gabriella insisted. "I've seen you somewhere, recently. I'm certain of it. I'm sure it'll come to me."

"Okay. So, how do you know Donovan?"

"His wife is my best friend."

"Then you're the perfect person to be here. Tell me about Dr. Little. Her favorite colors, her food preferences, whatever you think will help make this party a success."

"Donovan didn't already go over that with you?" Gabriella gave her an incredulous look.

"He did, but you know how men can be." She gave a warm smile.

"I do." She laughed. "Do you do party planning, too?"

"Yes." She nodded.

"That's good to know. I'm sure Donovan will let you know if he needs your help with that."

Tatiana sensed that Gabriella hadn't taken a liking to her. Gabriella had a serious demeanor and was not very conversational.

"Do you have the menu?" Gabriella asked.

"It's right here." Tatiana handed it to her.

Gabriella reviewed the selections. She first skimmed the hot and cold hors d'oeuvres: coconut chicken tenders with ginger plum sauce, Savannah crab cake with smoked red pepper coulis, roasted fingerling potato and smoked salmon with crème fraiche, and salmon caviar with chives. For the soup, lobster bisque with fresh lobster and caviar garnish. The salad, classic Caesar salad with shaved reggiano and croutons with Caesar dressing. The entrée was pan-seared chicken breasts, garden vegetables, rock shrimp risotto with a light lemon and garlic cream sauce.

"Sounds delicious," Gabriella assented.

"Thank you. We aim to please. Will you or Donovan be doing the taste test?"

"I'm not sure yet. Most likely it'll be him. I'm just the back-up."

"Understandable."

They both laughed. Gabriella seemed to be a bit more relaxed. She stood and said, "Thanks for your time. It was a pleasure meeting you."

"Same here."

After Gabriella left, Tatiana wondered whether Gabriella had remembered her from the restaurant. Gabriella hadn't given any indication as to whether she had. Then Tatiana wondered whether she had gone too far by calling and hanging up on Dr. Little. A part of Tatiana felt remorseful for what she had done. Yet, another part of her wanted revenge. She thought about how Jasmine would feel about her if she knew what Tatiana was capable of. She knew exactly what Jasmine would tell her. *Vengeance is mine, saith the Lord.* But Tatiana was torn. Reggie had dogged her and hurt her feelings. He seemed to have more regard for Dr. Little than he did for her. She wanted Reggie to pay for playing with her emotions. Even if it meant causing chaos in Dr. Little's comfortable little world.

Gabriella left the incubator and immediately noticed a shiny, red Corvette parked in the lot. She furrowed her brows, wondering how she missed seeing the car when she pulled up. Then she remembered where she had seen Tatiana. "Oh my God. That's her. The woman from the restaurant. Why was she staring so hard at Sky?" Gabriella had an uneasy feeling. She took out her cell phone and snapped a picture of the car and the license tag. She immediately got in her car and called Donovan on his cell phone.

"'Ello," Donovan answered.

"Hey, it's Gabriella."

"How'd the meeting go, Gabby?"

"Fine. The menu looked good," she paused. "Look, Donovan. You and I are friends, right?"

"Of course we are. What kind of a question is that?"

"Donovan, I think the world of you and Sky. The two of you are like family to me. I love you both. Something isn't sitting right with me, though."

"What's going on?"

"The caterer. When Sky and I were having lunch, she was there."

"So? What's the big deal?"

"The big deal is the way she stared at Sky. It made us both uncomfortable."

"Did you ask her about it?"

"We didn't have to. She came up to us at the restaurant and told us that she thought Sky was someone she knew. We dismissed it, but when we went out to our cars, Sky's tire was flat."

"Gabriella, I appreciate your concern. I can understand why you'd find that strange, but to me, it's merely a coincidence. Don't read too much into it. A guy I work with highly recommended her."

"I hear you. I hate to even ask you this, but I need to hear you say it."

"What?"

"Are you having an affair?"

"Absolutely not! I love Sky. We're very happy. We're trying to have a baby, remember?"

"Yes. I believe you. I'm sorry if I offended you."

"I'm not offended. It's a good thing that Sky has a friend like you."

"Okay. I'll talk to you soon."

She hung up the phone and drove off. Something about Tatiana didn't sit right with her. She trusted Donovan, but not Tatiana. If Tatiana was up to something, Gabriella was determined to find out. She wasn't about to let Skyler end up blind-sided and broken-hearted. Not if she could help it.

She secured her earpiece and called her friend, Nate, a private investigator. Nate used to work security at a night-club she and Kevin frequented prior to starting his own investigation firm. He had a solid reputation. She was convinced that if there were anything to be found, Nate was the man to find it.

"City morgue. You kill 'em, we chill 'em," Nate said.

Gabriella laughed. "Why did you answer the phone like that? What if I was a client?"

"Ever heard of caller ID? What can I do for you, pretty lady?"

"I need a favor."

"I'm listening."

"There's a woman doing some catering for my best friend's birthday party. I think the woman is trying to put the moves on her husband. Would you check her out and let me know what you find?"

"I'm involved in a case right now, but I'll put my rookie on it. He can handle it."

"Thanks so much." Gabriella provided him with Tatiana's name, physical description, office location, car type, and license plate number. Then they discontinued the call. "Let's see what you're up to, Tee," Gabriella said to no one in particular.

CHAPTER FORTY-THREE
Monday

"Mom," Alexis said. "How many times are you going to change clothes? You look fine."

"I don't want to look 'fine.' I want to look great," Monday explained.

"You looked terrific in all four of the outfits you tried on."

Monday continued to check herself out, at model perfect angles in the bathroom mirror. She wore a black skirt and white shirt with loose-fitting sleeves. Alexis clasped a large, white, beaded necklace around her mother's neck. She was nervous because it took her two weeks to plan this get-together with her entire family. It was difficult getting Paige to agree to break bread with Stan, but she finally relented.

"Now that looks good." Alexis complimented her.

"I think you're right. I'll keep this on."

"About time. You and Dad have been spending a lot of time together for the past two months. Could it be? Do I dare say? Are you guys in love?"

"Whatever, Alexis. Get out of here and go get dressed, please."

Alexis laughed and did as she was told. Monday couldn't stop the smile from widening on her face. Alexis was right. She was in love, and it felt good. Real good. Larry turned out to be everything she had ever wanted in a man. Even though Monday had a full-time job and was fully capable of paying her bills, Larry still provided. He was generous, showering her with expensive gifts, like a diamond tennis bracelet and tanzanite earrings.

Throughout the day, Monday found herself thinking fondly about Larry. The feelings were mutual, as he would call her "just because." She loved it. It made her feel appreciated and valued.

The way Larry got along with Alexis was the marshmallows in the hot cocoa. He spent quality time with Alexis. They would go to the movies or out to dinner together. He'd open doors for Alexis and tell her, "If you go out with a guy, and he doesn't open doors for you, leave him alone. You're a lady and whoever you date needs to treat you as such." Alexis soaked up Larry's fatherly advice like porous magma.

Monday finished getting dressed so that she could go downstairs and wait for the guests to arrive. Since Paige and Stan hadn't been in the same room with one another for many, many years, Monday invited Skyler to act as ringmaster. Monday was certain that with Paige in the house, it was bound to become a circus.

In the kitchen, Monday had set up a long buffet table draped in a white linen cloth. Chafing dishes containing baked chicken, macaroni and cheese, collard greens, blackeyed peas, and candied yams were displayed on the table. The kitchen smelled like a soul food restaurant. Larry was the first person to arrive.

"What's up, handsome?" Monday greeted as she closed the door behind him.

"Hi, gorgeous." Larry kissed her on the cheek and followed her into the kitchen. "The place looks great. And the food, well . . ." He smiled. "You put your foot all up in it!"

Monday laughed. "Alexis is getting ready. She'll be down in a minute."

"Is she excited about the party and going to Job Corps?"

"She seems like it."

The doorbell rang again. It was Paige and Malik, Monday's brother. Malik stood six feet tall. He had a low-cut fade, mustache, and goatee. Dressed in baggy Rocawear gear, Malik looked like he belonged to the hip-hop generation. Monday let them in, and they joined Larry in the kitchen.

"What's up, bro-man?" Malik asked Larry, giving him daps.

"Nothing much. How have you been?"

"Working hard. I been working at UPS for a few years now."

"Cool." Larry turned to face Paige. "Nice to see you, Paige. How are you?"

"Another day, another dollar. You know how it is. What you got to drink?" Paige directed her question to Monday.

Monday opened the refrigerator door and scanned the contents. "We've got a little bit of everything up in here. Iced tea, lemonade, soda, fruit juices. What do you want?"

"I'll take a glass of lemonade," Paige said.

"Anybody else?" Monday asked.

"No," Larry and Malik replied automatically.

"Hi, everybody," Alexis said as she entered the room.

"Hey, Lexi," Paige said, giving her a hug only a grandmother could deliver.

Alexis made her way around the room, giving hugs to her dad and uncle, too. It wasn't long before Skyler arrived. Monday was glad to have her there and couldn't wait to introduce her to Larry.

"Everybody," Monday said. "This is Dr. Sky, I mean, Skyler Little."

Skyler smiled. "Sky will be fine. Nice to meet you, everybody."

Alexis, Larry, Malik, and Paige introduced themselves to Skyler before migrating into the living room where Monday put on an old-school R&B CD.

"So, Dr. Little," Paige said. "Monday tells me you're her shrink."

"Well, I don't consider myself to be a shrink. I prefer the term psychoanalyst," Skyler said tactfully.

"Same difference." Paige smirked and took a sip of lemonade. "Do you interpret dreams?"

"Sometimes."

"I had a dream about—"

"Ma," Monday interjected. "Sky is here for a celebration, not work." She looked at Skyler and said, "Sorry about that. Would you like to see the rest of the house?"

Skyler stood up and said, "Sure. I'd love to." She excused herself.

Monday showed Skyler the upstairs bedrooms and bathrooms. The master bedroom was decorated in brown and turquoise. Alexis's room had burnt-orange-colored walls, and a sheer covering draped from the ceiling onto the bed posts and enclosed the bed. The guest bedroom had a safari theme, complete with a leopard-print comforter and carved wooden animal statues. They came back downstairs.

"Your home is lovely," Skyler commented. "It really shows off your sense of style. I like the custom blinds in every room."

"Thank you. Was that the doorbell?" Monday asked.

"I think so."

Monday opened the door and greeted Stan and Loretta. "I'm glad you could make it."

Loretta was full-figured, and dressed in a long black skirt and dark blouse. Her hair was shoulder length and curled inward at the ends.

"Thanks for inviting us. This is my wife, Loretta," Stan introduced, as he handed Monday a wrapped gift. "That's for Alexis."

"Thanks," Monday said as she accepted the present. "Come on in." Smiling, she motioned toward Stan and said, "Stan, this is Dr. Skyler Little, *my psychoanalyst.*" Then she gestured toward Skyler and said, "Sky, this is my father, Stan."

"Nice to meet you," Skyler said, shaking Stan's, and then Loretta's, hands.

"You, too," they said in unison.

They followed Monday into the living room. Paige and Larry were sitting next to each other on the couch laughing, and Malik and Alexis were sitting on the love seat talking.

"Hey, everybody. Stan and Loretta are here," Monday announced.

Monday placed the gift on the table. The room became silent. Paige's jaw dropped. Although Monday had forewarned Paige that Stan would be attending the party, Paige seemed surprised to see him.

"Hi," Stan said, smiling and waving, trying to melt the glacier that had frozen over in the room.

Larry and Alexis got up and walked toward Stan.

"I'm Alexis." She extended her hand to Stan and he shook it. "Nice to meet you. What should I call you?"

"Whatever makes you comfortable. We brought a gift for you. I hope you like it."

"I'm sure I will." Alexis smiled and introduced herself to Loretta.

"You're a beauty," Loretta commented to Alexis.

Blushing, Alexis said, "Thanks. I can tell we're going to get along just fine."

"Stan, I'm glad to meet you," Larry said, giving Stan a firm handshake. "I'm Alexis's father."

"Oh, the pleasure's all mine. This is my wife, Loretta."

Larry kissed her hand and said, "It's a pleasure."

"What's he doing here?" Malik asked. His eyes were bulging, fist clenched.

"I invited him," Monday explained.

"Have you lost your mind?"

"No. Alexis wants to get to know him. You need to sit down and chill out."

"Nah, sis. I don't break bread with perverts. I'm out."

Malik kissed Alexis on the cheek and left. Monday called after him, but he ignored her.

Grabbing Monday by the arm, Skyler said, "Let him go."

Frustrated, Monday let out a pained sigh. "Fine."

Larry wrapped his arms around Monday's waist and said, "You okay?"

"Yes." Monday felt bad about her brother's outburst. She expected Malik to be uncomfortable being in the same room as Stan, but she didn't expect him to be so rude. *I'll bet Ma didn't tell Malik that Stan was going to be here. That seems like the type of vindictive thing she would do.* Monday gave Paige an incredulous look. She seemed to be sitting back reveling in all the drama. Loretta and Stan held hands. They seemed to be embarrassed.

"If you want me to leave . . ." offered Stan.

"No way," Monday said. "This is a party. Let's act like it." Monday was determined not to let anything or anyone ruin Alexis's going away celebration. "We've got delicious food, cold drinks, and music. It's time to get this party started. Larry, would you bless the food?"

"I sure will. Would everyone gather around in a circle and hold hands, please?"

Paige joined the rest of them in the kitchen and held Alexis's and Monday's hands.

"Paige," Stan said. "You're looking lovely."

She ignored him. Monday squeezed her hand, indicating her displeasure. Everyone closed their eyes.

"Heavenly Father," Larry prayed. "Thank You for this food and fellowship today. Bless Alexis in her endeavors and direct her steps. Keep her on the right track. Give us restoration and healing. Mend these broken relationships and make them better and stronger. Show us how to love one another the way Jesus loved the church. Give us forgiving hearts and forgive us for our sins. In Jesus' name, we pray. Amen."

"Let's eat," Monday said.

They all fixed their own plates. Stan, Loretta, Alexis, and Larry ate together in the dining room while Monday, Paige, and Skyler ate on serving trays in the living room.

"Ma," Monday said. "Why didn't you tell Malik that Stan was going to be here?"

"I forgot."

"You forgot? You don't forget something so important."

"So what if I did? People do forget, you know?"

Monday shook her head.

"I think Monday's upset because this could've been a lot worse," Skyler explained. "Without any type of warning or heads up, seeing Stan again was a shock for Malik. Thankfully, Malik didn't become violent."

"You two are overreacting. Malik isn't the violent type," Paige said, stuffing a forkful of food into her mouth.

"That's not the point, Ma. You should've told him."

Skyler patted Monday's hand. "Calm down. It's over. Release it. How do you feel about having your father here?"

"It's better than I expected. He and his wife seem like nice people," Monday said.

"What about you, Paige? Are you all right?" Skyler asked.

"So now you want to analyze me?" Paige said sarcastically. "Thought you weren't working today?"

"I'm always working," Skyler admitted.

"You want to know what I'm feeling?" Paige said. "I'm

hurt, angry, and disappointed. When I saw Stan, I felt like going upside his head. He standing up there looking all happy with his new wife. I wanted to throw up. I'll never forget the day I found out he molested Monday. I wanted to kill him. Do you hear me? I wanted to kill him with my bare hands. The only thing that stopped me was fear for what might happen to my kids. You have no idea how much I suffered. I didn't trust myself. That's why I never got remarried. How could I? I couldn't see Stan for what he was, so how could I ever believe in another man? It wasn't like he was Monday's stepfather. She was his flesh and blood. My God . . . I know I was guilty of hurting Monday too, saying she was to blame for being victimized. It was wrong, but I was so angry. I needed to blame someone when I knew all the while I was the one to blame. I should have known. I should have known!" Tears flowed down her cheeks.

"It wasn't your fault," Skyler assured. "Stop blaming yourself. You weren't foolish or stupid to trust your husband. When you found out what he had done, you did the right thing. You put the needs of your children above your own. That's all anyone could ask of you, including Monday. She doesn't blame you for what happened."

"That's right, Ma. I don't blame you for what Stan did." Monday walked over to Paige and gave her a hug. "I love you, Ma."

"I love you, too, baby."

Monday felt as if she had made some progress with Paige. She was glad Paige had finally expressed feelings. Usually, Paige was hard-core and unapproachable. Today, she seemed vulnerable, and Monday appreciated it. She promised herself that she'd try to be more patient with Paige. Until now, she never considered how Paige may have felt about the incident or why she never remarried. Monday prayed that her mother would forgive herself and Stan so that she could free up her heart to love again. She knew firsthand that releasing the past was the key to moving on and having a more productive future.

Figuring that Paige would want to spend some time alone with Skyler, Monday went into the dining room with the others. Everyone was finished eating. They were laughing and seemed to be having a good time.

"You guys are having way too much fun," Monday joked.

"Dad was in here cracking jokes," Alexis explained.

"Is that right?" Monday said. "A real comedian."

"Well, you know, what can I say?" Larry said in his best Jimmie Walker impersonation.

With her hands resting on Larry's shoulders, Monday said, "Anybody up for a game of Monopoly?"

"Count me in," Alexis said.

"That's my game. I always get Boardwalk," Stan replied. They laughed.

"I haven't played Monopoly in years," Loretta confessed. "You can count me in. I don't have a problem whooping on youngsters."

"Oh, no," Larry said. "I got dibs on the thimble." He laughed.

They went into the family room and sat on the floor. Monday retrieved the board game.

"Since it's my game, I get to be the banker," Monday announced.

"You just like to steal the money," Alexis said.

They all chuckled. Everyone was having a great time trying to make his or her way around the board so that they could start buying up the property. When Larry purchased Park Place and Boardwalk, the others dreaded going into the "high rent" district. It was over after Larry started putting up hotels.

"That was fun," Monday said. "Let's open presents."

Monday handed Alexis the gift from Stan and Loretta. It was an African Heritage Bible.

"This is nice. Thanks so much," Alexis said, rubbing her hand over the red leather cover. She gave Stan and Loretta each a hug.

"You're welcome," Loretta said.

"I left my present outside," Larry announced. "Follow me." He led Alexis out the front door.

"Daddy, is that for me?" She sounded surprised.

"Yes," he said excitedly, grinning.

There was a black Honda Accord parked in the driveway.

"Thank you, Jesus. Thank you, Jesus. Thank you, Jesus," Alexis repeated.

Monday, Stan, and Loretta rushed outdoors.

"I can't believe you got her a car," Monday said, beaming with pride.

"Congratulations, Alexis," Loretta said.

Skyler and Paige joined the rest of them outside.

"What's all the commotion?" Paige asked.

"Grandma, my dad got me a new car." She jumped up and down, hands covering her mouth.

"That's nice, baby," Paige replied.

Larry promised to take Alexis for a drive. They all went back inside and sat in the living room.

"May I have everyone's attention please?" Larry said, taking Monday by the hand. "I have an announcement to make. Being around all of you today has been good for me. I feel like I'm a part of a real family. It's true that things come together in God's timing. I have Monday and Alexis back in my life, and I've never felt better. I love both of my girls." He kissed Monday on the cheek. "Recently, I was blessed to acquire my own radio station."

"What?" Monday asked.

"Baby, it's true."

Throughout the room, "Congratulations" and "I'm so proud of you," floated about. A line formed as everyone waited for his or her turn to give Larry a hug.

"Thank you, guys. You're making me feel real good." He took a deep breath. "There's one more thing I want to say." Larry looked Monday in the eyes and asked, "Will you marry me?"

Immediately, Monday began to cry. She was so choked up that she could hardly get the words out. She had dreamed of this moment all of her life. Now that it was here, she couldn't believe it. The thought of her and Larry becoming a legally recognized union and legitimizing their daughter meant more to Monday than words could ever express. Finally, "yes," escaped from her lips. Larry reached inside of his pocket and pulled out a five-carat, pear-shaped yellow diamond ring. He slid the ring on her finger.

Monday admired the ring. When she looked up, she noticed that every woman in the room was crying.

"I'm so happy for you, Mom," Alexis said, giving Monday a hug. Then she hugged her dad and said, "I love you."

If anyone had told Monday that one day she would be this happy, she would've called him or her a liar. Dreams seemed to come true for other people, not her. She looked at Skyler and realized that their work was done. She walked over to Skyler, gave her a hug, and whispered, "Thanks for everything."

"You're welcome. You deserve this happiness. Enjoy it."

Monday felt so much love that she cried even more. Her life felt complete. God had been so good to her. She was marrying the man she loved, her soul mate. Alexis was on the right track. She even had a better understanding of Paige. Because she had forgiven Stan, she had inherited Loretta, who seemed to be a decent person, into her family. All she could say was, "Thank You, Lord."

CHAPTER FORTY-FOUR

Skyler

"Good morning, love," Donovan said. "Happy birthday to you."

"That's right. It is my birthday." I smiled and nestled my head in his chest. Being in Donovan's arms always made me feel blessed.

"How are you feeling?"

"Pretty good. I'm looking forward to my day of pampering at Spa Sydell."

"I'll bet you are. What all are you and Gabby having done?"

"We're getting the works. Facials, massages, manicures, pedicures, and eyebrow waxes."

"Alrighty then."

He covered my mouth with his. We shared a morning of passion. Afterward, I took a quick nap while Donovan went downstairs and cooked breakfast. He returned carrying a serving tray.

"Wake up, sleepy head," Donovan whispered.

I sat up in the bed and removed the lid from the plate.

"Honey, this looks so good. An omelet, bacon, toast, and a side of fruit. Wow! You really outdid yourself."

"Don't forget the freshly-squeezed orange juice." He smiled. "Nothing's too good for my baby." He kissed me on the forehead.

"You're so sweet. I love you."

"Love you, too."

There was plenty of food to feed the both of us, so I cut into the omelet with my fork and slid a piece into Donovan's mouth. We took turns feeding one another. The phone rang, and I answered.

"Happy birthday to you. Happy birthday to you. Happy birthday, my precious Skyler. Happy birthday to you," my mom sang into the receiver.

My mom sang "Happy Birthday" to me every year. I looked forward to it.

"Thanks, Mom." I laughed.

"Happy birthday, sweetie. What do you have planned for today?"

"As a birthday gift from Gabriella, she and I are going to the spa."

"Sounds like fun. What did Donovan get you?"

"I don't know." I looked at Donovan, who was looking incredibly sexy. "He said he'd give it to me later."

"All right. Did you get our present?"

"Not yet. What did you send me?" I smiled and traced my finger along Donovan's pectoral muscles.

"I'm not going to tell you. You should get it today."

"Okay. Where's Daddy?"

Donovan wrapped his arm around my waist, causing me to fall back on the bed. I stifled a laugh.

"He's right here. Hold on," she said.

"Happy birthday, pumpkin."

"Thanks, Daddy." Donovan kissed me gently on the neck. I closed my eyes and said, "I love you."

"Love you, too. How are you feeling? Feeling any older?"

I opened my eyes and pushed Donovan away so that I could sit up. "Pretty good. And not really."

"What did you get?"

"Gabby and I are going to the spa." I felt like a little girl going on a play date.

"Good. Will Donovan take you to dinner?"

I smiled. "Yes." Donovan always took me to a nice restaurant for my birthday.

"Okay. Enjoy yourself. Here's your mom."

"All right, sweetie," my mom said as she got back on the phone. "Enjoy your day and have lots of fun. Give Donovan our love. I love you."

"Love you, too, Mom."

I pressed the "off" button on the cordless phone and placed it on the cradle. "I need to put some clothes on."

"You don't have to," Donovan flirted with me. "You can stay here with me just like that all day."

"As tempting as that sounds, I'll have to take a rain check."

I went into the bathroom and brushed my teeth. Then I took a shower. When I got out, I put on a robe while I pulled my hair back into a loose ponytail. There was no need to put on any makeup since I was getting a facial. I sat on the chaise in my bedroom and applied moisturizer.

"Baby," Donovan said as he came back upstairs with his hands full. "The UPS guy had a few deliveries for you."

I loved getting presents. Donovan placed the packages on the floor in front of me. I stopped rubbing vanilla-sugar-scented lotion on my body in favor of opening the gifts. I couldn't resist. The first box that I unwrapped was from my mom and dad. It was a heart-shaped diamond pendant dangling from a gold necklace. I held up the jewelry. "Pretty."

"It sure is," Donovan said. "Want me to help you put it on?"

"Sure. Thanks."

I stood up and turned my back toward Donovan while he secured the necklace around my neck.

"Done."

I touched the pendant with my right hand as it rested against my chest. It sparkled delicately from the morning sun peeking through the windows. I sat back down and continued opening boxes. The next parcel was from Donovan's parents. It was a lovely candle set. Those closest to me know how much I enjoy taking relaxing, candlelit baths. The third and last box didn't have a return address. After opening the package, I discovered lingerie inside. Puzzled, I searched the contents and found a card. The note read:

Dear Sky,

You haven't responded to the notes, cards, and token gifts that I've sent you. I can't help but feel as if you're ignoring me. Anyway, happy birthday.

From,
Your secret admirer

I nearly dropped the card.

"What's the matter?" Donovan asked. "Who's it from?"

I was at a loss for words. Ever since the bird incident, I suspected Tatiana had been prank calling me. I tried to ignore her. Then it progressed to tiny trinkets, like flowers and candles outside of my office door, and handwritten notes on my car. I hadn't discussed it with anyone because, in most cases, stalkers want attention. If you don't give it to them they usually go away. Now this. The fact that she had the gall to have a package delivered to my house showed me she was stepping things up a notch. I handed Donovan the card and watched as he read the note silently.

"Is someone stalking you?"

"I think so."

"Why didn't you tell me?"

"I didn't want you to worry. Most stalker cases are harmless and aren't even worth filing a police report. I thought that if I ignored the stalker, she would go away."

"She? She who? How long has this been going on? Tell me everything."

"Well." I paused to gather my thoughts. "Remember the morning I found the dead bird on the doorstep?"

"Yes."

"That's when it started. Sort of."

"I don't understand. What do you mean 'sort of'?"

"Reggie, you know, our lawn guy. He was involved with an emotionally unstable woman. She must've followed him here and created a distorted romantic notion about Reggie and me. I later found out that the bird belonged to Reggie."

"You mean to tell me some psycho is stalking you because she thinks you're messing around with Reggie? Who is she?"

"According to Reggie, Tatiana faked a pregnancy. Somehow, she blames me for Reggie rejecting her."

"Tatiana?"

Something I said seemed to resonate with Donovan. He had a deeply concerned look on his face. "Reggie never told me her last name."

"We need to call the police." He walked over to pick up the phone. "Do you still have everything she sent you?"

"No, I don't want to call the police. And yes, I still have every note and gift."

"Why don't you want to involve the authorities?"

"Because I don't think she's a threat to me. This isn't a romantic attraction. If it were, she would've done something by now. She knows where I work and where I live, yet she hasn't initiated any face-to-face contact."

"Baby, don't you understand? This woman sent you lingerie. She's probably gay and obsessed with you."

I felt my insides quiver. Donovan had a point, but I refused to give Tatiana any power over me.

"You can't be too careful when it comes to people like this," Donovan warned. "We need to do something."

"Honey, I'm not going to allow anyone to ruin my birthday. She sent this gift for shock value. Nothing else. If I had thought for a second that I was in danger, I would've called the police immediately. She's simply trying to get my attention."

I pulled out a cardboard box from my closet containing all of the correspondence from my stalker and placed the latest addition inside.

"May I see that?"

"Of course you can."

I placed the box on the bed. I kissed Donovan on the lips and finished getting dressed. I could tell by the serious expression on Donovan's face as he sat on the edge of the bed carefully reading one of the letters from my stalker, that he wasn't convinced that I wasn't in danger.

"I promise I'll be careful," I assured. "Call me on my cell if you need me."

Donovan hugged me closely, and I could feel his love exuding from every fiber of his being.

"I love you, baby," he said. "Please be careful."

"I will."

Then I left and drove to Spa Sydell at the perimeter location. I walked in and noticed Gabriella sitting in the waiting area, flipping through an *Essence* magazine.

"*Hola, chica,*" I said.

"*Hola.*"

We hugged and checked in at the front desk. Our first stop was a couple's Swedish massage. We took off our clothes and draped ourselves in white garments provided by the spa. Two female massage therapists entered the dimly lit, aromatherapy-infused room. We were instructed to lie face down on the massage tables. I felt like talking about the stalker situation, but didn't want to mess up the flow. This was time for rest and relaxation, not profound thoughts and analyzing. I figured we'd have plenty of time to talk about that later anyway. I allowed myself to release and let go. The massage felt so good, I ended up succumbing to a light slumber.

Next, facials. The room was also dimly lit with aromatherapy in the air. There was the calming sound of a meditation fountain in the background. Gabriella and I were each assigned skin specialists who thoroughly cleansed our skin. They even extracted blackheads that weren't visible to the naked eye. The pressure from having zits squeezed in my face was enough to keep me awake. However, when they finished, our faces were literally glowing.

We finished up the day with manicures, pedicures, and eyebrow waxes. We left feeling pampered and refreshed. By that time, I was famished. We decided to have lunch at La Madeleine because they served delicious French cuisine. As soon as we walked through the door, we were greeted by the mouth-watering aroma, relaxing décor, and soft classical music. I ordered shrimp Crêpe Florentine with mango tea, and Gabriella had a chicken cordon bleu sandwich with raspberry lemonade. We sat at a round, wooden table near the fireplace. It was like visiting the French countryside.

"I really enjoyed myself at the spa," I said.

"I'm glad. I had a nice time, too," Gabriella said. "I'm so pleased we could do this for your birthday. You were there for me during all the drama with Kevin, and I thought this would be a nice way to show you I really appreciate you and your friendship."

"I got a strange gift today." I looked her in the eye.

"Really?" She raised a brow. "What was it?"

"Well, it was lingerie sent from a secret admirer."

"A secret admirer?" She scrunched up her face.

"That's what was written on the note," I explained. " 'A secret admirer'."

"How long has this been happening?"

I told her about the situation with Reggie, Tatiana, and the dead bird on my doorstep. Then I told her my suspicions about Tatiana calling and hanging up. I went on to tell her about the letters and gifts.

"I must admit, I thought Tatiana would stop at phone calls. I didn't tell Donovan, but I was surprised to receive letters and gifts. And the lingerie has forced me to reassess this whole situation."

"Tatiana, huh? She sounds weird to me. Maybe she's in love with you." Gabriella had a strange look on her face. I could tell she was deep in thought.

"That's the same thing Donovan said. At first, I didn't believe that was the case. I thought she was a woman scorned. But now, I'm not so sure. The lingerie makes me think it could be something else."

"You need to be careful." Gabriella gave a thoughtful look. "How do you know Tatiana is the one stalking you?"

I took a sip of tea. "That's a good question. The phone calls started after the dead bird incident. It was the only thing that made sense. I never considered the possibility of it being someone else."

"Anything's possible. If I were you, I'd call the police."

"Like I told Donovan, most stalkers want attention. I'm not going to give it to her. Once whoever it is realizes that they don't have any control over me, they'll stop."

We finished eating our lunches. The thought of someone other than Tatiana stalking me thoroughly confused me. I couldn't get it off my mind. Had I made a mistake by not involving the police? What if she wasn't the stalker? Could I really be in peril?

Later that evening, I got dressed in a black, halter-style dress because Donovan said we were going out to dinner.

"Baby," Donovan said. "Would you mind wearing this blindfold?"

I was hesitant at first, but I completely trusted Donovan. I didn't think he'd do anything to cause me harm, so I agreed to wear the scarf around my eyes. Once in the car, I noticed that my sense of hearing was heightened. It was exciting and frightening listening to the car horns honking and brakes screeching. Whenever Donovan tapped the brakes, my heartbeat sped up. The car finally stopped. I figured we must've reached our destination. I heard Donovan unbuckle his seat belt, and open and close his car door. He walked around the back of the car and opened my door.

"We're here," Donovan announced.

I unfastened my seat belt and attempted to remove the covering from my eyes.

"No, no," Donovan said, moving my hand away. "I've got you."

He assisted me with getting out of the car. He held my arm and led the way. We stopped walking and Donovan uncovered my eyes. We were in a private banquet hall.

"Surprise!" The room full of people cheered.

There must've been at least one hundred people in the room. Gabriella and Kevin were standing up front. I couldn't stop smiling.

"Thank you, honey," I said as I gave Donovan a hug. "I really appreciate this."

We walked in together, hand-in-hand, and I greeted as many people as I could. The room was elegantly decorated in black, white, and silver. The seats were draped in silver covers, and the round tables were covered in long, white linen tablecloths. The food table was set up in the back of the room. The presentation of the food was impeccable. It looked and smelled savory.

"Were you surprised?" Gabriella quizzed.

"Yes. Why didn't you tell me?"

"Oh, come on. I wasn't going to ruin the surprise."

"Hey," Donovan interrupted, "may I borrow Gabriella for a minute?"

"Sure," I said.

Donovan kissed me on the cheek before walking with Gabriella through the crowd.

CHAPTER FORTY-FIVE

Gabriella

At lunch with Skyler, Gabriella couldn't let on that she, too, had reservations about Tatiana after making the connection that Tatiana was the same woman who had stared at Skyler in the diner. She was glad she called Nate to check out the situation after she met with Tatiana at her office.

"Gabriella," Donovan said. "I need to talk to you because I think you were right about Tee. This morning, Skyler told me she was being stalked."

"She told me about it while we were eating lunch. She mentioned Tatiana, and I knew it was the same Tee catering the party. I didn't tell her that I hired a private investigator to check her out."

"What?" He seemed shocked. "You did?"

"Yes. I told you I didn't trust her. I didn't tell Sky because I wanted to discuss it with you first."

"What did you find out?"

She stepped closer to him so that no one else could hear. "That she was on trial for murder in Texas."

"Murder?" His mouth flew open.

"Yes." She peeked over her shoulder and when she didn't see anyone, she said, "She killed her fiancé, but she was acquitted. Crime of passion. I didn't get the details. She spent some time under psychiatric care. Since she's been in Atlanta, she hasn't gotten into any trouble. At least not until now."

"I can't believe this." He shook his head. "Murder?" Donovan rested his back against the wall and seemed to stop breathing.

As if on cue, Tatiana walked into the hallway. "Hey, how's it going? Did you like the food?"

"Tatiana, I'm glad you're here," Donovan said. "We need to talk."

"You sound serious. Is something wrong?" Tatiana asked.

"I don't know. You tell me."

Tatiana raised her brow.

"Look," Gabriella interjected. "Have you been stalking Sky?"

Tatiana seemed appalled. "Stalking? What are you talking about? I've never stalked anyone in my life!"

"Were you dating Reggie?" Donovan said.

"Yes, but . . ."

"Did you leave a dead bird on our doorstep?"

Tatiana became silent.

"Have you been prank calling and sending gifts to my wife?"

"Wait a minute," Tatiana said. "I don't know what's going on, but I can assure you I'm not stalking Dr. Little or anyone else."

"Don't play games!" Gabriella yelled. "We know about your past."

"My past? What are you talking about?"

"You killed your boyfriend," Gabriella said.

Tatiana's jaw dropped. "You've got it all wrong. I don't know what you think you know, but I'm not a threat to anybody. I'm sorry if someone is harassing Dr. Little, but it isn't me."

"Yeah, right," Gabriella said.

"Fine." Tatiana looked at Donovan and said, "Yes. I left the bird on your doorstep. I'm sorry. I was angry and not in a good place emotionally about my break-up with Reggie. I thought Reggie and Sky had something going on but realized I was wrong. And yes, I did call and hang up on your wife a few times, but that's it. I swear."

"Why should I believe you?" Donovan said angrily.

"Because it's the truth. I realize my behavior was immature. Again, I'm sorry. I never should've blamed Dr. Little for my problems with Reggie. It was irrational, and I was wrong. I'm over it now and have been for a while."

Donovan stood inches away from Tatiana's face and said, "For your sake, you better be telling the truth. If Sky receives any more anonymous phone calls, letters, or gifts, heads will roll. I'll be all over you like stank on chitlins."

Tatiana was visibly shaken. She hurried into the women's restroom.

"That should be the end of that," Donovan declared.

"You know, I'm not so sure she's the stalker. I mean, the way she reacted. She seemed shocked."

"Yes, she did. Maybe she's just a good liar."

"Hope so. Let's go back and join the rest of the party."

Tatiana splashed cold water on her face and pat-dried with a paper towel. She heard the toilet flush from inside of a locked stall.

"Hey," Jasmine greeted as she exited the stall. She turned on the faucet to wash her hands.

She caught a glimpse of Tatiana's reflection in the mirror and could tell she had been crying.

"What's the matter?" Jasmine asked as she dried her hands.

Tatiana bent over, checking for other sets of feet. When she was convinced they were alone, she told Jasmine about her encounter with Donovan and Gabriella.

"Wow! I'm shocked. Are you all right?"

"Yes."

"If it's any consolation, I don't believe you stalked Dr. Little."

"Thanks. It means a lot to me to hear you say that."

They hugged.

"Come on," Jasmine said. "We need to go check on the food."

Tatiana gave a faint smile and followed Jasmine out the door. Tatiana wasn't paying attention to where she was going and bumped into Reggie.

"Excuse me," Tatiana said, still not looking up. "I'm sorry."

"Tatiana?" What are you doing here?" Reggie asked.

"Oh, Reggie."

Jasmine backed up to stand beside Tatiana.

"I'm catering the party," Tatiana explained. "Since you're here, there's something I need to tell you."

With everything she had been through, she decided to take Jasmine's advice and straighten out some of the wrong in her life. She was tired of plotting and scheming because, in the end, she was the biggest loser.

"Forget about it!" Reggie said as he was about to walk away.

"Reggie, I'm sorry!" Tatiana yelled behind him.

He turned around.

"The way I behaved was inexcusable, and I apologize. I'm sorry about Rufus. It was an accident. I shouldn't have been in your place when you weren't at home. That was wrong. I know you think I lied about being pregnant, but I didn't. It was your child, and I had a miscarriage."

"It's the truth," Jasmine confirmed.

"Who are you?" Reggie asked.

"This is Jasmine," Tatiana introduced. "She's the one who called you while I was in the hospital."

"I hate that we had to meet under such circumstances," Jasmine said, "but she's not lying about the baby. She was on bed rest for a week afterward."

"Oh, I'm sorry about your loss. You okay?" His tone softened.

"I'm fine. Thanks for asking. I want you to know you don't have to worry about me. I won't be bothering you anymore."

Reggie nodded his head. "Take care of yourself."

"You, too."

They went their separate ways.

CHAPTER FORTY-SIX
Skyler

I walked outside to get some fresh air. Large crowds tended to generate heat, and the atmosphere inside was stifling. The night air felt soothing against my bare arms and back.

"Skyler, you look radiant tonight," a male voice whispered in my ear, startling me.

I turned around immediately. I didn't like this guy being so close to me that I could smell his lunch. "What are you doing creeping up on me like that? Scaring me half to death," I quipped.

The mysterious stranger stood approximately six foot six. He didn't appear to be a guest at the party, as he was dressed in baggy jeans and a hoodie.

"I'm Nigel." He extended his hand to me, and I hesitantly shook it.

"Nice to meet you, Nigel. How did you know my name?"

"I've been watching you for months."

My smile faded. I felt as if I were trapped in a horror movie. "Excuse me?"

"Happy birthday, Skyler. Did you like your gift?"

"The–the lingerie was from you?" I stuttered.

"You got it. I would've delivered it in person, but I wasn't invited to the party." He chuckled, but at the same time seemed hurt.

I felt like running back inside, but I knew he'd grab me. So, I said, "Thanks for the present. It's starting to get chilly," I rubbed my arms. "I don't have a shawl. I'm going back inside. It was nice meeting you."

I walked backwards toward the door, never taking my eyes off Nigel. As I reached for the door, he said, "Why are you walking away from me? I love you."

I attempted to run, but he lunged for me. "I've waited all these months to be with you, and this is how you treat me?"

I screamed, and he covered my mouth. I bit his hand and tried to claw at his face. He picked me up by the waist and I kicked him with all my might. He released me and I ran. He sprinted after me like a linebacker, shoulder down, gaze affixed on his target, ready to topple. He hit me squarely and I fell to the ground. I slammed my knees and palms on the gravel. There was a large hole in my pantyhose, revealing the bloody scrape on my knee. Pain radiated through my leg.

I turned over, trying to crawl backwards. "Please, let me go," I pleaded as he jumped on top of me.

"Stop fighting me."

He pinned me to the ground and attempted to kiss me on the mouth. I turned my face away from him.

"What's wrong with you? Why are you fighting me?" he asked with a hint of disappointment and disbelief.

I spat in his face and shoved him as hard as I could. He toppled off of me. I scurried off the ground before running inside of the building, yelling and screaming.

"What's wrong?" Donovan hollered as he ran toward me.

"There's a man outside dressed in baggy jeans and a hoodie. He tried to kidnap me."

Donovan, Kevin, and a few other men from the party ran

outside. They searched the premises. Gabriella retrieved her cell phone from her purse and called the police. I was scared and thankful to be alive. I could get over the bruises.

About thirty minutes later, the men returned with the culprit. I cringed when I saw Nigel again. In the light, I could clearly see the crevices in his forehead and deep laugh lines around his mouth. Blood was oozing from the scratch I had given him. His round eyes narrowed in on me, sending frightening chills throughout my body. I felt as though I were looking into the eyes of the devil. I turned away in fear.

"We found him hiding underneath a car in the parking lot," Donovan said, as he held me in his arms. "You're safe now."

I cried. Not long afterward, the police arrived and took my statement. I was glad when they took Nigel away in handcuffs. I thanked God for sparing me, because the devil thought he had me. But I had fooled him. I had long divorced the devil. He was no longer a part of my life.

Reading Group Discussion Questions

1. Did you view Skyler as a sort of sage?

2. How did you feel when Ambrosia died? Were you concerned about her children, Mateo and Destiny?

3. What did you expect Kevin to do about Mateo and Destiny?

4. Were you surprised that Kevin and Gabriella reconciled? What would you have done if you were in Gabriella's shoes?

5. Could you identify with any of the characters and their plights? If so, which one(s) and in what way?

6. What did you think about Larry? Were you supportive of his relationship with Monday?

7. Did you agree with Monday's decision to forgive Stan? Why or why not?

8. What was your initial impression of Paige? Did Paige's confession change your opinion of her? Did you believe she was sincere when she apologized to Monday?

9. Did you believe that Tatiana was stalking Skyler? Were you surprised by the outcome? Please explain.